PENGUIN BOOKS

The Blue

Mary McCallum was born in Zambia, and has lived in New Zealand since she was four. She has worked as a broadcasting journalist in New Zealand and Europe, and continues to work as a freelance writer and reviewer. *The Blue* is Mary's first novel. It won her the New Zealand Society of Authors' Lilian Ida Smith Award and an MA with distinction at Victoria University's International Institute of Modern Letters. Married to Ian, Mary spends much of her time raising three children in their house by the sea and writing her second novel.

The Blue

Mary McCallum

PENGUIN BOOKS

PENGUIN BOOKS
Published by the Penguin Group
Penguin Group (NZ), 67 Apollo Drive, Rosedale, North Shore 0632,
New Zealand (a division of Pearson New Zealand Ltd)
Penguin Group (USA) Inc., 375 Hudson Street, New York, New York 10014, USA
Penguin Group (Canada), 90 Eglinton Avenue East, Suite 700, Toronto,
Ontario, M4P 2Y3, Canada (a division of Pearson Penguin Canada Inc.)
Penguin Books Ltd, 80 Strand, London, WC2R 0RL, England
Penguin Ireland, 25 St Stephen's Green, Dublin 2, Ireland
(a division of Penguin Books Ltd)
Penguin Group (Australia), 250 Camberwell Road, Camberwell, Victoria 3124,
Australia (a division of Pearson Australia Group Pty Ltd)
Penguin Books India Pvt Ltd, 11, Community Centre, Panchsheel Park,
New Delhi – 110 017, India
Penguin Books (South Africa) (Pty) Ltd, 24 Sturdee Avenue,
Rosebank, Johannesburg 2196, South Africa

Penguin Books Ltd, Registered Offices: 80 Strand, London, WC2R 0RL, England

First published by Penguin Group (NZ), 2007
3 5 7 9 10 8 6 4 2
Copyright © Mary McCallum, 2007

The right of Mary McCallum to be identified as the author of this work in
terms of section 96 of the Copyright Act 1994 is hereby asserted.

Designed by Vivianne Douglas
Typeset by Egan Reid
Printed in Australia by McPherson's Printing Group

ISBN 978 0 14 300723 4

A catalogue record for this book is available from the
National Library of New Zealand.

www.penguin.co.nz

ARTS COUNCIL OF NEW ZEALAND *TOI AOTEAROA*

The assistance of Creative New Zealand towards the production of this book
is gratefully acknowledged by the Publisher.

Dedicated to my parents Norma and Lindsay McCallum; my husband Ian Stewart and our children Paul, Adam and Isabel; and the real whaling families of Arapawa Island past and present – all heroes in their own lives.

TORY CHANNEL

NEW ZEALAND
1938

1

It was the start of the day and the calling of the chickens. Lilian loosened the gate of the run and ducked her head to enter, giving a thin high whistle at the back of her teeth as she did. It was either that or the clang of the scrap bucket against the gate post, but by the time she looked up they were out of the hen house and running across the hard earth. It didn't take much, only the smallest whistle and the single knock of a bucket, and Lilian was besieged by birds.

She counted them, all twelve, the Leghorns, the bantams, Russell the Rooster, and Molly standing listlessly to one side. There was a frost and the puddles had rinds of ice, but the shove and scatter of the girls, and the intimate way they prodded her calves, sheltered Lilian somehow from the worst of a bitter morning. She took the bucket over to the heap by the fence and tipped it up, watching as the birds fell on the scraps – all except Molly. Lilian fed the old hen with her fingers and went in to look for eggs.

Four wasn't bad for the time of year, but there was nothing coming out of Molly unless she was hiding them. Lilian stood a moment, hearing the chickens outside. She always had a sense – and she couldn't decide if it was menacing or not – that the light in there with its sediment of feathers and grains and straw was also intent on absorbing her. She wondered what would happen if she stayed long enough, how quickly and painlessly she might disappear.

The shift back to the run again made Lilian suddenly clumsy. She caught her head on the frame of the shed door and tipped one of the eggs from the basket. It cracked without a sound, and lay there leaking. Lilian bent down to scoop it up, clicking her teeth at her own ineptness. If she was careful she could save the yolk.

It's how an egg falls that determines if it breaks or not, Ed used to tell her. Throw it high enough and it'll fall on its end so you can keep it. He'd talked like that in their early months together but it was only an excuse to juggle while she warmed the pan. Of course she didn't believe such nonsense. 'Ed, that's breakfast!' would fly from her mouth, and he would catch them one by one and put them in the box. 'It's scrambled eggs, then, Lily.' He never threw one without catching it, so she never saw if it was true or not, and she couldn't bring herself to do it, even now. An egg was an egg when all was said and done.

The distant water was pale and still, and where air and water met there was a blur of white instead of a clear horizon to sit a boat on. Closer up, in the narrow waterway that was Tory Channel, the sea was still dark and waiting for the sun. Between the light and the dark there was more water, for it was a world brimming with water in a constant state of unease, the land nothing more than the tips of long-drowned valleys struggling for a handhold. There was little else, bar half a dozen gulls at the mouth of the channel.

Gulls were Lilian's least favourite birds but there was something about them on a fine day. They hung on the air currents like celestial washing. White to white. Wing-tip to wing-tip. As high as they could go. *Iris*, she thought, *you've been busy*.

A tui gargled and let loose a string of low notes. That and the smoke from the coal range reminded Lilian it was time to get on.

Behind the green curtains, Billy was sleeping. She'd looked in on him before feeding the chooks and doubted he'd woken since. He'd had the usual dream – something dark and formless, and he was chasing it – and Lilian had heard him in the early hours calling out to her. She'd found him slick with sweat, his legs wrapped tight in his bedding, more excited than frightened. As the morning yawned and stretched at the high ridge of Arapawa Island and slid down into Tory Channel, Billy wouldn't know she'd gone out and come back in, and was putting the fresh eggs into the egg box with one eye on the stove. He'd have uncurled a little and settled himself up higher in the bed, his mouth relaxed and his blue pyjamas all askew. Maybe he could feel her humming through the wall. Humming, yes, she was humming: *It's only a Paper Moon*.

Down the hall, Ed was stirring. The rooster had woken him, crowing without break in a fit of vanity. Ed's eyes would snap open and he'd turn on to his back with a grunt, one arm above his head.

There they were, the three of them in the house on the hill. Somehow they would come together as the morning stirred itself. Maybe the boy and his father would rise at the same time and brush past each other in the corridor on their way to the outhouse. As it happened, they settled together at the kitchen table, each with a plate of eggs and bacon and fried bread, waiting for the tea to draw. There was little conversation

11

but it was comfortable enough. Ed had reached for Lilian's hand when she'd put the plate in front of him. He'd given it a small squeeze and said, as he did every morning, 'Now that's what I signed on for.' Lilian had smiled as if to say, 'You silly thing.' And then, 'Eat up, don't let it get cold.'

And why did she say that? Not so much to make him get on with it as to have something to say. The gesture of the squeezed hand made her brisk. When Lilian began clearing away the dishes, Ed and Billy knew it was time to get a start on the chores. Always it was like this, thought Lilian, scraping vigorously at the egg stuck to the rim of Billy's plate: the detritus of breakfast, the detritus of early morning, broken through the middle and thrown away.

By mid-morning, the waters of Tory Channel were slick with light, and the surface was wrinkling like the skin on milk that's about to boil. Lilian was in the wash house counting out the socks and matching them together. He was in the garden in his jacket and cap as if he was going somewhere. But he wasn't going anywhere. He was standing, as he'd been every day for two weeks now, looking through his binoculars. He was watching for a pulse in the water. No, not watching for it, willing it.

Through the fly-specked window, he seemed further than he was, and smaller. How still he stood, she thought, but with no stillness in him. Lilian knew the feel of the small tremor in his shoulders, down his spine and up the back of his neck. She patted the socks down firmly in the basket, not once but twice, and picked it up.

Inside the house, Billy was sitting in front of the range with his back to her. Lilian put the basket down and stretched her arms, locking her fingers together and yawning. 'Have you done your sums, Billy?'

'Yep, and I got them all right.'

'Did you, love? Are you sure you've checked them? You were very fast.'

'I did it the quicker way,' said Billy, looking at her over his shoulder.

Lilian could see the slate on the table and the numbers dashing across it. 'Tell me, Billy, do you do anything the slower way? Being fast is good, but sometimes you need to take a little care.'

'But they're right.'

She leaned closer and smiled. 'They are all right, yes. Good boy.'

And she went to kiss him, but Billy moved, so she missed and kissed the air instead. There was something there about the movement of his head and the soft brush of hair and the empty air in front of her mouth that stopped Lilian for a moment. She stood at a loss.

'How much years is it from six to a hundred?' said Billy. Lilian felt him tug at her hand, and again. 'Mummy? How long till I'm a hundred?'

'Well,' she said. 'The answer to that would be ninety-four. Now off you go and get some fresh air.' Lilian gave him a squeeze on the cheek to release him, and Billy took off outside. He'd want to do something like chopping the kindling and would pester his father until he was allowed to do it. It'd be good for the both of them. There was plenty of time for lessons.

*

The morning was over. How many times had Billy run across that stretch of grass to ask his father to come and chop wood with him? Only once did Ed move, when he stretched and grunted and walked back inside for lunch. By then Billy had given up. He was piling up stones and throwing a ball to knock them over and pretended he hadn't seen his father walk past. He tried to ignore his mother too, but lunch was ready and he must be hungry.

The three of them sat in their places at the table and ate fresh bread and four-day-old vegetable soup that Lilian was glad to see the last of; and after she'd washed the dishes and Ed had gone back outside, she hung up her apron and smoothed her dress with her hands. They'd go and see Susan.

Out on the front step, Billy sniffed the beginnings of a southerly buster while Lilian tied a scarf over her hair. The strait was getting choppy and the distant thumb of the North Island was almost obscured. There was still time to get to Fishing Bay and back if they got a move on.

Ed was pacing at the edge of the garden, and they walked towards him, their faces unintentionally resetting themselves.

'We're off then,' Lilian said, and he turned, his eyes still focused elsewhere. She'd seen the puzzlement, and the effort it caused him to turn around. He squinted at them both and tried to smile.

'We're going to see Susan,' Lilian said.

'I'm going to catch a fish,' said Billy, holding up his rod. 'Maybe a whale.'

'Hah!' Ed looked closely at Lilian for a moment and turned back to his binoculars. 'Be careful on the track.'

'I will.'

She took Billy's hand and they started walking to the gate.

'We go over to the Lookout tomorrow, first day back.' Ed was talking to the water, not to her, but Lilian knew he wanted her to hear.

She slowed her step. 'That's good news,' she said. 'You'll be pleased.'

Lilian was thinking now of the people who'd be milling around the whale station and how it would be harder to slip in and out. Maybe they should stay home. She'd nearly reached the gate, though, and Billy was climbing up the fence to open the latch. He'd be disappointed.

She watched as the gate swung open cleanly and hung there. There was still a shine on the new hinges, and the fresh paint adhered to the pine wood Ed had split and sanded over summer. He had gone to extraordinary lengths to give it as smooth a finish as possible. In ten minutes, he'd smashed the old gate to kindling and delivered it to her in the kitchen, his hair wet with the exertion.

'Well, that's that,' he'd said.

Through they went, Lilian and Billy, quickly past the bank of pine trees, one walking, the other skipping backwards. The track was firm enough here, but in no time it started to become slippery with overnight rain. Lilian felt anxious for Billy, who was running now as fast as his legs could carry him. Three times she told the boy to slow down, and the fourth time she yelled it: 'Slow down, Billy, you'll kill yourself!' He looked back briefly then returned to the job at hand, walking as fast as walking would allow and running his hand along the tops of the gorse that flanked the path, just missing the sharp spikes. Then he stopped all of a sudden to turn over a rock to look for slaters.

Lilian hadn't had a chance to think about the news that the whale season had started up again. Truth was, the months Ed was farming he was a man without a place to hang his cap. He did what had to be done and would go the extra mile if required, but he was restive in the doing of it and never able to settle. The day the whales returned was a different matter. Lilian saw him transform in front of her: his face stoked, his body solid and defined in its movements and holding its weight again. Admittedly, he spent the next three months out on the whale chaser and only came home to eat and sleep, but when he was home you felt him there. He was more substantial, a happier man.

Lilian reached out to grab one of the yellow gorse flowers and crushed it between her fingers, lifting them up to smell.

'I'm going the quicker way!' Billy called, and he was off again, scrabbling up the hillside behind two frightened sheep, grabbing on to the grass with one hand and holding the fishing rod over his head. He knew this walk better than she did and could probably do it on his own in the dark. She wasn't worried about him, really; you just never knew after heavy rain what the track was doing.

Lilian quickened her pace too. Seeing Susan was a good idea. At eighteen, her daughter was so young and still so new to marriage and motherhood that Lilian almost expected to be given water in mussel shells and small stones on leaf plates rather than a real cup of tea and a biscuit. In fact, she knew her daughter to be a good mother and a good wife who'd understood what she had to do from the start. Lilian remembered the day Susan had brought Ben up home, holding his hand without a hint of shyness or embarrassment, and looked Lilian straight in the eye as if to say, *This is it, I have not a shred of doubt.* Lilian had wondered what to make of it. Had that been her twenty years before? Delivering Ed to her father like a parcel she'd packed? If she'd appeared confident, she hadn't been. At least Susan had known Ben for some months before she made a decision – and *properly* known him, face to face. Although Lilian suspected that if she mined her daughter's reasons for marrying Ben they would come down to his being uncomplicated and kind and close to home.

Billy was around the bend, back on the path, and throwing stones down the steep hillside. He turned and grinned, holding out something he'd fished from his pocket. It moved. Then, slipping around the next bend, he was out of sight. He'd wait at the turn-off. He knew to wait.

There was something in the water. In the middle of the deep channel, in the roiling water that was like milk about to boil, there was something dark and purposeful. Lilian stopped and watched. Nothing for a moment or two, then an enormous black back broke through the white spume and rolled forward, massive and relentless. A puff of fine spray hung above, and water clung to its sides as if reluctant to let the great beast go. For that's what it was. A humpback was in Tory Channel. Had Ed seen?

That's when she slipped.

Grabbed at the grass but instead grabbed air, grabbed again as she started to slide down the bank, got a handful of sheep dung, slid further down to where it got steeper, a rocky drop into the hissing sea. And she was hissing herself, hissing through her teeth, biting her lip, grabbing at anything to stop herself. She could feel beneath her a small ridge running down the bank like a backbone. She gripped it with her knees; her dress rucked up around her thighs. But it was bucking her off, making her slide, and there was nothing to hold on to. Fear

17

was warm and threatened to spill; her breath was ragged and shocked. And then she stopped. Her knee throbbed deeply and her hand stung. She was shaking and cold. She could feel her heart.

It was quiet after all that falling and rustling and grabbing. Looking up, Lilian could see where the edge of the path had collapsed with the rains. What had she been doing, walking so close? She was all right, though. If she worked slowly and carefully she could pull herself back up. But dear God, her knee ached and there was the blood.

Choosing carefully, Lilian grabbed a rock and tried to pull, but she was shaking so much she had to stop. Her right hand was grazed and stuck with grass and soil. She remembered the handkerchief in her coat pocket, and pulled it out to wipe the hand and wrap it up a little. Billy must have reached the turn-off by now, surely? The possibility whispering before but now shouting at her in the face was that he'd slipped like she had and been unable to stop himself hurtling to the sea.

'Billy!'

Little Ellie, last winter, went right off the end of the whale station and into the sea. That noisy bundle of child had dropped like a stone. No one knew why she'd kept on running or how it could have happened without anyone seeing. The next day they'd found her, wrapped in kelp and reeking of whale offal. Lilian could still hear the cry from the mother when they pulled the body in.

'Billy!'

A sheep cried out in a similar tone to Lilian's, its flat eyes fixed on her, its body impossibly balanced against the slope of the hill. Lilian could hear the small stones she'd knocked with her feet scrabbling behind her all the way down to the water.

She didn't dare look. The thought of the sliding steepness with barely a hand-hold stabbed a needle into her stomach. There was no sound of Billy.

Exhaustion overcame her. She had to blink her eyes hard to clear them and her body was still shaking, but she needed to start moving. Handful by handful, Lilian started to pull herself painfully back up the bank.

The track wasn't as far away as she'd thought. Lilian grabbed a final hank of flax and pulled herself on to it. Sitting there, hunched inside her coat, she looked at her knee. The hem of her skirt, she noticed, was ripped, but the knee wasn't too bad once she'd wiped the blood away with the handkerchief. There was a cut, half a finger's length only and not too deep, and some bruising. The palm was grazed across its surface. Lilian was still shaking, though, with a chill that hovered on the surface of her skin but didn't penetrate. Somehow she got to her feet and started walking.

Now this was where she should see him. A little way on was the small track which wound its way down to the small clutch of whalers' houses by the shore. The main path continued on round the next hill to Tar'white. But where the two diverged there was nothing. Her feet faltered a moment and her face flushed with apprehension. She just couldn't see him, that was all; he was somewhere there. Lilian's eyes traced the track.

The missed kiss in the morning suddenly seemed very important. Billy was one of those children who loved to be kissed. He'd nuzzle up and squeeze her face and stare at her ferociously. But just lately he'd been doing it less and less, and choosing to spend his time away from her. She would come upon him on his stomach in the grass, prostrate with boredom but within coo-ee of Ed who seemed wholly unaware of the attention. She'd hold her hand out, and sometimes he'd come to her and sometimes he wouldn't.

Lilian remembered the feeling that had brushed by her with the hair on Billy's head. A feeling of being tipped from something into nothing, the 'oh' she'd said, like a last breath. Loss. It wasn't Billy she'd thought of then, it was Micky. He'd slid away from her much earlier than his younger brother – his chin leading the way and boots on his feet two or three sizes too big. At the age of six he'd be out all day with his father and would barely have a single word to say to his mother when he came in the door. It was no surprise when Micky left Arapawa the day after his fifteenth birthday. The only surprise was his boots finally fit him.

It was Micky she'd thought of at that moment when Billy had slipped by her earlier, because for a moment Billy was Micky. The two boys were peas in a pod, by looks if not nature. They had the same dark unmanageable hair, and the same gap between the end of their eyebrows and the tips of their eyes which gave them a delicacy of expression that many would call innocent. Sometimes for a moment, a tiny split moment smaller than an apple pip, she'd think she had Micky back with her again. That she could, perhaps, make everything right. That the 'oh' with its soft endless aspiration would become something buoyant and replete. But Billy wasn't Micky. He was a boy with a whole different life behind those delicate eyes. He was her happiest child, the one she'd done the best by. She should have kept a better eye on him.

Lilian found herself looking gingerly over the edge of the path to the rocks and the claw of sea, and she felt a small bubble of panic at the back of her throat. *Please, not this one.*

'Billy!' she cried.

Just then, Lilian felt rather than saw something, and turned sharply. Wasn't that the top of the fishing rod coming out of the grass near the turn-off? 'Billy! I can see you!' She didn't want to frighten him.

Nothing happened for a moment, but then he stood up. Flushed with relief, Lilian waved and put her hands to her mouth to shout, 'Stay where you are!' She couldn't see his face clearly, but she could see him and the straightness of him, and she knew when he turned to go he would move with a low lope as if he could travel for miles. And in his pockets, among all the bits and pieces, there'd be a worm, a flat stone and his best marble. Below his lip, almost faded, would be the small white scar where he'd fallen last winter and his teeth had gone through and he'd bled all over her apron with the primroses. He was there, self-contained, ineluctable. Lilian smiled at the word, for it was one of Ed's mother's and she'd never thought she'd find a use for it. 'Lilian,' Iris would say, 'I'm afraid that is the *ineluctable* truth.'

Billy was turning as she watched him, itching to be gone. There was no point in calling again. He was at the safest part of the track and nearly to the baches by now. She just wanted to keep him in her sights.

At the turn-off at last, Lilian stopped a moment to rest her leg. It was throbbing painfully around her kneecap, but it was localised pain that she could manage. It was a matter of thinking herself away from it and keeping on. With rest and a poultice, the swelling and bruising would go down and the pain would ease. Thinking she might have lost Billy – that's where her anxiety rested. And her husband, where was he? They must have seen the whale by now. There was no sound or sign to show that, though, no flag on Lookout Hill.

2

The Friar knew the first whale of the season was upon them the minute he woke that morning. It was the crawling sensation that started at the base of his neck and crept through to the top of his bald head, finishing just above his eyebrows. It wasn't a premonition – he'd never had any truck with such things – but rather a shivering scalp brought on by an obscenely crisp morning. That meant that even though it wasn't yet June, it was cold enough for whale.

As soon as he was up, he put Annie's hat on. The thick brown wool was matted now, but he refused to wash it, and not just because he wasn't sure how to without ruining it. It had been touched all over by her and he wouldn't want to wash that away.

Annie had never called him the Friar; it was not a name anyone used back then. Annie had called him Owen. Smooth, almost one syllable, like a bird in the bush. The tonsure surrounded by a thick white fringe of hair that had given the Friar his name had come upon him the day after he'd been left alone. It was the shock that did it. He'd separated like a broken egg, and it was as if half of him hovered over her unbelieving and the rest of him went about life as usual. The next morning he'd woken to a nest of black hairs on the pillow, and what hair he had left was pure white.

The crew at the whale station had got into the habit of not meeting his eye, but when he got back to work something had changed. One by one throughout that morning they came and patted him on the back without a word. Just that, a hand on the back and the smallest transfer of pressure and warmth. Later, at smoko, young Charlie had called out, 'Hey, Friar Tuck! Pass us the milk.'

All eyes had shifted to the man sitting on his own. Slowly, deliberately, he'd stood and carried the milk tin to Charlie, set it down before him and then put his hands together as if in prayer. 'It's all yours, Brother.'

With three whales to process before the day was out, the Friar hadn't had a moment to think about what had happened. His new name cast a different light on things too. Calling him 'Friar Tuck' made it clear he wasn't Owen any more; calling him 'Friar Tuck' closed the door on Annie and made it all right for the crew to joke with him again. So it had stuck. Friar Tuck he became and, more often than not, just the Friar.

Annie hadn't much liked the whaling. She'd liked fishing, but then there were so many fish, she'd say, just look at them all. She'd row out on a morning with three hooks on each line, throw them in and within minutes return with half a dozen cod still wriggling. It was like they wanted to be caught, and their deaths were mostly bloodless and quick. Whales were a different matter, Annie said; their size meant they were an almighty job to kill – there was violence involved and gallons of blood. Fishing Bay became an abattoir.

She'd gone off on her own once to do some twilight codding, and a whale had come out of nowhere, shouldering the water aside, pushing up against the dinghy like a recalcitrant dog. She'd been terrified but she'd had enough sense to start rowing for shore. The whale was not the usual humpback, she said, it was long and lean and pale, and it had stuck by her, measuring its speed to her speed, continuing on the clumsy course she was setting. When she was almost there, it had turned suddenly and headed back out of the bay at speed, towards the mouth of the channel and the deepening dusk. It spouted before it dived, and the vapour had been tall and alive with phosphorescence, lighting up the whole of the exposed body and half of the bay.

How long Annie had sat in the tilting boat, she couldn't say. It was as if (here Annie had blushed, he remembered, blushed!) the whale had wanted to communicate in some way. It had the whole of the ocean to choose, but it had followed her.

The Friar had laughed because he couldn't help himself. He knew for a fact, for he'd seen them dragged out through their gullets, how small a whale's brain was compared with its enormous body and how they weren't big enough in the midst of all the blubber to have anything much to *think* about let alone *say*. He couldn't believe Annie talking like that.

Not long after, he'd lost her. And how he hated now to think of the sound of his voice in that conversation and the way she'd skidded into silence and stayed there.

The Friar was drinking tea, standing outside his door, watching the sea lap on the beach and the sun lap at the tips of the hills surrounding the narrow bay. It wasn't enough to warm things yet, but the tea was doing a pretty good job on him. He could feel the creaminess in his throat warming him from the inside out, and the stewed bitterness of the tea leaves was enough to wake the dead. *The small pleasures, the things I still like.* It was going to be a good day in Fishing Bay.

He finished off the last drop, licked the lip of his cup and sighed. Smiler appeared beside him then and took the edge off things.

'Dog, you stink.'

Ben was picking his way between the Friar's bach and Jimmy's, looking skywards. 'It's another nice one,' he said.

'It certainly looks that way,' said the Friar, pushing Smiler away with his foot.

'Bloody oath, he smells bad. I saw him rolling in something down on the beach. Baby shark. There were a couple of them down there yesterday.' The boy was grinning at the dog as if he'd done something good for a change.

'That'd be right,' said the Friar and, stepping back through his door, he ran his hand down the hunk of bull kelp hanging there. He looked a moment at the moisture on his fingers. 'According to this, we're in for some rain. Doesn't say when it's coming, though.'

'Shame. I thought it was shaping up pretty nicely.'

The Friar took his cup to the sink, rinsed it and left it upside down on a clean bench. On the table was his pipe. But first he folded the letter he'd written that morning, pressing the single sheet firmly with the palm of his hand to make the creases. It wasn't a long one, he didn't have much to say these days. He slipped the pipe into his pocket.

'What do you think then? Whale today?' said Ben, as the Friar pulled the door shut. The boy was smiling, busy smoothing his hair at the front where he'd combed it and plastered it flat with water.

'I thought so when I woke up, I'm not so sure now,' said

the Friar, also managing a smile, not at the prospect of a whale but at the young man standing in front of him, a husband and father at twenty-two but still unsure how to deal with unruly hair and who'd asked every morning that week, with the same unrelenting enthusiasm, 'Whale today?' He was a tonic was Ben.

They walked along side by side with their hands deep in their pockets, one square and sturdy, the younger one tall and loose – so loose it looked sometimes as if he might drift to the side of the path and rest there. But still they matched step for step, the dog trotting behind them, along the small beach to the whaling station, stopping while Ben lit up, and then continuing to the collection of corrugated and wooden buildings huddled where the rock had been hacked to make room for them. The windows were open and they could hear three or four men yarning inside, Gunner out-talking the lot of them.

No one could talk louder or longer than Gunner. This was explained to everyone's satisfaction by the fact that his father had come from Italy. For that same reason, but with less evidence, the Friar believed, it was generally agreed that Gunner could sing. He was leaving the building now, cursing emphatically.

'Having a party without us?' said the Friar. 'Good thing Ben did his hair nice. I can't do a thing with mine, so the ladies will just have to take me as I am.' He took off his hat and exaggeratedly stroked the bare top of his head. The pipe smoke came in one long even stream from the side of his mouth.

Gunner was looking at the ground. 'We're not anywhere near ready. The equipment hasn't been fully checked, not everyone's out from town yet, there's no sign of Tommy, and my two lads are still in Picton trying to get the *Moana* fixed. First day back and we'll have whales lined up out of the bay waiting to be processed.'

He stalked off, his arms moving as if he were deep in conversation, and then stopped by the slipway. The Friar followed him. Gunner was looking down at the thick brown bull kelp moving just below the surface.

'You know, as far as I see it,' said the Friar slowly, 'it's been like this every year since you started out. Somehow we get there.'

'Somehow we get there.' Gunner tried each word and then smacked his lips as if they tasted all right to him. 'Yes. Yes. Of course. Of course. We get there.'

'First things first,' said the Friar. 'The digester and the boiler.' And he steered his boss towards the digesting room where Tommy was waiting for them.

'Are we winning?' said Gunner hopefully.

'Haven't even started,' said Tommy. 'Bugger of a job cleaning this thing up. Looks like it hasn't been touched since last winter.' He walked along the side of the digester – a vat, the height of two men – tapping the metal sides as he went. 'Chewing, vomiting, shitting thing, there must be a better way to get oil out of a whale.'

'You find it, Thomas, I'll buy it.' Gunner was proud of his digester, ridiculously so in the Friar's book. He was up close to it now, laying his hands on its iron flanks like a man with a thoroughbred.

'Good to see you, Tommy,' said Ben from the doorway. 'How's Picton been? Missed us?'

'Picton is Picton. It's best to be away from there for a while.'

'A girl,' said the Friar and Ben together.

Tommy closed his eyes in assent and mock exhaustion.

He wasn't what you'd call good-looking, his nose had been broken and mended askew, but what Tommy had was a large pair of eyes that seemed to do all the work for him.

'You need to settle down, lad,' said the Friar, slapping Tommy's back. 'Time to think about somebody else for a change.'

'That's just what I want, Friar. It's the ladies that don't want a man like me.'

'Who was it this time?'

'Trixie Bertram – a little pony. Lots of brown hair, kissable lips–' His eyes glittered. 'High pointy tits.' Tommy pitched the last words high, and mimed it to Ben who sniggered.

'What was that?' said Gunner, emerging from behind the digester. 'I missed it.'

'Tommy's new girl looks like a horse,' said the Friar.

'Hah!' said Gunner.

'A pony,' said Tommy, 'there's a world of difference.' Then he lowered his voice and indicated the others should come in closer. 'You know you're lucky I made it to Arapawa at all this year.'

'Go on,' said Ben.

'There's a saying in Picton: "Don't mess with Trixie Bertram – she's got too many brothers."'

'Never heard that one,' said Gunner, his ear to the flanks of the digester now. He thought he could hear a murmur in there like a weak heart or lung. 'Bertram,' he said, more to himself than anyone. 'I don't think I know the family at all.'

'The father owns the *Shearwater*,' said Tommy.

Gunner shook his head.

'All six of the sons work it with him. Anyway, I got an invite to a Sunday roast and I thought I had it made, but when I got there I could see it was going to be a hard road. Turns out each one of her brothers is built like King Dick – they had not a word to say between them, and took it in turns to watch my every mouthful. It was hard to swallow at first but I was able to ignore them after a bit in favour of the feast laid out by my blushing Trixie. There was a mountain of spuds, buckets of gravy, a whole pig with the *best* crackling.' Gunner and the Friar nodded: that wasn't bad at all. Ben's eyes were fixed on Tommy. 'Trouble is, Trixie probably talked the leg off that pig we ate. Her mother's the same. And they don't say anything in all that noise.' Tommy sighed – for Trixie or because of her, it was hard to tell. 'She wears me out.'

Ben and Gunner and the Friar exploded then with laughter so loud the digester seemed to swallow it into its bowels and spit it back out on to the concrete walls. Get Tommy back to Picton for the summer and he always came back with more than enough stories for the hundred days of whaling.

'Susan and the baby all right?' asked Tommy at last.

'They're apples, mate,' said Ben. 'I just hope my little Emily doesn't turn out like that Trixie. It's a mean trick of God's, a beautiful woman with a runaway tongue.'

Tommy nodded.

'Except for the roast, of course. If Em grows up able to make a good pork roast, I'll be a happy man.'

'. . . happy man,' echoed Tommy, blinking.

'Susan says to come for tea,' said Ben, suddenly remembering.

'I'll be there.'

Gunner sat down heavily on a benzine box by the water, gesturing for the Friar to do the same. The Friar pulled out his pipe and started scraping it. Gunner put the makings for his cigarettes on his lap.

'How many years has it been?'

The Friar said nothing and didn't look up.

Gunner pulled out a single paper and tapped a line of tobacco along it. 'Eleven, twelve years? If you ask me, it's not just the young ones need to have a face to look at on the other side of the bed.'

There was no sound at all for the moment except the slop of sea at the foot of the whale ramp. The Friar stopped with his thumb in his pipe.

'It isn't my business, but you're not short on advice when I need it,' said Gunner. 'Have you thought it might be time for you to shift your boat from that wharf you're tied to?'

The Friar looked at his friend as he rolled his cigarette tight and licked it closed. He couldn't think when Gunner had needed anyone's advice on anything. He had a good wife, two strapping sons in Charlie and Stew, a grandchild on the way at last, and a successful whale business. If small things did go wrong, it didn't take much to set Gunner right. A smoke or a drink would do or, even better, a spot of goat-shooting up on the ridge. The Friar liked this about him, and not replying just then wasn't because he was uncomfortable with the line the conversation was taking; it was just that he had nothing useful to say. Gunner knew how long it had been as well as he did.

The Friar began filling his pipe while Gunner flipped the cigarette into his mouth and lit it. One hand in his pocket holding the lighter, he nodded mildly in the Friar's direction, his eyebrows raised and waiting for a reply. When there wasn't one, he cleared his throat.

'My father used to say: *Bacco, tabacco e venere riducono l'uomo in cenere* – wine, women and tobacco reduce a man to ashes.'

Gunner released the smoke in small puffs. 'He had a bad run of luck, though. The family fishing business and all his brothers destroyed by a storm, and then his fiancée gives his ring back. So he sails away through the Straits of Messina and a year later washes up at the ends of the earth. *Alla fine del mondo* you can't go any further, you just have to stop where you are and hope your troubles don't come after you.' Gunner jabbed at the air in front of him. 'The point is, he didn't let them come after him. He moved on and made himself a new life. When he discovered the sardines round here, he started fishing again and never looked back.' Gunner loosened his legs; his cigarette had gone out. He lit it again and huffed the smoke out over the water. 'Then I came along and found bigger fish to fry.' He chuckled. It was an old joke of his but a good one.

The Friar took a moment to light up, then a moment or two longer to be sure the pipe was under way. 'If you hear of any wharves with room for a leaky old boat, let me know.'

'Hah! Good on you!'

Their eyes met, and the two men grinned frankly at each other. Just then the Friar's pipe fired and he sucked on the stem as if his life depended on it.

As soon as they heard the thud of small boots on the hard earth outside the building, they all knew they were finished with waiting. It was the quick and insistent nature of them – whoever wore those boots had something to say. But it was Gunner who yelled the words, his hand on the shoulder of the small boy beside him: 'There she blows!'

They ran then – the four men setting up the whale station, and Jimmy, Gunner's driver – and as they ran, they laughed and shouted things that didn't make much sense, and jostled each other for the sake of jostling, and Gunner was shouting louder than the rest, and little Billy Prideaux ran behind them, silent and proud. The Friar slowed down a little to get his breath back and then walked the rest of the way to the end of the whaling station where its nose faced into Tory Channel. There, standing on the rocks, the men fell quiet, craning their heads to see what was happening across the heaving channel water, up on the highest point of the narrow spit of land across from them, Lookout Hill.

Old Jock was over there. If he was standing with his back to them and Tory Channel, he'd be looking into the Pacific Ocean. They couldn't see it, but they knew it was there. That heaving, breathing expanse of blue water would be stretched outwards like a dog in the sun to the promise of the tropics in the north, South America in the east and Antarctica in the south. More than likely, though, Jock was turned side on to them with his eyes scanning the brew of Cook Strait. He wouldn't think to turn and look inside the channel.

'Nothing,' said Gunner, and with that he ran for the *Balaena*, bellowing for Jimmy to join him. They'd go anyway and trust what the boy said he saw. Gunner hadn't checked everything over or readied the boxline, he'd have to do that out in the channel, but at least he wouldn't have to do it in open waters. If the boy was right, the whale was close by.

'Light a fire!' bawled Gunner over his shoulder.

'Tell the wife!' cried Jimmy, his red hair flaring and his face with it. Any excitement or exertion and you could count on him to go the colour of a boiled crayfish.

The Friar caught up with Tommy down on the beach scrabbling for driftwood with everyone else. He started telling him what needed to be done with the boiler, but he could see the boy wasn't listening. First they'd light a fire to signal to Jock there was a whale out there, then they'd see to the boiler. The roar of the whale chaser as it plunged from its mooring made the Friar turn. There was Jimmy at the wheel, rolling his eyes, and Gunner beside him, his hand held over his head and clenched in a fist. The Friar lifted his arm in reply.

The driftwood had already been gathered into a pile on the beach and Ben was throwing on the kerosene. Just moments after the boat crew had gone, the fire was lit.

Billy started throwing small stones from his pocket into the water.

At last, there it was, pulled tight by the growing wind.

'The flag!' cried Billy. 'He's seen it! He's seen the whale!'

And then the first wisps of smoke curled upwards from Lookout Hill. Like their fire, bold and furious now, Jock's signal fire told where the whale was. It was facing into the channel.

'She's here,' said Ben. 'She's come in from the strait.'

'I told you,' said Billy. And Ben squeezed his shoulder.

'Easy pickings,' said the Friar, smacking his lips.

Without warning, the whale heaved itself up into the air. Almost all of its great body was thrust free – gleaming and spilling and streaming with seawater, crusty with two-foot-wide barnacles, its white belly and corrugated throat laid bare. Two long fins, almost a third of its body length, were thrust out either side as if to pull the whale up from the deep water. Its head was pointed towards the sky and, like an afterthought on a body that size, Lilian could just see one watchful eye. For a moment, the whale balanced on its tail, as if it could stay there all day, then slowly and with apparent relish it flipped sideways, a perfect curve that became a free-fall, ending with the whole of the giant body smashing into the water.

Lilian had to put her hands out to steady herself. Her head was light. She closed her eyes and then opened them. Breathing deeply, she caught the scent of the gorse and the tang of sheep. Steady, now. It was something to do with the fresh gate, the injured knee, the worry about Billy, the vertigo – all had unbalanced her somehow and left her feeling anxious. And then there was the whale she'd seen and the eye of the whale. She needed to get home and treat her leg and rest a while. Billy was a one running off like that.

Lilian began walking again.

She knew before she heard a sound that it was coming, and then through the gap in the gorse she saw the *Balaena* careering out of Fishing Bay and into Tory Channel. Once, she'd have run up the hill with the other women to sit and watch a whale hunt close to home. They'd made a sport of tracking the chasers and picking out the men on deck – tiny and emphatic when the light was good, they'd fade to almost nothing at dusk. Then in those last moments before darkness fell, when their eyes knew nothing for sure and Iris would bleat 'They've lost it', the chasers and whale would blend and the whale hunters would become whale riders. It was Iris who'd declare it so, sighing and flapping her hand in front of her face as if chasing moths. Huddled together against the evening chill, the other women would nudge each other and giggle like girls. Lilian had thought nothing of it at the time. It was just what you did when the whales came.

Nearing the end of the track, she heard a cheer over by the whaling station, and across the channel she saw the flag, and smoke from the Lookout signal fire. They'd seen it, then.

The baches were in front of her; she could hear the sounds

of the whaling station starting up, the cluck of chickens, a baby crying. Lilian moved as quickly as she could with her sore leg, her head tipped forward and her scarf like a hood obscuring most of her face. Susan and Ben's house was behind and a little apart from the others, and she was nearly there. Billy was waiting at the path his sister had made with shells and stones. His face was flushed and he grinned when he saw her hurrying unevenly towards him.

'It was me,' he said. 'I told them.'

One thing Lilian knew for sure as Susan cleaned her knee was that as soon as the whale had been called, Ed had begun running – running and every muscle taut, running and his body powerful again, running down to the sea, the gorse breaking under his feet. And he was probably already on the water, rowing like six men, nearly out to the chaser moored in the bay.

Soon she would hear the engine gunning, and then the rocky finger of land they lived on would clench itself into a fist and punch the men and their boats into battle.

3

Susan made tea. Lilian sat with her head propped on the open palm of her good hand, watching her daughter. Susan's hair had once been so lush and heavy she'd complained of a headache if it was tied up for long. Now, in Lilian's opinion, it was fly-away and cut too short. And the dress she was wearing wasn't long for the ragbag either. Susan put the tea things on the table, tucked her hair behind her ears three times, then stooped to pick up Emily from her cradle. There were biscuits Lilian didn't recognise and a slab of pale, almost fruitless fruit cake.

'Give her to me,' said Lilian, holding out her arms and already rising to her feet.

But Susan was settling them both in the rocking chair. She smiled vaguely up at her mother and yawned. 'She needs a feed. Why don't you pour me a cuppa?'

And Susan sighed then, and her eyes rolled back in the way young mothers do when they are able to stop a moment but all they really want – are crying out for – is to go to bed and sleep for a month.

'Let's give it a minute.' Lilian put her hands on the tea cosy and felt the warmth of the pot. The house was cold – did they not have enough coal for the stove? Lilian could see dirt under her fingernails and in the cracks around one of her thumbs – it looked almost impossible to shift. The skin on the back of her hands was loose and discoloured. She removed them from the teapot and went to get up.

Susan was watching her. 'Are you all right, Mum?'

'I'm fine, love.'

'Ben should take you home in the dinghy.'

'I'm fine, love. Really.'

Lilian went over to the sink. There was a slab of soap and a small wooden brush. She started with her nails and then moved on to the rest of her hands, carefully avoiding the sore palm which Susan had dressed. She dried each hand carefully and held them to her face to smell the freshness. Better.

Susan was still watching her when she turned around.

Billy had been joined on the beach by the four children who lived in Fishing Bay. The Friar had seen them gather around the bonfire, and despite the work crying out to be done he'd stayed outside by the ramp, turning his pipe over in his pocket and watching them play. It was a favourite game of theirs; the Friar had played it himself as a boy. The first one to spot the incoming whale called out 'Thar she blows!' and the prize was the best skimming stone to be found. Everyone knew Billy usually won.

It was going to be a long wait, and soon the children would tire of the game and head off round the rocks with sharp sticks to harpoon the bull kelp. They'd tried cooking it on a fire and eating it once, but everyone had run away screaming after the first bite – except for Billy. Today, it looked like they were listening to the story of the whale he'd spotted, because he was gesturing to the sea and spreading his arms wide.

The boy's mother mustn't be far away.

Fishing his pipe out, the Friar tried to relight it. She wouldn't come down to the beach, not if she could help it. He'd heard the young jokers talking about her, and the names they had. They clearly thought he was a deaf old fool or they wouldn't have been talking quite so loud – either that or the pipe smoke must sometimes render him invisible. But surely that was her, close by, calling Billy's name? The surprise of it made the Friar step back suddenly. Did she know he was there? He couldn't see her yet, but her voice was so close. It was difficult to move without drawing attention to himself. The rest of the men were inside preparing for the whale and he was the only one standing here like a tick on a hairless dog.

She was walking tentatively along the beach, stooped against the weather. He couldn't see her face because her scarf was pulled forward. She stumbled again, and he stood stock still. Could she see? No, that wasn't a stumble. She was limping slightly. What had happened?

She stopped, and was calling the boy again. She had to call three or four times before he came. Billy's voice was sharp with disappointment and became clearer as they walked towards the whale station.

'We only just got here.'

'It's my leg, Billy.'

'I didn't do any fishing.'

'You can do it later, love, off the wharf.'

'Can I row then?'

'No, it's too rough for you. Ben should be able to take us. You go and ask him.'

Billy looked up and saw the Friar. He rolled his eyes and the Friar stared for a moment before he thought to wink. She didn't look; she stayed like that with her head turned away.

The whaler slipped through the doorway into the digester room. 'Your mother-in-law wants you,' he said to Ben, and Ben looked blank for a moment before he went to see.

In the dinghy, Lilian and Ben talked about the wind getting up. Billy trailed one hand in the sea and flicked stones from his pockets with the other.

'We'll ask Sarge if he'll take you out fishing,' said Lilian, patting his leg. 'You enjoyed it last time. I might even come too.'

'I don't want to fish with Sarge.'

By the time they reached the edge of the bay and Ben started to pull round the point, the wind was pushing hard against them. It was a flood tide too and seawater was pouring into the channel, gallons and gallons of it, pouring into the cups of the small bays, pushing hard against the bow of the rowboat. It was hard to keep going forward, but Ben braced his feet and pulled harder on the oars, his whole body leaning to it. Billy still had his arm over the side, but he made a face at last and pulled it in.

Lilian was relieved to be out of Fishing Bay and on her way home. Above her, she could see only a ribbon of blue sky left like the slick of still water behind a whale. Everywhere else was heavy, restless cloud. She pushed her head back as far as it would go to put pressure on her neck which was aching too now. It helped a little.

'Doesn't know whether it's going to laugh or cry,' she murmured. And almost immediately it started to cry.

4

Williwaws. The manic winds sucked mouthfuls of seawater and spat them back, sucked again and spat them back, dropped to an eerie calm and then resumed their frenzy. There were twenty-foot-high plumes of water like the exhalations of a dozen whales, and out of the white-out the whale chaser came, dark green and sleek as a seal.

'Mother of God!' cried Sarge, his hands gripping the wheel of the *Chance*, his mouth as wide as it would go, his head tossed back on his neck. Roaring through the rough water, knifing the flood tide, leaving the water on the back of a wave to meet the air head on. What a beauty.

Sarge was in the cockpit, the kauri deck at chest height, a small window between him and his gunner. He embraced the helm and embraced the boat, the noise and size of him almost overpowering the roar of the engine at his feet.

Ed, kneeling on the deck while he prepared his weapons, was closed and silent. His oilskin flapped like a wing, his wide-brimmed felt was tucked low; and though he couldn't see his face, Sarge knew his gunner's mouth would be as tight as a bird's. Ed was coiling twenty-five fathoms of boxline in front of the harpoon gun which was fixed to the deck beside him but able to swivel wherever his hands wanted it to go.

There was nothing between him and the sea except the spray that stung his face and hands. Wiping his eyes, Ed checked the run of the rope – the tail end of the three hundred fathoms of line that lay below deck. Then, body braced, feet straddling, Ed addressed the harpoon gun. He opened the breach and fed in a brass shell filled with blasting powder, then pushed a wad of newspaper down inside the gun barrel to give the shell something to work off. He slid the harpoon in next and swivelled the whole thing into position, its aim just to one side of the bow.

They were well out of the bay and in the middle of Tory Channel, and it had started to rain. Sarge had stopped laughing. He could see the *Nautilus* still hadn't made its way out of Tar'white two bays along, and they'd lost sight of Gunner and Jimmy who'd taken the *Balaena* deep inside the channel. What they needed to know was where in all this water the whale was. Out in Cook Strait, they had eye contact with Lookout Hill and could see the fire Jock had built there to show them where to go. A fire to the right and that was the way to turn the boats; up high and they had to come in. Inside the narrow neck of Tory Channel, the Lookout was fast receding and Cook Strait had gone from view. It was up to them.

Ed was oblivious. Half-crouched, his legs apart, his knees taking the thrust of the boat, he laid the wires from three hand-bombs along the deck to Sarge. Then, slowly and methodically, he checked everything once more. He refused to hurry.

Sarge was laughing again by the time his gunner had finished. Despite the wild waves and the spray, he'd spotted the whale spouting, and he was pushing the boat towards it. It was the bushy spout of the humpback. He called Ed's name once, sharply like the bark of a seal, and when Ed turned, Sarge pointed.

It didn't take long. Five or six minutes and the whale was back at the surface, exhaling softly into the cold air just ahead and to the right of them. Ed braced himself against the movement of the boat, holding the harpoon gun in position, content that everything was perfectly ready, and laughed as Sarge had done. 'It's coming,' he called. 'It's coming.' And unless the other chasers got there fast, it was all theirs.

Ed's right hand went out to show Sarge where to go and he leaned his whole body back, preparing to take the kick from the gun when it fired. Sarge pulled the boat to starboard, slowed down and peered forward. Ed released his left hand and indicated Sarge needed to take the chaser back a little more. Then he clasped the gun again, his body a counterweight.

There it was, the familiar broad head with the double air holes like massive nostrils and the back with its finger-like fin. The big man let out a whoop and punched the steering wheel. As if echoing him, the massive black and white patterned tail with its nicks and tears slapped the water sharply three times before the whale rounded up and disappeared below the choppy water.

Bugger, thought Sarge, he knows we're on to him. Big fella, too. A good ten foot longer than the chaser – he'd measure forty-six foot at least. Hah! Probably not a fella then after all.

Ed was leaning forward again, still attached to his gun, looking for the smooth circles the tail leaves on the surface. He patted his right hand downwards, telling Sarge to slow. They would wait.

Within seconds, it surfaced again behind them. Sarge had seen the shadow rising, and he grabbed the wheel and hit the throttle before it let go its first spout. Ed's head snapped around, and he muttered something Sarge couldn't hear but could guess at. For a brief moment, he saw the gunner's face – eyes narrowed to a point, lips set in something approaching a snarl. The whale started to panic. It took off, and Ed told Sarge to do the same, rotating his hand at shoulder height as fast as it would go. This was the fun part. The driver accelerated; water shot up over the bow and flooded the deck. They were as wet as west coast wetas. They were on the tail of a whale. Life was a fine thing.

Any other gunner would have looked back briefly to share the moment with the driver but Ed didn't work like that. It didn't bother Sarge. Friends since they got big enough to work out how to climb the fence between their two properties, Sarge knew Ed as a single-minded gunner and a private man who'd learnt the hard way that it was best to keep yourself to yourself. None of this being cobbers on shore after a hard day's hunting, sharing a beer or playing a hand of cards.

Slower. Ed was patting down towards the deck. The whale had sounded again and all they could see was water. Sarge slowed. They'd followed the whale a long way into Tory Channel and it was tired; it wouldn't go far. Then Sarge heard a chaser hurtling in at port: the *Balaena* had turned back and was a mile away, approaching fast. He heaved the *Chance* in the direction of the whale.

The second the whale was up again, it started to heave around haphazardly in the water. 'Fasten the bastard,' Sarge muttered, pulling the chaser in as close as it would go. Ed was tugging at the brim of his hat to get some of the rain off his eyes. It seemed to be difficult for him to get a fix.

Sarge held the chaser where he was told, just behind and to the left of the whale. Over-run it and it would turn. Ed was good at judging these things, and Sarge trusted him to do it right, but at the same time he was getting impatient. 'Fasten it,' he hissed into the air, 'fasten it.' The *Balaena* was closing in.

All at once, Sarge heard the spark hit the powder, felt the gun recoil, saw Ed recoil, saw a flash of harpoon in the air, saw it flash above the bare black back of the retreating whale, knew without seeing that it had pierced the giant's skin and bank of blubber. The harpoon head exploded on impact and Sarge howled. Shuddering, slowing, the whale paused a moment as if its great body needed to absorb what had happened before it could continue. Neither man moved. Blood darkened the water. Then, all of a sudden, the massive tail flukes flipped up like arms in surrender and Ed was whirling, grabbing and dropping a bomb, his fingers wet, gripping now, throwing. Hard.

The flukes slapped the water, just in front of the chaser, and the whale sounded. It was gone, and the bomb had missed.

The boxline was still attached to the harpoon and running freely along the deck and out into the sea, and Sarge was using his hands to break the speed of it around the loggerhead beside him. His skin was chafing but it wasn't the fastest he'd seen – there'd been times the rope had caught fire. Sarge guessed the harpoon was lodged somewhere near the base of the whale's tail, which was like shooting a dog in the bum.

Ed had pulled in the bomb that missed and was getting another one ready. He turned and caught Sarge's eye. They were both thinking the same thing: where were the other two chasers when you needed them?

When it surfaced, the whale was heading back to the mouth of the bay, back out into the channel. Sarge was on to it. He pulled the chaser round and drew it in close and steady. It was an easy shot: Ed let go the second bomb, and the moment it hit the back of the neck Sarge touched the contacts together to fire the explosives. The great beast convulsed. Waves heaved around the *Chance*, and Ed and Sarge hung on, but the whale wasn't done yet. Incredibly, it started to move again and Ed scrabbled to ready another bomb. *Close in*, he gestured to Sarge. Alert to trouble, the driver came in as close as he could to the dying whale and held it there as best he could for Ed to drive the third bomb into its side.

The whale breached. It reared up, its flippers outstretched, embracing the sea and the hills. Sarge hadn't seen that before, not in its death throes, and it seemed to him that the flippers were like the wings of a giant angel. It gave him pause, but the thought just as swiftly left him. For the angel had gone, it had fallen on its side on to the surface of the water and was floating there, bleeding. The same exulting, pirouetting whale Lilian had seen while the day was still fresh exhaled one last time.

Ed thrust in the air-spear. Sarge pressed the compressor pedal and air flooded down the hose with a hiss. No longer sleek or beautiful, the carcass floated buoyed by compressed air, its skin puckered with rain.

The *Balaena* pulled up beside them, and then the *Nautilus*. The crew's faces were red with cold and irritation.

'What's the hurry?' called Gunner. He pinched his eyes and squinted. 'Well, it's a bloody good size. The *Moana*'s not back from Picton yet. You okay getting it in on your own?'

Ed looked back at his driver. 'What do you reckon?'

5

Annie. Annie. Annie. He'd call her name three times, four times, five times and still she wouldn't come. Annie. It's me. *Annie*. They were far enough from anyone, at the place he'd taken her to, at the far end of Tar'white, which was at the far end of Fishing Bay and even further from Whekenui and Okukari: too far for anyone to hear him calling.

As the Friar remembered it, when Annie came to Tar'white the other families were in the process of moving back to Fishing Bay for the whale season. Dick Groves stayed because he always stayed, but he was across the other side of the bay and as deaf as a doorpost. The Friar hadn't wanted to move anywhere. He much preferred to row round to the whale station every morning and back again at night and have Annie to himself. In all honesty, they didn't have a choice, but he liked to think they did.

He'd worried about her, of course he had, on her own all day, nothing around her but the scrubby hillside and the tide scouring the beach. Would she hurt herself and there'd be no one there to help? Where did she go when he wasn't at home? Each time he returned to an empty house, his heart would leap to his throat. Checking the beach and then climbing the track calling her, he would struggle to keep calm. And just when he was thinking the worst, he'd hear something like, 'Yes, that's me, and who might you be?' In that teasing way she had, her voice like the small stream that gave the bay its name. Te Awaiti. Dick Groves had told him what the name meant, and he should know. Five generations of his family had lived in the bay, from before the time of the first white settlers and the first whale station, before the first whales most likely. Dick never used the name Tar'white; he said the name was pig-Maori and meant nothing at all.

'It's Owen,' he'd say – who else could he be? – and she'd send his name back to him. Not 'O-when' as the whalers said it, or 'Say-when' as they preferred it to be when they were downing a few; what Annie said was close to 'Own', with the smallest trip between the w and the n. He remembered the time she'd laughed and pulled him to her: 'Now, what can I do with a name like that?'

'My mother called me Owny.'

'Well,' she said, 'I am not your mother. It will have to stay as it is until I think of something else.' And there'd been a moment. 'But I like Annie, it makes me feel a different person. Younger,' she'd giggled, 'and sweeter.' She'd whistled the last word through the small gap in her teeth, and he'd felt the giggle rather than heard it, for he was lying against her chest. He was so close to the inner workings of her body he could hear the small but certain whooshes of her heart. 'My mother will be turning in her grave, though.'

'She wouldn't like "Annie"?'

'She believed you should use the names your parents gave you – not chop them up or garnish them like a fancy dinner.'

'If you're mutton, you stay mutton,' he said, and he felt her smile. It was the way her muscles loosened under his cheek.

'Never lamb,' she said. 'Or Johnny or Al or Madge. Even if people insisted, even if that was the only name they'd known, my mother would change it back to its original *mutton*. She believed – and would tell people without hesitation – that the devil resided in decoration, and it wasn't just the names. We had the plainest house in the whole of Picton: there were no frills on our net curtains, no cushions on our lounge suite. My hair was scraped back into plaits that were like weapons they were pulled so tight.'

Annie had tightened up again too, and the Friar watched her hand as she talked – open, shut, cupped. He liked the way her hands were square and compact, and useful.

'I always had one curl by my left ear that would resist her,' Annie said. 'She tried clipping it and wetting it with spit or water or whatever came to hand, but when it dried, there it was again.' Annie said nothing for a moment, and then her hand opened and she started slowly stroking his hair. 'You know, one day she grabbed the curl and pulled me into the kitchen. She hacked at it with a bread knife until it came away in her hand, and then she threw it on the fire.' Annie took her hand away and he was sure her heart missed a beat or maybe her movement covered up the sound. 'It sizzled to nothing. She'd nicked my scalp. There was blood. It dried all around and inside my ear and I picked it off for days.'

He didn't know what to say to that. It was told so matter-of-factly; she seemed so fine. 'So now you don't like to tie it up too tightly.'

'Yes. That's it.' She sounded surprised. 'My mother got something wrong with her throat in the end. She couldn't speak, she could only swallow, loudly like water draining. I hated being at home with that, so I'd go roaming and stay out until I was too hungry to stay out any more. It was worth the hidings.'

There were times when Annie didn't call out, when he'd felt absolutely certain she'd changed her mind and taken the track home. But somehow he always found her, and somehow she always seemed surprised. 'Were you calling me? I didn't hear a thing.' She kept him on his toes all right.

Once he chanced upon her and she didn't know it. He'd gone straight up from the bach, quite a way up the hillside, and was making his way back. And then there she was, less than ten feet away, facing away from him, squatting behind a gorse bush, the dark green of her dress tucked up so anyone could see, by way of contrast, her white thighs which were surprisingly heavy and dimpled. The back of her neck looked pale too against that dress, and had the look of something plucked, the way the fine hairs were pulled upwards and twisted loosely into a single clip high on her head. His nostrils caught the sharp tang of urine and he heard the rush of her water.

It didn't feel right spying on her like this, and yet the Friar felt it was she who really offended the natural order. Squatting animal-like, she was not the woman he knew who held her head a certain way and who undressed in the dark, her clothes making muted sounds as they fell. He hadn't seen the way her thighs bloomed from her body like that, not really.

It seemed a dog's age before she finished, and then she was jiggling a little, and standing. She had her back to him and her legs apart, and she fanned the skirt of her dress in front of her as if drying herself off. She started walking down the track.

It was a moment before he realised. She hadn't reached down to pull anything up; she'd just walked away, her dress swinging slightly and, he imagined, a little damply. He started to move then, almost sliding down the track after her, past the steaming urine and the flattened grass. Calling her name, again.

6

The end of the day, and the coal range was cooling and hissing and ticking, dampered down for the night. Lit at first light before she fed the chickens, it had burned all day, and here was Lilian for the first time sitting in front of it. She had the stove door open, watching the coal burn down.

Billy was in bed, tucked up and fast asleep. The dishes were cleared and the mutton stew was cooling on the bench. Lilian's hands as she sat in the old chair were loose, her wrists resting on the wide wooden arms where you could leave a cup of tea and not be concerned. With the lamps unlit, the room faded off into darkness. She could read, she had mending to do, but Ed still hadn't returned and the air seemed thinner and less reliable without him. She was all right in the day, but when whaling took Ed away after dark the air would stretch and wheeze in an alarming fashion and she was unable to concentrate. She hated the risks the whaling crews took on a dark ocean in a heavy wind. But they'd say the whale was at the end of a rope and it would be a crime not to finish it off, or they'd be out so far that even if they turned back in daylight they wouldn't be home until after dark. All she could do was sit as she was now, staring at the dying coal, the house neat as a pin.

Ben would have told him of her fall, no doubt, but he'd have said she was fine and not to worry. Which was true, Lilian supposed. She was fine, only knocked about a bit. She'd told Ben to go, even though he'd offered to stay, and had deliberately waved and smiled as he'd rowed away. Now Ed would be coming in the door soon and she wondered if he'd be concerned. She suspected not. He'd have himself to think about: stiff with cold and wringing wet, salt brine flaking from his cheeks.

Every season he took on the guise of a whale to fight a whale, perpetually sluiced and sodden, looking at the world through a curtain of water. He even rubbed whale oil into his coat and boots, which seemed to Lilian to be as much a way of disguising himself as a method of waterproofing. Despite Ed's best efforts, his feet would be pallid and wrinkled, and while he was waiting for the bathwater to heat he'd sit on his chair and put them up for her to tend. In the early days, Lilian used to rub them dry with a towel and tuck them under her blouse to warm them with her skin. She couldn't think when she'd stopped doing that thing with his feet. Maybe it was the small children needing her, and it was easier just to give him a bowl of hot water and Epsom salts instead. Maybe it was just the way things became.

Ed never had much to say about the hunt, but he had even less with his feet in the hot water. He'd sit there while she busied herself readying his bath. 'How many this time?' she'd say over her shoulder in the same way she'd throw a towel there, and the answer from him would be brief. If she felt like pressing, he'd come up with a tale about the hunt, like the one about the whale cow they'd killed out by Lucky Point and the bull that had stayed with her even as the first harpoon pierced its skin. 'A cow wouldn't do that,' Ed would tell her as if he'd never told her before. 'Kill a bull in a pair of whales and the cow is off to save her own skin.' The story seemed, perversely, to please him.

They'd hauled this one through the dusk. Lilian had been outside pulling up carrots when she'd seen them silent on the water far below. The rain had gone and the sun was coming through in the final minutes of the day as if cheering them in, and there on the back of that broad sea was the small but powerful *Chance* dragging the whale behind it.

It was the whale she'd seen dancing on the water. It wasn't the whale she'd seen dancing on the water. It was the whale she'd seen dancing on the water. It wasn't the whale she'd seen dancing on the water. And the light was dancing on the water, and the water was dancing on the water, and the boat and the whale and the slender shapes of the men on board were all broken into strips by the sharp light, and it was as if each of the separate pieces were dissolving in front of her. Lilian's eyes had hurt, and her knee had hurt, but she'd been unable to look away.

They'd be well past the bride cut now. Blankets of blubber would be peeled off as the moon rose and giant fillets would be hacked from the whale skeleton. Then the digester would do its job, and what a stink there would be as the mess of blubber and guts and bones was ground up and boiled into a giant stew. She'd smell it up here. Everyone on this part of the island would smell it, in the air, in their clothes, in the tiny hairs on the backs of their hands. And by morning there'd be oil.

It helped Lilian while she waited for Ed to think of their family. She knew by now Billy had probably kicked off his quilt in the next bedroom, and at the bottom of the hill Susan would have done the same, especially without Ben in bed next to her to hold on to it. Her son-in-law would be feeding the digester still, blank with tiredness. Over in Picton, Jenny would be tucked up in her aunt's spare room with its faded bedding and seafaring pictures on the walls and nothing of Jenny except for three books from home and a hairbrush with her mother's initials on the back. On the other side of Cook Strait, Micky's face would be crushed into his pillow, an alarm set for an early start at the fish shop, his trousers ready to step into on the floor by his bed. How little she knew them all, really.

It was time to bring Jenny home, she thought, using her good hand to pull her chair in closer to the range. She's missing me. I'm missing her. She could do the lessons again with Billy. It would be no different teaching two. She should never have listened to Ada about the girl going to school. What did her sister know, for goodness' sake? She had no children of her own. And Micky. Lilian wished she could bring Micky home now too, just write to him and tell him it was time. But Ed would have a thing or two to say about that.

Lilian had no sense of how much Ed missed the children when they weren't with them, for he never said. When he was away fighting and they were courting, his postcards had been only four lines or five, and one of the lines was always the same: *I miss you* – three small words on their own. And the three small words had given her an unexpected glimpse of his feelings and saved those postcards from being a disappointment. The rest was written as if writing were something new to him and he had to try it out first on simple things. He always put in a word about his brother Jack and his cousin Owen. Sarge he didn't mention until later. And there could be something about what they got to eat, getting her nice letter, no complaints. Then *I-miss-you*, those three words chained together like buoys, stopping each other floating away, giving her hope, anchored to the single word below: *Ed*.

When he'd returned from the Great War, he hadn't gone home to his island but had come straight to her house, walking from the wharves of Picton with her letters in his kit bag and a proposal of marriage tied up in his tongue. She'd said 'Yes' just like that, and laughed, and said 'Yes' again. He'd laughed too, deep in his throat, surprising her, and looked at her in that way he had, with a small frown as if he were listening closely to every word. 'I-missed-you,' he said, but she knew what he meant. She'd allowed her hand to reach up and touch his fresh-shaved face, the dark skin shiny with cold. She liked his shyness and the height of him and the way he had to bend to kiss her. But she was slightly unsettled to see his eyes gazing back like that. Lilian had forgotten the way he looked at things; she'd forgotten a lot about him, in fact.

They'd been married the following week, Lilian dressed in something blue her best friend Jeannie had lent her and, draped over her shoulder, her dead mother's dark red fox fur. After the ceremony, Lilian had packed her things in a portmanteau, the fox fur last of all, and she'd gone with Ed the two-hour boat ride to the island where his family had lived and farmed and caught whales for almost a century.

There was a lot Ed hadn't told her. The bach up the track from the beach at Whekenui Bay was barely more than two rooms back then, and had no electricity and no toilet to speak of. All it had was a beckoning view of the sea. She'd stood there in the middle of the lounge, her things unpacked all around her, unable to speak or cry or even look at him, twisting the fox fur in her hands as if strangling it over and over.

After a while, Lilian had taken the ridiculous fur with its sneering face and hung it at the back of the big oak wardrobe in what was to be their bedroom. She'd never worn it again.

Lilian kneaded her knee gently with her hand in the hope of diffusing the ache in there. Not only had the fall made her anxious but it seemed to have softened her mind. Fancy thinking about her wedding! Jeannie's dress. The fox. What good did that do her or anyone? The past was best left where it was.

Lilian regretted not having made a poultice for her leg when she'd returned home, but she'd been so weary. It was stopping for the day and sitting down that she'd started to really notice it. There was no doubt she'd been lucky, though – and what a throwaway word that was for all the weight it carried. It said things could have gone either way but for some flick of the tail of chance, and the word itself sounded like the flick of the tail, not the weight of disaster that she'd avoided.

She still wondered why there were some who'd called Ed Lucky when she'd first come to Arapawa and then just as quickly stopped. She'd assumed at first it had come from her husband's luck with the whales, but then she realised from something his mother said that it was a new name to him that had come out of the War. There had been an uncomfortable aspect to it, and no stories attached. Just a stiffening around his lips when it was used. She'd understood Ed wasn't the sort to have a nickname, but then there it was: Lucky. She'd liked the comradeship it implied and the lightness in its construction that wasn't present in the bare bones of Ed. She'd laughed up at her husband, relieved to find out this thing, waiting for an explanation. But there was none forthcoming. Later, she'd tried it herself, tentatively. And his lips had tightened to white.

'Ed will do,' was what he'd said.

With that, Lilian fell fast asleep, upright in her chair, her head bent towards her chest as if she were listening to it.

7

Micky was the only one on the deck of the *Tamahine*, his hands in his pockets and his hat low over his face, apparently oblivious to the whip of wind and rain in the rising dark.

'Picton,' he said under his breath. What kind of a name was that? It was what his Nana called a tick-tock of a town. Tick and you were in it, tock and you were out. It was trapped between the water of the Sounds and the surrounding hills, and both the southerly and the nor'wester were relentless in seeking it out. There was barely a day when they weren't scratching and poking and prodding.

Micky had passed the whale station an hour ago and seen an outline of activity in the dusk. Smelt the smell of boiled whale, of naked industry, of bare hills. Wondered again why he'd come. He'd asked to be let off at the entrance to Tory Channel, but the letter must have gone astray because there was no one out there to meet him. The boat waited ten minutes and then continued to steam its way to Picton.

In Wellington, thought Micky, lighting another cigarette in the cup of his hand hard up against the cabin wall, you felt the energy the minute you got off the boat. People moved faster and thought faster, and when they got to the end of a road they'd insist on building a new one to take them around the next corner or over the next rise. No turning back and shaking their heads, *oh well*. Everywhere in the capital you could see where the shape of the hills had been changed to put in houses and roads, where soil and rocks had been dumped into the harbour to make more flat land for ship cargo and shops and offices. Nothing was the same from one day to the next. Coming home now, after a whole year away, Micky knew he'd find everything exactly as he'd left it. God knows why he was going back. Probably the same reason he'd stayed on deck for the trip over, his eyes picking over the surface of the sea like a wool-buyer.

The ferry berthed without fuss and Micky heaved his swag over his shoulder. At the top of the gangway, he looked towards the shops and the hulking outline that was The Federal. Six o'clock swill was well over, of course, and the place was dark, but even if the doors were open he'd still have to stand outside licking his lips like a mongrel dog with no place to go. It was plain stupid – he was old enough to work for a living, almost old enough to fight for his country, but he wasn't allowed to raise a jar with the men.

Micky set off towards Aunt Ada's. He'd doss down there and make his way out to Arapawa tomorrow. Ada always had her sherry and a bottle of Christmas brandy in the kitchen cupboard, and she wouldn't mind sparing a drop or two for a mongrel nephew. The sea air had left him dry as a bone.

The window of the kitchen at the back of the house looked out not at the sea but at the pine trees, the shed and the dunny. There was an old sink there for gutting fish, and in the morning sun its concrete sides shone with a bluish sheen from collected fish scales. Lilian was rubbing butter into flour with her fingers, making scones for Susan. Her daughter had promised to come up with the baby to see how she was. Well, she was fine enough, but it would be nice to see Susan.

No, that wasn't quite right. 'Fine' wasn't the word to use. Lilian paused, hoping it would come to her. No, she didn't know how she was.

Ever since she'd fallen, there had been a strangely suspended quality to her thinking, as if the things she lit on were highly polished and she could only slide over them. She wondered again if she'd jarred something in her head, knocked it and not realised. She felt alert enough. Too alert in fact: memories that she worked so hard to keep under control were crowding her now, as illusory as fish scales and as difficult to dislodge.

Lilian tried to decide then whether to put out gooseberry or blackberry jam with the scones. The jars of three different jams and two different chutneys and whole golden peaches and whole tomatoes filled two shelves in her pantry. She stared at them all, unable to come to a decision one way or another but wholly taken up with what she saw in front of her. All that industry at the end of summer had left her exhausted but pleased with herself, and each time her eye caught what Ed called the fruits of her labours she felt as if she'd been bottled herself. A plump self-satisfied peach.

After nearly twenty years on the island, Lilian knew by now the best thing to do was to keep busy. *Idle hands*, Ed's mother used to say, standing uninvited in Lilian's kitchen, her eyes skimming over window sills and benches and the top of the coal range. *For a woman who knows what she's about there aren't enough hours in the day*. From the outset, Iris made no bones that she suspected Lilian of lacking the steel needed to live on Arapawa – what with her Picton upbringing and losing a mother young – and she had taken it upon herself to demonstrate what was expected.

Iris had a term she'd got from her grandmother: 'bottoming'. She insisted Lilian do this once a month, and it included pulling down all the net curtains to wash and scrubbing the sea-crusted windows. In between, they starched tablecloths and darned clothes and made their own soap. At the tail end of summer, Iris got Ed to bring up a preserving pan so her daughter-in-law could bottle the leftover fruit and vegetables. Not a minute of the day was spent sitting still.

'Your house has to be immaculate,' said Iris. 'Not cleaner than any other house on this island, immaculate. There's always someone out there who wants to catch you out. Keep your head down and your ears clean and even the biggest, nosiest neighbour will have trouble making dirt stick.'

Then one day Iris stopped coming on a daily basis. It was something Lilian had said to Ed about it being Iris who made work for idle hands. His mother had a habit of letting herself in, and this time she was just inside the back door putting on her apron when Lilian spoke. It was a flippant remark brought on by the looming curtain ritual – Lilian's arms felt sore just thinking about it. Within seconds, Iris had her boots back on and was seen leaving with her apron ties flapping.

Lilian believed that Iris had grown tired of supervising her son's household and needed an excuse to leave. Ed said Lilian had as much as called his mother a devil and should apologise. Lilian said she was doing nothing of the sort and Iris should learn to knock before she walked into another person's home like that.

The housekeeping didn't change when Iris stopped coming. The truth was, Lilian had become used to it, and she also found in the constant activity an antidote to the soughing of the pines. She'd always felt there was something vaguely sinister about pine trees, the way they grew so straight and tall, ignoring the slope of a hillside, their dark spiky branches ineffectually combing the air and finding it wanting. And the dozen or so up the back of the house seemed to want to remind her that indeed there was nothing, nothing but her up on that hillside, until Ed came home.

The chooks came around the side of the shed and fanned out across the grass. Three of them headed for the fish leavings that had been washed down the open hole at the base of the old sink and on to the grass. Molly wasn't there, and she usually led the pack. Lilian had given the old girl some warm mash that morning to perk her up, but it clearly wasn't enough. Her back was being well picked over by the other hens; she needed to be separated from them for a while. Lilian had held off doing it because she knew what Ed would say. To him a sick chook was a chook whose time had come.

At first glance, the kitchen was silent, but in fact there were four distinct sounds that rubbed together and blended like the butter and the flour. There was the sound of finger on finger and the flour in between, the rush of fire in the stove, the creak of branches, and then, far off, the swallowed roar of the sea. And somehow, without her hearing, Micky walked in with his swag on his back and stood at the kitchen door.

Feeling a shift behind her, Lilian turned and shrieked and ran forward to hug him, and then stopped, remembering. She held her fingers splayed in front of her, covered with butter and flour.

'Micky! Why didn't you say?'

He leaned forward awkwardly to kiss her on the cheek. 'It would have spoilt the surprise.'

Lilian frowned. 'How long?'

'Two weeks.'

'Goodness!' She looked at him searchingly for a moment before she smiled. 'That's wonderful, Mick. You certainly pick your days. Your father's at the Lookout – first day back – and he's crowing because he's already got himself a humpback.'

Micky didn't seem to have heard her. He moved to the kitchen table but he didn't sit down; he just stood looking at the room. Lilian went to wash her hands.

'He crowed?' Micky said in that way he did.

'Well, no, of course not. He was very happy, though.'

'Was he?'

'Of course.' Lilian looked at him. 'Is everything all right, Micky?'

'What have you done to your leg? You're limping.'

'I had a fall. It's nothing much – just a small cut and a bruised knee to show for it.' She dried her hands. 'But you're so thin! You haven't been eating.' Lilian went over and put her arms around him, squeezing accusingly. 'I can feel bones. Aren't you getting the parcels?'

Micky patted her back with the flat of his hand and then gently shrugged her off. He yawned.

'Sit down,' said Lilian. 'I'll make you something.'

'The food parcels?' There was something about the way he said it, Lilian thought, that made her feel defensive.

'Yes. The food.'

'We're out of the slump, Mum. You can buy food in Wellington, you know.' His face softened and he yawned again. 'Ari likes your fruit cake.' It was as if there were other things to say, but that was the best he could come up with.

Lilian cut two thick slices from the loaf of bread. 'Ari?'

'Aroha.'

Lilian waited, but Micky was rubbing his eyes.

'Stayed at Aunt Ada's last night,' he said. 'She says to say hello.'

'Did you, Micky? How are they? How's Jenny?'

'Good, but she doesn't want to stay at Aunt Ada's any more.' He leaned forward and started unlacing his boots. It was only then Lilian noticed he'd worn them inside. He sighed as the boots loosened and he drew his feet out.

'Why would she want to come back now? Ada says she's doing well at the school.'

'She hates it. She wants to come home.'

Lilian was buttering the bread. 'She loves school. She learns more there than she would with me.'

'Well, you did all right with me and Susan. All I know is she wants to be home.' He took the bread and butter, and in two bites and a swallow it was gone. 'Now, where's Billy-boy?' Micky was already out of the kitchen and down the corridor, calling his brother's name. Lilian heard him throw back the door of each room, his voice rising into playful whoops. Then he was outside in the garden, heading for the pines.

The scones were in the oven when Lilian's two sons appeared at the kitchen door. Billy was stuck all over with pine needles and clasping the length of Micky's arm to his small chest. Micky was stooping to accommodate him.

'We're going fishing!' said Billy.

'Maybe catch a whale!' they said together like they used to – how long ago was it? And they laughed, and then Micky wrenched his arm from Billy's grip.

'Oy! Get off me, you little octopus, you'll make my arm fall off.'

The boys were out the door and halfway to the shed to get the lines and the bait when Lilian opened the kitchen window and called, 'Susan's coming!'

They waved without looking back.

At least there'd be fish for tea.

Billy was allowed to row; it was calm enough, and the tide would take them anyway. Micky told him where to go: 'port', 'starboard', 'keep it straight'. He appreciated that Billy needed to show him what he'd learnt since he'd been away from home; besides, he was strong for a kid and his co-ordination wasn't bad. 'Good work, Billy,' he said. 'She's a tough one rowing round here. If you can row this, you can row anywhere.'

Looking at the shore, and then over to Wheke Rock, Micky lined the boat up. 'This is it,' he said. And dropped anchor.

While Billy shipped the oars carefully, Micky got out the lines, baited the hooks and dropped them over the gunwales. Almost immediately the lines started to twitch, and Micky and Billy were hauling in blue cod, and re-baiting and hauling in more blue cod, and it was how it used to be: the two of them side by side, nudging each other, grinning, letting go shrieks in their excitement, winding in the winged fish with the gaping mouths, dropping one down the other's jersey, the boat tipping in the struggle to get it out, filling the boat with cod, flat-eyed and flapping.

The waves were getting up. 'Hey, Billy-boy,' said Micky. 'We've got a lorry-load mate, let's get them home.' And that was the signal: without arguing, Billy started pulling in the lines and coiling them at the bottom of the boat. When they'd finished, he picked up the oars and started to row. It was harder returning against the ebbing tide, and the dinghy lurched with his efforts. Micky looked at his brother's neck, and the way the curls clung to it, wet with exertion and wet with the sea. He saw the sharpness of his shoulder blades and heard his small uneven breaths.

'Hungry, Billy?'

The boy nodded, pausing a moment.

'Me too,' said Micky. 'I reckon I can smell those scones.' Then again: 'Need a hand, cobber?' Micky's hands closed firmly over Billy's. He felt the boy relax and hand over the weight of the ocean. He heard him counting the fish on the bottom of the boat until he got muddled and stopped.

'Nearly there,' said Micky, peeling the small hands off the oars and replacing them entirely with his own.

He'd always meant to be there for Billy, but things hadn't worked out. Still, Billy seemed to be getting along fine without him. He was a different sort of boy, really, not bothered by anything much – in his world, people were mostly to be trusted. When their mother came into the room at night and whispered to Billy, 'Sleep tight, little angel,' and kissed him on the forehead, he went to sleep immediately and slept like – an angel. When she'd done the same with Micky as a child, he'd felt only dread. He didn't know what he had to protect Billy from, but he knew it was wrapped up in those four words.

'I knew he'd be back for the whaling,' said Susan, holding the net curtains back so she could watch them from the lounge window. She could see the dinghy slowly making its way to the beach, and then she couldn't because she'd blown the smoke from her cigarette straight at the glass.

'I don't see why,' said Lilian, flicking her fingers in and out of the baby's clutching hands. 'He has a job now.'

'All right if I go and meet them? Could you mind Emily?'

There was a split second before her mother waved her away. 'Of course – off you go. Emily's happy.'

So Susan left the house. The chickens were pecking at the weeds. Susan saw where Billy had been piling up stones in little pyramids. Funny boy. Her mother had been pruning the roses and the spiky branches were left there ready to burn. As if sensing an audience, Russell the Rooster mounted one of the hens, his body pumping, the small hen struggling feebly to stop herself being flattened. And then Susan was out. Out of the garden, clipping the old gate firmly behind her and turning to walk down the path cut into the grassy side of the hill, the one that took her down towards Whekenui Bay.

Without Emily, her legs seemed longer somehow. Her hair sprang from her head, trapping sunlight and small insects. Susan heard her brothers coming before she saw them, the younger talking in quick gusts, the older grunting back, but then she heard the baby. Inside Susan something tweaked as if it were attached to a thread tied to the door of the house which had just then pulled tight. She paused but didn't turn back; instead she hugged herself and waited. 'Micky!'

The little boy's chattering stopped, and there was Micky calling her name. She would wait, for Micky was her baby too. She was the one who'd spent hour upon hour minding him in the house and the garden; and then there was the time he'd wandered off and she'd walked the hills for what seemed like half a day to find him. She remembered it so clearly, although she must have only been six or seven. There was the panic she'd felt because her mother wasn't there – was it when she was sick? – and her father was out on the farm but she didn't know where. The paddocks seemed to go on forever, as big as the world, but she had no map for them.

In a gully somewhere, and she couldn't say how long it had taken her to get there, Susan had heard his voice. It was frightened and didn't sound like Micky at all. He'd run at her, and she'd scooped him up and held him so tight he'd cried. She'd tried to piggyback him, and he was light for four or five, but she'd had to put him down and make him walk, hitting him and dragging him sometimes to keep him going.

When they'd got home, finally, muddy and exhausted, he'd fallen or rather slipped to the ground, and had lain there, frighteningly still. But there'd been a flicker, his eyes had snapped open and he'd cried out in a surprisingly loud voice, 'Suzie found me.' As if there was no reason to worry all along. After all, she was his care, his safety, his abiding love. Parents got distracted; Susan never did. And she stood now and waited for Micky to join her.

8

Muttonbirding had been Annie's idea. They'd borrowed Dick Groves' runabout and headed for Cabbage Island, surging towards the mouth of the channel, under the brow of Lookout Hill. Dick had been going to come along but he'd stayed behind with a toothache. The Friar had tried to hide his pleasure at the news because Annie had been concerned – taking the old man some herbs and a special tea for his tooth before they'd left – but she'd seen him smiling and gone crook at him for thinking only about himself. Which wasn't true: he thought about Annie, he just didn't care a bean for Dick.

Now they were two, and nobody, not a soul, within cooee. He'd wondered about the Lookout. It was still too early for whales, so it wasn't likely anyone was up there, but he'd heard Old Jock and a couple of others talking about going over for a recce. He hated to think of them sprawled on the grass watching him and Annie like you'd watch a couple of dolphins – the effortless way they'd muddy it.

Annie had seemed oblivious. Her eyes were elsewhere and she was smiling into the light wind with her chin up and her hair streaming back around a single ineffectual clip. The Friar concentrated on piloting the boat. The squalling waves of the strait were playing havoc with the water pouring out of the channel, and while Dick's boat was about the size of a chaser it didn't have nearly the same horsepower. The Friar was relieved to be clear of the channel at last, and on their way to Cabbage Island.

There, Annie had known exactly what to do. Dropping to her haunches beside a hole, she'd buried her arm up to its shoulder. She lay prostrate like that on the peaty earth with her eyes closed and heavenward, looking for all the world like one of Sarge's precious saints. Her face distorted as she hit a tree root, and again when a flea bit her, then her whole body contracted and she was holding a good-sized shearwater chick. A downy thing with loose legs. She twisted its neck and threw it into a flax bag. She moved on to another burrow. And then another and another. The Friar had trouble keeping up.

By the time Annie had had enough, there were over a dozen muttonbirds in the flax bag and she was standing looking at them, sweat pricked out on her forehead.

'We could feed the whole of Arapawa with this lot! Let's have a party!' She was going to go on, he could tell, but she stopped herself and stood there silently, frowning and staring at him, wanting him to rescue her somehow. He felt daunted.

'A party? You're mad. There's barely enough for me.' And he'd rubbed his belly and she'd laughed, and then she took him by the hands and, dropping on to her knees, pulled him down to her. He felt he did it rather clumsily, for it was unexpected. And she kissed him on the throat, which was also unexpected because no one had ever done that before, and she leaned her full weight against his chest as if collapsing on him, and he put one arm around her and his other arm did its best to prop them both up. Sitting awkwardly by the bag of dead birds on an island that was barely there, she'd told him she was happy. No, she'd said she was happier than she thought she'd had the right to be. And she didn't need a party, which was a good thing, because nobody would come. Except Dick, of course.

The Friar had murmured back something to assure her he felt the same and that he wanted her all to himself anyway, and he wasn't sure about inviting Dick. He said that in his opinion their neighbour was an old man with nothing much to offer except a couple of old boats, questionable advice on where to get seafood, and a mouth of rotten teeth. What's more, he laughed too much. The Friar had returned home twice to the sound of a man's laughter. The first time he'd found Annie in the kitchen looking puzzled when he burst in and Dick outside mending the washing line, and the second time he found Dick sitting at the kitchen table like he owned the place. A solid, muscular man, Dick had a flattened profile that made him look perpetually stunned; and while he didn't have a lot to say for himself, he had a ready laugh and could turn his hand to anything. The Friar knew enough about women to think Annie didn't mind having that around her at the bach rather than being on her own all day.

'Hello Owen,' Dick had said, his leg tapping on the floor the only sign that he'd been considering getting away before the Friar returned. 'Can I get you a cuppa?' And he'd tapped the old teapot then as if it were his pot, and his tea to offer. 'It's hot.'

When the Friar had gone to hang up his hat, there on the single hook at the back of his door was Dick's hat, waiting for its owner to fish it off and return it to his head. The Friar stared a moment, unsure what to do. He was clearly too early home.

'We've been talking about muttonbirding,' said Dick.

'Have you?' said the Friar.

'Eh?' He tapped his ear.

'I see,' yelled the Friar.

'We were saying how the season's coming up and you could take my runabout out to Cabbage Island if you wanted to, as long as I can come too.' Dick had lumbered to his feet then and left, but not before giving Annie an unfettered smile.

If the Friar were honest, what he'd felt just then on Cabbage Island with Annie was anxious. He thought at first he was worried about what he was going to do with all the birds, but then he realised it was the slight strain between them that had caused it. Where had that come from? Was it the way she'd been so skilled at twisting the necks of the muttonbird chicks? At least she didn't bite their heads off like Dick did. Was it that? Or was it the concerns he had about their neighbour hanging about the place?

No. He guessed it was something about her, and the sheer nerve of her, when he'd expected something else. Truth was, if he thought about it, she made him feel as if he was always running to catch up. Deep down he trusted Annie, but somewhere else, off to one side, he had in mind the image of them both arriving at Tar'white for the first time, furtively, in the dark, with Annie tripping over tree roots. Had they started out so wrong it could never be right?

The Friar had shifted his body to try and hold Annie's weight better, but his arm was hurting and his back was slightly twisted. He could make out a scattering of adult shearwaters against the sky just above the horizon. He watched them and Annie watched them.

'You know,' he said, 'it's unnatural, birds leaving their chicks unprotected like this for days on end so they can go and find food on the ocean.'

'Is that what you think, Owen?' She shifted herself off him but didn't move away. 'It's unnatural? That's why they use these islands, isn't it? They think the babies are safe or they wouldn't go. Which mother would?'

Her voice had become strident.

The Friar picked up a handful of the soil and crumbled it in his hands. The whole of Cabbage Island was like this, crumbling, broken open by birds. The smell of the peaty soil climbed to his nostrils. He thought of Annie alone all day while he worked on Gunner's farm and how much worse it would be when the whale season began. No wonder she'd made friends with Dick. He felt suddenly acutely sad for the woman sitting beside him. He leaned over and kissed the top of her head.

'Of course you're right. Before mankind came along there'd be no predators on an island like this. And they're not to know about Annie. You know, the one that looks like a girl out for a picnic with her handsome lover, then *bang* she's killed over a dozen chicks and she's still got a bloody great smile on her face.'

'And then *bang* she kills the handsome lover because she wants a bit of peace and quiet and he talks far too much.'

'And she's still smiling?'

'She is, as a matter of fact.'

And his heart swam because she was.

'Well, it just goes to show, you can never trust a woman who suggests muttonbirding.' The Friar was so overwhelmingly grateful that she was happy again, he knew he was grinning foolishly and his gestures were bearish and big. 'Now, if it's all right with you, I think I'll get a drink of tea on.' And, stretching and grunting, he shambled off to collect driftwood to light a fire for the billy.

*

The Friar needn't have worried about what to do with the birds. The minute they reached Tar'white, Annie was hard at work plucking them. He had been touched by the concentration on her face and the preciseness of her fingers and the way she carefully kept the feathers to one side. She'd clipped the legs and wings, and dripped wax on the carcasses to get rid of the last of the down. Some she salted and strung up near the range, others she boiled and packed into kerosene tins in their own fat. She shook her head when he offered to help but was happy enough for him to watch.

The bach stank of the birds, but she'd been so absorbed, Annie, so happy; at one point she'd started humming, a song he didn't know that seemed to go on a bit. When she'd fallen into bed beside him, she reeked of those fishy birds.

'It's good to be busy,' she said.

He had been lying on his back in the dark waiting for her. He turned on to his side when she spoke and sniffed her. 'Mmm, muttonbird.'

'I'll have a bath in the morning.'

He picked up one of her hands. He couldn't see it in the dark, but he knew well the square fingers and short nails and what they were capable of. Licking the palm first, he took each of her fingers one by one into his mouth. Putting that hand back on the eiderdown, he picked up her other hand and did the same thing to the palm and each finger. He slid down under the blankets, then, all the way down to her toes. There was a small giggle as he licked them briefly, pretended to gag at the savoury flavour and then started on the bones of her ankles. There was something very fine about her ankles, something remarkable. To think they could hold a whole body up.

As he climbed her, he wasn't surprised to find that every one of her surfaces tasted of muttonbird and had the slight graininess of sand or salt. It made his tongue dry, but the awkwardness had gone. He rolled her nightgown up as he went, peeling it off over her head when he reached her throat. Then there was her chin and her lips. But it seemed she had fallen asleep. The Friar hung over her a moment.

'Love,' he said.

He heard her hair rustle against the pillow as she lifted her head. The kiss was like someone sipping from a soup spoon. She was surprising and insistent, and then all of her was lapping at him and there was nowhere else for him to go.

When she was asleep, the Friar tucked the blankets around her and climbed from their bed. In the dark kitchen, gulping water by the glassful, he felt like a man freshly emerged from the sea.

The next day, Annie was triumphant. She'd found some cape gooseberries up the back, enough to make a few jars of sticky yellow jam. There were not as many as she'd like, but after a morning of jam-making she'd put the jars on the shelf near the salted birds and clapped her hands lightly together. 'Look!' And as if she'd just that moment thought of it, 'I'll take some to Dick in return for using the boat.'

'He doesn't need them, love. His wife filled his shed with preserves before she died. Some say she finished the job off by preserving herself, in parts of course, so he had something to remember her by.'

Annie had sniffed and screwed her eyes up. 'That's an old story. You pinched it.' And she'd gone anyway.

The Friar recalled that her jam had used up all the sugar so he'd had none for his tea that morning. He'd never gone through so much sugar so quickly, ever – not that he was complaining. It seemed a sign of the way his life had been civilised. With Annie, sugar took on a myriad uses he had not entertained in his house before – cakes, preserves, sauces, jams. His trousers got tight and Annie had to let them out.

Then there was the first day he returned home and Annie wasn't there to be found. She wasn't up the back, she wasn't on the beach. He stood looking at the water – it was almost high tide and the sea in front of him was disturbed by a southerly. Surely she wouldn't go now? They seemed so settled, in hibernation almost, with enough food to see out the winter.

The Friar realised he was staring at the sea in the hope of finding the answer there. It was the thing that took the eye here, that drew a blue line through everything. The land was peripheral. What could it know?

A cry from the other end of the beach made him turn. She was making her way back, struggling with something heavy. He went to meet her, trying not to hurry but hurrying all the same, his excitement a feeble thing.

'Thank goodness you came! I thought I'd have to give up and leave it all behind. You should see the mussels we got, and the kina!' She dropped the sack and squeezed her hands to get the blood back into them. 'We went to Wheke Rock. Have you heard what Dick says? "When the tide's out, lay the table!"' Annie's eyes seemed to reflect the water. Were they usually quite so bright? 'He's got an old dinghy and he says I can borrow it to go fishing when you're working. He's got to patch it up a bit – it was his wife's. The *Periwinkle.*'

'You went as far as Wheke Rock?'

She looked at him full in the face for a moment and her eyes quietened down. 'I didn't know what he had in mind, but we were there and back in no time. There wasn't a soul outside the whale station.' She smiled, but didn't glow, didn't *reflect.* 'You must have been hard at work.' Annie went to turn away but stopped. 'Do you know why the kina from Wheke Rock has red roe instead of orange?'

The Friar was trying to match her lightness but just then it seemed an impossible thing to do when she was so intent on mocking his caution. 'No, no, I don't.'

'According to Dick, an ancestor of his killed a giant octopus in Whekenui Bay. He hacked at it with his axe and there was so much blood it filled all of Tory Channel,' Annie was grinning at him now. 'It turned the kina red.'

She waited for a reaction, but the Friar was still fighting his bad humour. He screwed his eyes up as if at the brightness of the sun, and waited. She's still brimming, he thought. He should be pleased, but all he felt was an impulse to poke a hole so the excitement would spill out and drain away.

'I knew about the octopus. I just didn't know about the kina.' He knew he was speaking too harshly; he cleared his throat to gentle it. 'The Brothers . . .'

He worried that what he had to tell her would disappoint somehow, and he couldn't bear that. He wasn't even sure he had the story exactly right. He could remember Jock going on about it up the hill, and he had a touch of the tar brush so he should know.

'Those rocks – ' he licked his lips – 'are the *eyes* of the octopus.'

'Really?'

Maybe it was the way he told it. She was frowning.

'Why don't you go and ask him then?'

Brusquely, the Friar hauled the sack on to his shoulders and started walking back. The weight he was carrying was nothing compared to the weight he could feel behind him. Why had she gone to Wheke Rock? She should have stayed here like he'd told her to.

'Tell me, why didn't Dick give you a hand with this?' he called back, and as he did he saw to his relief she was following. 'He's full of stories, that old Maori,' he grumbled. 'Forgets his bloody manners.'

'I told him I could manage,' she said, picking up a shell from the beach and putting it in her pocket.

After that, they ate jam and bread for breakfast and muttonbird or shellfish or cod for tea with stored potatoes and fresh carrots or tinned peas. It was better than the Friar was used to, and the meat that fell from the bird bones was more succulent than anything he'd eaten in his life, and Annie licking every last shred from her fingers was more succulent than anything he had seen in his life. The muttonbird would have to be his favourite. He was happier than he thought he had a right to be.

When she told him she was pregnant, the Friar felt himself relax. The promised child held Annie to their bit of shore in a way he couldn't on his own. Being pregnant also gave her something to do even when she was doing nothing. With the baby inside her, she began staying closer at hand, and he'd often find her inside the bach absorbed in feeding the fire or out on the beach watching the water. Sometimes she was knitting or reading or both. What a miracle it was, the growing baby and the way she stayed.

When Annie started planting a vegetable garden, leaning over the drum of her belly and letting out small grunts from the effort, he went off then and there to shoot a goat for tea. And when he got himself a good-sized buck after only half an hour, he took it as a sign that everything was going to be all right. Annie was his now. Everything was good.

The week she began on a cardigan for the baby, she talked about getting some chickens and ordered two sacks of sugar. Soon they'd be settled in the bay, properly settled, with a bunch of children of their own.

Not long after that, and just ten months after she'd come to Tar'white, she gave birth to Robert.

9

The Friar was polishing whale bone. He was rubbing sandpaper in small circles on a piece the size of his forearm. Despite the delicacy of the job, the muscles in his arms knotted and unknotted as he worked, and the muscles in his face and neck did the same. He seemed to be smiling and then frowning, and now and then he'd mutter something, and sometimes his face would go still. He and Micky were the only two out the front of the whale station on the narrow walkway between the buildings and the small drop to the sea. The Friar was filling time before the next whale, and Micky was just filling time.

The boy watched the older man, smoked and looked out over the water. There was nothing else to do, and he could feel boredom stretching out inside him and threatening to fill all his cavities. It was pushing on his lungs now, making him yawn.

'How's your mother?' The Friar's voice was surprisingly quiet but at the same time quite distinct, as if he considered every word before letting them out. *How's. Your. Mother.*

'Fine,' said Micky.

'She was limping . . .'

'Yes, she had a fall when she was walking, but it seems right enough.'

'Oh, is that it?'

There was something about the shush of the sandpaper, and the shush of the water. It made Micky think of Ari, who used to say *shush* a lot, blushing, holding her hand flat over his mouth. She'd say it up close to him like a kiss but then look horrified if he turned to try and give her what she seemed to be wanting. Micky inhaled deeply, and as he released the smoke through his nose and mouth and (could it be?) ears, he dropped the fag end to the ground and crushed it slowly with his boot. He thought of her – of course he thought of her, he couldn't help himself. Micky liked the way she smelt – the smell of a small clean animal – and her teeth were so white, too, and straight.

There was a tattoo on the Friar's right forearm. It was crabbed a little with age, but it was still clearly a sailor's knot, and wrapped around it were the names *Owen* and *Annie*. Micky saw how the two names moved into and away from each other with the movement of his arm. How could you ever feel enough towards a woman, thought Micky, to want her name permanently engraved on your skin? At the same time he remembered: *Ari + Micky*, and the two of them cutting into a pohutukawa tree at New Year. Ari had taken such care with Micky's jack-knife, her tongue tucked to one side of her dark mouth, the tip sticking out through those white teeth. She'd taken so long, he'd suggested they could leave it at *Ari + Mic*. That way they'd have enough time for a swim in the river and a cuddle afterwards to warm themselves up.

Shush, her hand on his mouth. *Shush you!* And her lips so close he could feel the warm air on his cheek. Then all of a sudden he'd thrust the tip of his tongue on to her palm and she'd cried out. 'Micky Prideaux!' Then, 'Keep your tongue to yourself and let me finish this,' and she was all flounce and

81

flutter. Well, that about summed her up, thought Micky. She wanted all the hearts and flowers but none of the other.

'How long have you been working that bone, Friar?' asked Micky.

'A month or so,' he said. 'It's from last season's catch. It's coming up nicely. I reckon I can start cutting the picture in soon.'

'Can I see?' asked Micky.

The Friar held it up and the boy moved closer. He frowned. All he could think of were Ari's teeth. 'Looks a bit yellow to me.'

'It's from an old bull whale. When we cut it open, we found a harpoon head in it from a whaler who used to hunt round Kaikoura in the 1860s. It was the oldest whale I've ever seen. It'll make a nice bit of scrimshaw.'

'Scrimshaw,' Micky said. 'Strange bloody word.'

The Friar grunted. 'There's a history of it with whalers, Micky. On those long trips on the whale boats it was good to have something to do with your hands. It was either carving bone or knitting.'

'Right.'

'I'm serious. Sailors liked to knit.' And the Friar's eyes met the boy's for a moment.

'Maybe that's something I should be thinking of taking up. There isn't much else for me to do here.' He yawned again, a big, unsatisfying yawn that didn't let anything out.

'Maybe you should.' The Friar paused a minute, his eyes off somewhere else. 'I've got some knitting needles if you need them.'

'Did you knit that hat of yours then?'

'Ah. No. Someone else did, as a matter of fact.'

'Annie?'

'Eh?' The Friar dropped the whale bone in his lap and seemed not to know what to do with his hands. Micky pointed at the tattoo.

'Oh,' said the Friar without looking at it. 'Yes, she liked to knit.'

'What happened?'

The Friar's eyes flicked around a bit before they settled on the water. His neck and shoulders reminded Micky of a boxer he knew. She's dead, thought Micky, has to be.

'Micky Prideaux!' It was Gunner. 'I've been waiting over half an hour for you to do those barrels. They need to be cleaned out by tomorrow. Get your tram-riding arse down there.'

'Mick here was just telling me he needed to get on and do that job for you, Gunner,' said the Friar. 'He's been hard at work helping me at the boiler and we just stopped for a quick smoke.'

Gunner looked sceptical. 'All right, all right. Come on then.' And the Friar winked at Micky, who shrugged back.

After they'd gone, the Friar thought about the boy. He was Ed's son, so was a cousin of sorts, but the Friar didn't know him at all. It was hard to get a fix on Micky because as he'd grown he'd started backing away from people, and then all of a sudden he'd upped and left. When he did look at you, the effect was surprising. It struck the Friar that he was a good-looking kid: a finer, darker version of his mother. Not much of Ed in him physically – hardly any Maori at all – yet there was something about him that reminded the Friar of Iris.

Iris's father, Ed's grandfather, was one of those Maori healers whose practice was declared illegal but who went underground and continued his work anyway. According to family lore, Iris had been flattened by the weight of that secret and as a result had become insecure and suspicious to the point where she'd come to mistrust herself. Was that Micky too – distorted by family secrets? What did he know about all that other business? What *could* he have known? He'd been little more than a baby. Then again, there he was, not quite whole somehow, not someone you could immediately like or trust.

The Friar hauled his mind away from speculation and back to the bone and the picture he would cut into it. He'd never claimed to be much of an artist, but then again the whalers in times gone by must have felt the same and gone ahead and done it anyway. Whales and dolphins, sailing ships and mermaids – the Friar had seen them at Mrs Grey's museum in Picton. Those who couldn't draw would simply cut letters into the hard surface: *I count the hours til my return, all my love Jacob.*

The Friar stopped his sanding. He'd do the old bull whale the bone had come from – breaching, with its flippers spread like they did. He'd seen it once or twice and it was a sight. In blue ink, not black. The mail boat was due tomorrow; most likely he could get the ink from Titch if he had it. More sandpaper too.

'It's the inanga,' said Ben, wiping his forehead with the back of his hand and sitting down hard on the whale to rest a moment.

Through the flensing-room door they could see the mail boat pulling up alongside the whale station and Titch Tasker at the wheel. He was a skinny man who looked like he'd snap in a Tory Channel wind, although somehow he managed to keep himself in one piece, year in and year out.

'That's good,' sniggered the Friar. 'Inanga! Skinny whitebait like him would feel at home with all those little fishies.'

Titch managed to tie up the boat in one brisk movement while the whaling crew came out to watch.

'Now that's the smell!' he said. 'Whale. I'd forgotten. I don't know how you lot live with it day in day out. All right if I park here for the afternoon?'

Tommy sniffed. 'It's not my whale station.'

'I need to do a bit of work on the boat, that's all. It shouldn't take long.'

'That's fine for now,' said the Friar, 'but you'll have to move when we get on to the next whale.' And he gestured out into the bay where a humpback was floating, half a dozen seabirds on its back, the shine going quickly from the blubber.

Titch nodded. 'Box of birds.' Then he leapt neatly back into his boat to ring the bell.

'I don't see why he insists on using that,' said Ben. 'Every-body knows he's here.'

'I heard a story about him and some girl in Queen Charlotte Sound,' said Tommy languidly, holding the word 'girl' long enough for the men around him to turn and listen. 'He'd ring the bell to tell her he was at the wharf. If her husband was there, she would do nothing and he'd know to stay where he was; if the husband wasn't there, she'd hang a tea-towel out of the kitchen window, and he'd be up that track faster than an old goat.'

'Nah, mate, you've got that wrong,' said the Friar. 'Old goat? He's boneless. A whitebait, remember?' And he waggled his pinkie at Tommy.

'Hah!' said Ben. 'That's a good one.'

'You're right,' said Tommy. 'And if he doesn't shut up I may have to get out my frypan and cook him up for lunch.'

*

Susan had seen the boat come in and was already down at the whale station with Emily tied in a shawl and tucked under her coat. In her bag were two books – the Tennyson and Mrs Gaskell's *Cranford*: her mother's books. *Cranford* was slender and green with gold writing on the spine, and Susan liked the feeling of picking it up and holding it in her hand, though she had no inclination to read it. There were illustrations, and one of them was titled: *endeavouring to beguile her in conversation*, with the bird-like Captain Brown in black leaning towards the pinch-faced, pinch-minded Miss Jenkyns in satiny gold. None of the men on the island looked like that, nor the women for that matter. The lives in the book were so very different from her own that Susan wished she could pick open the pages without yawning and focus on the small clever words for a while. It was Emily who'd made this impossible.

Susan had to stop a moment and look through one of the whale-station windows. Up on a good-sized humpback, astride a swathe of blubber that had been cut from the whale and peeled back, he was calling for something. Ben. In his left hand was the largest of his precious set of knives, its blade bloody; his right hand was gesturing to someone she couldn't see. He was stripped down to his string vest, and the slick of blood and sweat on his skin made him look darker, sprung with muscle.

Susan liked catching him unawares like this. She flushed with pleasure to think she was his wife.

What she knew, and no one else did, was the way Ben would beg to take the baby from her even after a long day with the whales. He said it calmed him as much as it calmed

Emily. If she was stiff and colicky, he knew just what to do. Gently, he'd lie her small body, stomach down, along the soft underside of one of his forearms with one of her cheeks on the palm of his hand. Like that, her tummy would relax and she could sleep. Up and down her husband would go with the little one balanced just so. *Moe moe pepe. Moe moe. Sleep, baby, sleep.* In their house in the depth of the night, with his rolling voice and way of pacing the floor, gentle Ben was a force of nature.

Sleep tight, little angel.

No, that was stupid. It was nothing like the phrase her mother had used with them. Ben's was calming; hers was a charm, a spell.

Susan leaned to the dirty window and Emily snuffled in close. There he was, her husband, stretching to take something, not a trace of vanity or self-consciousness about him, a man at ease with himself.

'Gidday,' said a small, light voice beside her ear.

Susan jumped slightly, embarrassed to be caught spying. 'My husband's in there.' She nodded towards the window. 'Flensing.'

'Ah,' said Titch. He took out his handkerchief and blew into it, a sharp honking sound, checked what he'd deposited, and then folded it carefully and put it back in his pocket. His mouth twitched. 'Disgusting smell when they cook the whale. How do you live with it?'

'I don't notice it, really, except at the start of the season.'

Titch's eyes slid across Susan and back to the window. 'Shame I don't see your mother. She's quite a reader. Did she like *Cranford*? I've just bought it and some others from the collection of the late Mrs James Haskell of Picton. She had over one thousand books. Did you know her?'

Susan shook her head.

'Your mother would have known her perhaps.'

'My mother doesn't go to Picton much,' said Susan.

'Where is it she goes then? For I certainly don't see anything of her when I'm here. I was saying to June the other day, she's one of my best borrowers and I've never met her.' His eyebrows were propped up above his eyes, accusingly.

Susan was quiet a moment and then came to a decision. 'I think you're wrong. She says you and she might have met.'

Titch frowned, and the effect on his eyebrows was startling. 'Does she say where?'

'A holiday somewhere? She doesn't remember exactly. She says the name's familiar.'

Titch seemed to retreat a little, his tongue clicking softly inside his mouth. 'Ask her,' he said.

Titch's lending library was stacked neatly on shelves, with rope tied along the front. Tucked in beside the books was his mail desk with cubby holes and shelves for the mail, and along the opposite side of the boat were bolts of cloth, wool, sewing materials, writing materials, underwear, socks, ribbons and boxes of boots. Susan's eyes ran over the shelves of what people of the Sounds called 'Titch's Bazaar'. At a pinch, he could also measure you up for a suit or a dress and take the measurements back to his wife June, who would produce something to rival the best fashion houses in Paris. Or so Titch said.

Where Titch was thin and sharp, June was built like a soft skittle with pins tucked absently in the corner of her mouth and across the front of her dress; they both had the same unhealthy-looking skin and tatty red hair. The whalers used to joke about the ferocious pride Titch had in his wife as if there was something a little tasteless about it.

'I thought June was coming out today,' said Susan.

She saw him startle. 'My wife isn't well. She decided to stay home. Next time, perhaps. Did you want a dress?'

'No, I sew for myself. I think my mother might want something, though. Her eyes aren't as good as they were and she'd prefer to save them for reading. She was wondering if June would go up to the house and measure her there? I can show her where it is.'

'I think that's possible,' said Titch. 'I'll make a note to ask her. My wife is not a great walker but I'm sure we could get her up the hill somehow. Maybe I should go too and meet your mother at last?' And he sniggered to himself. 'Is there a horse we could use perhaps?' The question sounded slightly indecent.

'It's not that far,' said Susan quickly. 'Or you could walk up from Whekenui, it's that bit closer.'

She could hear the other women from the whaling settlement approaching the boat.

'Anything else? Socks, writing materials? What about another book?' Titch was standing too close, really. Susan stepped back, shaking her head.

'No, thank you. I have everything I need. But my mother would like some more Robert Browning, please, and she ordered a Jane Austen.'

Titch went behind his desk to the Reserves shelf. 'Interesting how people can seem so different but have much that is similar under the skin,' he said. 'There are always the ratbags, the busybodies, the upstanding citizens – in novels and in real life – wouldn't you agree?' He tapped the spines of the books as if the sound they made would alert him to the correct one. '*Persuasion*! Here it is.'

Emily let out a small muffled snort, and Susan stroked her back.

'We can find something for you, too, I'm sure,' he said.

'No. Thank you. Maybe another time.'

'As you like.' He seemed to be pouting. He banged *Persuasion* to remove the dust, and filled out her mother's name on the card with his fountain pen. He found *Palgrave's Golden Treasury*, mumbled 'Some Browning in here,' and filled out the card for that one too. On the deck above, they could hear the three other women and half dozen children from the whaling houses; you'd think there were twice the number the noise they made. Looking put out, Titch went to his cubby holes to pull out Susan's mail and a week of newspapers. 'Time for these?' His tone, it seemed clear to Susan, was not at all pleasant. She signed the account he slid across the makeshift bench at her, gathered up the books, newspapers and mail, and pushed them into her bag.

Susan climbed on to the wharf and took a deep breath. In the middle of the bay a dead whale was lolling with blind eels sucking at it, and a small shark was circling unremarked. She could hear Ben coming, and she turned. He was talking to the Friar, and Gunner and Micky were walking behind. They walked in the way men did, thought Susan, as if they were trying to make headway. A group of women walked as if they were trying to balance something between them. All of a sudden they were on her, and Ben was coming forward with a kiss, apologising for the blood and making Susan think of wet, worm-tilled earth. As her husband pressed against her, the small child in the jacket whimpered again and Ben jumped.

'I forgot!'

Susan giggled and touched his cheek. 'What did you think I was carrying here? An eel?' She turned to her brother. 'You all right, Micky? Want to come and have a cup of tea with me?'

Micky looked uncomfortable. 'Maybe later, Suzie. I have some things to do here.'

Ben took the newspapers from her and leaned close, his lips moving against her ear and then nibbling it so she squeaked. The other men peeled off to visit the mail boat and some settled themselves down on benzine boxes, stretching copies of the *Express* in front of them and peering into the dense print to separate out a story they wanted to read. The women were starting to settle too, with their letters, magazines and newspapers. There were exclamations, unwrappings and running children. It was like a party. The Friar carefully put his newspapers in order before he started.

Tommy was the first to speak. 'Things are getting hot again in Europe.'

Gunner grunted. 'Yes. Jerry's up to something. First the Rhineland, and now those troops along the Czech border—'

'I don't trust them as far as I can throw them,' said Tommy.

'The politicians seem to have it in hand,' said the Friar.

'Appeasement is what it's called,' said Micky. 'And it's exactly what it sounds like. Piss. They should go in and deal with them now before it's too late.'

The Friar turned towards him, surprised. He wanted to say, 'What the hell do you know about it?' But seeing the way Micky's face was clenched, he said, 'Who have you been talking to?'

'It's all those newspapers he gets to read while he's waiting for the fish to fry,' said Gunner. 'It's given him opinions.'

The Friar coughed, Tommy laughed; Micky stood up,

muttered something, kicked the box he was sitting on and walked off.

'Now listen–' started Gunner, but the Friar shook his head. Micky had gone, walking to the rocks at the end of the whale station where he lit a cigarette, tossing the smoke up into the air.

The Friar watched for a moment and then turned back to his paper. There were no two ways about it, the boy unsettled him. How old was Micky now – sixteen, seventeen? Ed hadn't been much more than that when they'd gone over to Gallipoli, and the Friar ten years older again – still young in anyone's book. There they were, two cousins who'd lived within a mile of each other on the same island all their lives, vastly excited at going somewhere, anywhere at all, and as green as they come.

Micky talked about showing Jerry the door, but what did he know? Only as much as he'd seen at Anzac Day parades in Picton at that memorial like a kids' castle. *Glorious Dead* above the gateway. What did Ed call them once? Leftovers at attention.

Ed had trouble getting along to those parades; he always had some excuse or other. The Friar remembered the boy Micky there, and his mother, and the disappointment in the cut of her mouth. *Galli'poli.* That's how Ed used to say it. Like 'gallop pony'. He used to have a funny way with words that he'd lost as he'd got older. Iris would tell people how he was so painfully shy he didn't talk until he was four and then when he did the words had just poured out. That was a huge exaggeration: words had never poured out of Ed. What did happen, and the Friar was there when it happened, was his cousin started talking one day in whole sentences as if he'd been doing it all along. He was looking out of the window and he'd said to the glass in front of him, 'The weather's turning, there's a storm on the horizon.' It was an odd thing to say for a person who hadn't said a known word before that moment. His mother stood there as if frozen. She couldn't speak herself for a matter of minutes (and that was a record for Iris), then she'd made such a fuss you'd have thought she'd just discovered her silent child was a genius.

That first sentence showed Ed had started as he meant to go on. He would only speak when he wanted to, and what he said did not always fit into other people's idea of a conversation. The Friar remembered arriving at Gallipoli and Ed and him looking at the narrow beach and steep hills and the firing going on from the Turks and the men dying in front of them.

'Welcome to Galli'poli,' said Ed.

'Give me The Federal any day,' said the Friar.

And they both had a laugh, and some of the other diggers joined in. It started up a bit of banter until someone put a stop to it. Ed didn't banter; he just kept his eye on the beaches. From that moment, he called Galli'poli as he saw it – or heard it – which seemed a vaguely subversive thing to do at the time. What was going on in Ed's mind when he did that was anybody's guess.

Then there was that phrase of his: 'Tootsies up.' He used it when a fellow was shot in front of them and lying there toes to the heavens. Ed had got it from one of the stretcher-bearers who came to treat trench foot. You could hear them calling it up the line so you'd know to remove your boots and socks and wait your turn.

The Friar remembered the boy collecting ice to boil so he could wash their feet. It can't have been Gallipoli then – it must have been the Somme, which came later. The two boys

– no older than Micky – had each carried a tin, one cut down on one side to make a foot bath, the other unmarked.

'What's in there?' said Ed.

'Smell.'

And both Ed and the Friar had leaned forward together and inhaled at the mouth of the tin.

'It's a sweet one,' said Ed, his eyes closed.

'Sweet,' said the Friar.

'I don't know about that,' said the taller of the stretcher-bearers. 'It's whale oil. The best bloody thing for trench foot aside of getting your feet back home and into slippers beside a roaring fire.'

'Or up your missus' nightie,' said the shorter one.

'It's a sweet oil,' said Ed, irritated, his eyes still shut. 'It's made from a newly killed whale and it's still fresh.'

'I don't know about that, but it does the trick. Now then, tootsies up.'

Ed had sat quietly while his feet were washed and the whale oil applied. Then it was the Friar's turn, and still Ed said nothing. Afterwards they'd both sat for a while not looking at each other. When the Friar glanced across at Ed, his face was stricken, and he knew he'd been back home too. It was strange the things that did that to you, and smells were the worst. The whale oil had taken them both back to Fishing Bay at the start of the season: the chug of the boiler, the stink of boiled whale, a creeping breeze, sharing a smoke down by the ramp, a child singing somewhere, Iris bringing scones. All so utterly – words escaped the Friar – nothing would do, really. So utterly.

'Tootsies up' came later then.

At Galli'poli there was no ice. It was stinking hot. The bodies were piled so deep in places they were used like sandbags, and lying there for weeks in the sun they were bloated and blackened and stunk to the heavens. One day a truce was declared and the men were given eight hours to bury the lot. Word went round that there were five hundred corpses to the acre in no man's land.

The stench was one thing, but dragging a rotten body by the arm and finding you've left most of it behind was another. It was clear the earth had started claiming the dead and wouldn't let them go without a fight. The Friar remembered the sucking sound below a sound, like an old lady swallowing tea, the warning creak, and then an unexpected lightness when the arm parted from the body. The horror he felt the first time. The numbness he felt at the end of an hour. Then there was smoko with Ed.

His cousin had trouble rolling his cigarette, and the Friar, despite the numbness, had felt a small surge of shock. Ed had got the shakes – his hands weren't steady, and there was a slight tremor in his lips and around his eyes that made the Friar think of their grandfather. At last he licked the thing down and smoked it hard and fast, rolling another one while he finished the first. He was better at it this time. The Friar had no problem filling and lighting his pipe. He held his hands out flat in front of him to see, but there they were as always – steady as a rock.

They'd said nothing to each other while they smoked, but stood there looking out from the scrubby hills, out from the cross-hatch of trenches and corpses and lines of exhausted men to a distant stretch of sea. The view was not unlike the view from Stony Knob on Arapawa; either way they were at the ends of the earth. In this case, hell was all around them, waiting. At home, well, it was heaven, wasn't it?

Ed spoke at last. 'What are we doing here?'

Did his voice shake too? The Friar thought so. That morning he'd watched his cousin stand in front of a sliver of mirror and shave his chin with soap and only a capful of water. The Friar could see a congealed cut on his cheek, and a rash where the skin had been scraped too hard. Ed's hand had been steady holding the razor, but since his brother had died in Snipers' Gully he'd been less resolute somehow, less certain of himself, so he'd shaved the skin three or four times when once would have done. He was barely twenty after all.

The Friar went to put his arm around Ed with the intention of calming him. The gesture was a clumsy one and Ed pushed him away. 'Piss off.'

The order came down that they should stop trying to move the decomposing bodies but scratch shallow trenches beside them and roll them in instead. Twenty at a time into single graves less than a foot deep. It would be temporary. There'd be reburials. Ed and the Friar tied singlets over their mouths and moved as fast as they could. The Friar made sure Ed stayed close.

Not too long after that, when the area between their trenches and the Turks was littered again, a shell had landed in a body near where Ed was standing. He'd been splattered from head to toe. It was days before he got down to the water to give himself a proper clean. He was a live corpse, he joked. His cheek had started to twitch by then in a manner which made it look as if he were finding the whole thing immensely amusing. It had unsettled the men.

That was the day they'd started calling him Lucky.

There'd be some in Arapawa would still remember that, many who wouldn't. Only a few knew where it had come from. Not Micky, not the boy's mother. He doubted Ed had said anything. And now it didn't matter because the name had quickly fallen into disuse once they'd returned home, like those funny phrases of his. The shaking had stopped too, eventually, as far as the Friar could see, although Ed still lapsed into what some of the boys called his 'thousand-yard stare'.

The land they'd cleared during the truce was never taken. The dead came back with the first rains.

The Friar watched Micky walk back towards them. The quality of light and the high polish on the water made him a silhouette. But the Friar knew without seeing the bruised look to his eyes and the way his hands were on the verge of shaking, and he felt a swell of anger towards the lad. He had a family, a mother who cared for him more than she cared for herself, a girl, all of his limbs and a whole life ahead. The Friar wanted to stop him then and there, hold tight to his arm and point to the picture-book day. He wanted to ask the boy what on earth could possibly be as bad as all that. What, on God's sweet earth.

10

Lilian was outside the chicken run hanging ribbons of whale blubber on the wire fence to dry, and the chooks were high-stepping around inside watching her. They liked dried blubber. Lilian remembered the way Iris used to cut it into squares and bake it in a cool oven until they became hard dark biscuits for the children to chew. When Lilian remonstrated that they looked like something you'd feed the dogs, Iris was firm: 'It'll make them as glossy as roosters! Good for their innards too.' She'd repeat this every time she made them, so they'd all remember, so they'd all *believe*.

Chewing on the blubber bars, as the children called them, gave their teeth a faint oily sheen, and made their lips glossy. Iris had had glossy lips – remarkably full and wonderful lips for a woman her age – and her hair was the same. It had been thick and still black when Lilian had first met her, and only faded a little before her death two years ago. That hair, those lips, her complexion were all Maori, and could have made her quite beautiful, but unfortunately they fell away to a sharp, unforgiving Anglo-Saxon chin. She could have opened tins with that chin. It came from her English grandmother, she said. The one who used the word 'bottoming'.

Lilian heard the report from the .22 and the breaking

glass; although she flinched, she knew it was Micky. She hadn't heard that sound in a while. There was a time when if she couldn't find him she knew he'd be up by the old farm wall going at it hammer and tongs. The wall was the perfect height to stand his targets – the old tins and beer bottles he'd scrounged from round about. His last year at home, Micky had used anything he could find. Every day Lilian would hear that pea rifle, the sound of broken glass or a dented can or the thud of something she couldn't name, and always a funny yelp at the finish. It was a strange musical triplet that seemed to get faster and louder as the year went on. This older Micky was silent when he got a hit, though, and that worried Lilian more than any noise.

The chickens seemed unfussed by target practice; in fact they were unfussed by most things. Molly was having a dust bath. It was good to see her comb had got some of its blush back – the warm pollard must be helping. But she was still being pecked. Where the back was bare, there were flecks of blood. She needed to be separated from the girls for a while. How things had changed – for so long Molly had been the queen of the chicken run, a feisty red bantam that laid consistently and never got sick. And what was she now, poor thing? Headed for the chop if Ed had his way.

Lilian remembered the box out in the shed, the one she used to cure the girls of their broodiness. It always worked: a short sharp stint in the dark to put a stop to all that silliness, and then they'd get back to laying eggs. If only there was something like the brooding box that would work for children. In a way, the fish shop was supposed to be that for Micky, but he was home again and no different from when he left. Did he need more time there? Or something else? More importantly, what did he want? For that's what it was, wasn't it? He wanted something.

Lilian picked up Molly and held her lightly under her arm while she left the chicken run and went to Ed's shed. The order he'd imposed was still present, though it seemed an age since he'd done any work in there. Jars were attached to lids nailed to the underside of a wooden shelf at eye level, and all the tools were hung on the wall beside the bench according to size and use. Lilian smiled and adjusted the struggling hen.

Someone had moved the brooding box, and she had to squeeze behind the old chest of drawers to find it. Molly didn't like that and began to struggle harder, but Lilian tightened her hold on the old girl and whispered up close to her head to calm her. That's when she found the jar with the whale in it.

Lilian hadn't seen it for so long she'd forgotten it existed. Through the sticky dust, she could see the outline of the whale foetus inside. Like a bird. The size of a seagull with small unfeathered wings. It floated in thick yellow whale oil. Baby Blue, Ed's father had christened it. There was something of a mystery surrounding its origins, as no blue whale had been caught around Arapawa in recent times, let alone a pregnant one. Ed's father had been silent on the matter.

Iris was only too happy to fill the gaps in the story over a cup of tea. As she had it, some distant cousins of her husband's had sent their children to stay during the flu epidemic. According to her, they were especially whiny children and after two days she was heartily sick of them. On the third day, Iris had a box of peaches to bottle, so she set to and told the whiny children they needed to run off and play.

They were all right for half an hour, but then, with the fruit bubbling and the kitchen full of sugary steam, one of the boys fell over in the garden and started crying. And did he cry! Who are these cousins anyway? she thought furiously. Didn't she have better things to do with her time? She'd gone out, though, picked up the child, given him a hug and put him back down again. But still he bawled. She told him to come inside and sit for awhile, but still he bawled. She gave him some sugar on a plate to dip his finger into, but still he bawled. Iris couldn't believe it. She'd had enough. She grabbed him by his ear and dragged him down the dark hallway and into the bathroom to wash his mouth out with soap. That's when he started screaming up a storm – rolling on the floor and kicking his legs.

'Cry-baby!' she roared. 'You're driving me crazy!'

And with one swoop Iris picked the boy off the floor, took him to the kitchen and bottled him.

Hah! Hah! How she laughed seeing their faces, all those people who believed she could do that – the same people who looked at that whale baby for an extra few seconds, just to be sure. Her laugh was as hard as a slap. She knew the whispers. *Cannibals, all of them, before they were civilised. Arms and legs all over the beach and heads in a pot.* And she took those whispers, checked them for sharpness and hurled them right back. *It tastes better than pork. And it's good for brains to eat brains. Didn't you know?*

When Ed's father died, they'd found a reference to the whale foetus in his papers. It seemed he'd cut open a pregnant blue whale when he was working on an Australian whale station for a year and had smuggled the foetus home. Susan and Micky, however, chose to believe the story of Iris bottling the boy. When she died, and Baby Blue came to their house, they started charging children a penny to see it.

Lilian thought Susan and Micky liked the story because

it cast Iris as a witch. They still blamed their grandmother for being there when their mother wasn't. It was Iris who'd told them when they were only four and six that their mother was sick at the hospital – too sick to see them – and then managed not to mention it again for a whole year. (That was Iris for you, good with secrets.) She certainly seemed to have wasted no time moving in, reorganising the kitchen and setting the rules. Her preferred punishment was to wash out the children's mouths with soap. She didn't beat them, she didn't yell much, she didn't bottle them, she just used the soap. Iris would have thought she was doing the right thing. They were her grandchildren and she was holding the fort.

When Lilian had returned, her mother-in-law acted as if nothing had happened. The house was immaculate, and the children too, and she'd simply packed her things and left. Lilian hadn't had the strength to detain her.

Later, Iris sat her down and told her about the children, most especially Micky. Five years old and he didn't know his manners. Over the year, she'd been forced to wash his mouth out at least a dozen times, if not more. It didn't help that he had a stubborn streak a mile wide. In Iris's opinion, Micky needed sorting out before it was too late. On the other hand, she had nothing but good things to say about Susan: how helpful the girl had been looking after her little brother, and how quiet she was. All the time.

Lilian had kept her mouth shut and listened. After all, if it hadn't been for Iris, who knew where the children would have ended up. Ed wouldn't have been able to manage on his own. She knew she should be grateful.

Lilian leaned closer to Baby Blue in his dusty jar with his pale, blotched skin. Biggest mammal on earth, she thought, and look at its little one. Iris was right: it could be one of ours.

Air pressed at the walls of Lilian's lungs but she didn't cry. She left Baby Blue where he was, picked up the box with her spare hand and walked out of the shed.

Billy was looking for her. 'Where have you been? I need to read you what I wrote about Captain Cook.'

'Could you get me some straw first, love? I'm going to put Molly in this box for a while until her back gets better.'

Between them they made the box snug, and put it in the porch with the boots. Ed might not even notice her out there. In the kitchen, Lilian filled the kettle and put it on the stove to boil. She would make tea for herself and mix up some pollard for the hen.

Billy began to read aloud, wrinkling his nose as he deciphered the words. He'd written about how he lived on the island where Captain Cook had first seen Cook Strait. He said he'd walked up to that spot with his brother. His brother was strong, he said, and good at shooting goats.

'It wasn't called Cook Strait when Cook first saw it,' said Lilian, kissing him on the head. 'You know that, don't you?'

'Silly,' said the boy, and he took the food for Molly.

When she sat down with her cup of tea, Lilian checked her leg again. The cut was healing well and the bruises were lighter. She knew she should be pleased, but she wasn't. It bothered her that Ed hadn't asked after her leg, and now, with the bruises healing, he never would. It seemed that when she'd said she was fine except for her knee, he'd heard that her knee was fine. He hadn't asked to see it, so she hadn't shown him. When he'd come home that day and put his feet into her lap she'd winced a little, but he'd said nothing and then there didn't seem a moment after that when she could fall easily into mentioning it without laying herself open somehow, looking as if she needed something from him he wasn't giving. She should just have lifted her dress, pulled back the bandage, and shown him then and there. Instead she'd simply kept the knee a secret and hoarded it with the others.

Lilian pressed the largest bruise gently with her finger, all around the edges and into the centre, liking and not liking to feel the tenderness there. As she did, she could hear Molly plocking quietly in the porch and Billy talking to her in a similar tone. Then he called out, 'But we won't keep her in here all the time, will we? We'll let her out sometimes?'

'Yes of course. On her own, though. She needs time to mend.'

There had been a time when nothing about Lilian had escaped Ed's gaze. She'd been aware of him down at the wharves for some weeks before they met. It was like walking into cold harbour water in summer. She took to turning quickly, sure that whoever it was would be there right behind her. But there was no one following and no one watching, just the usual people going about their business.

Sometimes Lilian would find something unexpected as she walked back from her father's boat – a small pyramid of white stones or a polished apple perched on a bollard. Then, one day, she'd dropped a bag full of supplies on to the jetty and they'd gone everywhere, and he'd been there, silently retrieving everything, putting them back in the bag. He had big hands that could grab two large potatoes at once. She'd watched them, not the face, and relished their competence. Then there he was standing to his full height, six foot at least, handing the bag back, saying nothing. Lilian had to stand too; she couldn't stay forever looking at the wooden planks where his hands had been. Then he'd cleared his throat. Lilian had found herself pausing a moment too long. She could hear his voice now: 'You have far to go with that?' It had quickened her breathing and she'd nodded towards her father's boat. His head had been inclined at such an angle and his brow creased in such a way that he seemed vitally interested in what she had to say. She noted the straight smooth planes of his face, the high colour on his cheeks. In short, everything was in its place and there was nothing exceptional: it was the face of any farmer or fisherman in these parts.

That face she had held to herself all the time he was away. There hadn't been enough time to find out much of what was behind it, but the face was a reassuring one, enough to keep her writing and hoping. It was the same face that returned to her, although she wasn't sure at first. She puzzled over it when he wasn't looking, and watched closely from the window of her house as he walked from her gate to the front door. It was the texture that was different, she decided, or the composition of the skin, perhaps. She guessed he was unhealthy after a poor diet as a soldier. But that didn't satisfy her. She lit upon the eyes – surely they hadn't been quite so deep inside their sockets? No, she'd realised at last, the change was structural. The face of her soldier was supported on different bones.

Lilian knew for sure on their wedding night when she took his face in her two hands and kissed it. She'd felt a tremor in there that she took for excitement, but the next morning when she woke she put her fingertips on his sleeping cheek and felt again. It was under the skin, inside the bones, barely perceptible but threatening to erupt.

Ten years later, the Murchison earthquake was felt on Arapawa and she remembered opening the kitchen window and hearing the tail end of people screaming. Sarge had heard about it on his crystal radio and came running to tell them. He found her sitting at the kitchen table, frozen, staring at her hands. 'The shake—' he said.

'I know,' she said.

'No,' he said. 'It's worse than that.'

How deep did her husband's tremor go? How terrible was it down there?

Those first months in Whekenui did nothing to reassure her. Ed was there and then he wasn't. She would be talking to him, and turn from her task to find him gone. He felt no need to tell her what his plans were for the day; he seemed to hate being bound by arrangements of any sort. Every lunchtime, she'd have a meal waiting and the table set, but Ed wouldn't arrive until it suited him. Sometimes an hour late, sometimes more. One day, Lilian decided to go and find him. She knew he was up the back somewhere, docking the lambs, so she took off her apron, packed the bacon and egg pie into a basket and started to climb. She was pregnant with Susan so she felt heavy and moved slowly, even though the baby was barely showing. She saw Sarge first, and felt a twinge of disappointment. He had his back to her and was holding a lamb belly-up on the top of the fence.

Ed was there too, though. On the other side of the fence. He had just cut off the animal's tail, by the look of it, and was using his knife to nip the ends off the tiny testicle sacs. Now he was burying his face in the animal's groin, jerking back and spitting the testicles into a sack. Mountain oysters. Lilian had seen them on her cousin's farm. They'd want to cook those up and eat them later. Ed said something that she couldn't catch, and Sarge chuckled back. It was his stock reaction: their neighbour had a suspicion of words that verged on the ridiculous. 'Come and I'll show you' was his favourite phrase, which could sometimes involve a half-hour horse ride to see what the problem was.

Lilian sighed and sat down on the grass. The lamb Sarge was holding was set down too. He did it with one hand, letting it slip off unsteadily into the paddock, then he scooped up another one and flicked it over on to its back with its legs splayed. For a man of such bluntness, he was surprisingly gentle.

Ed was cleaning the knife on his trousers. He sliced then at the tail of the lamb, detached the testicles and waited for the next one. The men were methodical and unhurried in their work, and the effect was calming. Lilian was aware, though, of the smell of egg in the basket beside her and the dampness of the earth feeling its way finger by finger through the grass. Her stomach rumbled and she put her hand there to silence it, but with the hunger came a small wave of nausea. Lilian swallowed, and had decided to call out when Sarge called it quits. Ed stopped then, too, and wiped the back of his hand across his face. He stood a moment, blinking, as if remembering where he was. Sarge seemed to lean on him then to get him moving, or maybe he was just telling him his wife was waiting for him. Ed's eyes settled somewhere near her and widened a little.

'Lunch already, Lilian?' he called. 'Have you been waiting long?'

While Sarge took the knife off to clean it, Ed had sat beside her, the full length of him, and tidily eaten a piece of pie. He'd commented on how good it was, the weather that was coming, how many lambs they'd got through. He asked what she'd been busy with that morning, and his head had dipped towards her to listen, offering his cheek. He smelt marvellous outside in the sun, like an old wharf, and the smell made her happy. She wanted to breathe it in and hold it there for those times when she sat alone in the kitchen with lunch cooling.

He'd gone on to talk about building her a hen house, and used his hands to show her the shape it would be. He held those big hands up against the big sky, cupping it, holding the blue inside a cathedral for hens. It should be spacious, he said, shaped like a house not a shed and high enough for her to stand. There was still something faintly unsteady about his hands, but there had been a light wind that day, so she couldn't be sure. He was getting better, wasn't he? Iris didn't think so. 'He's been chipped and badly mended,' she'd said to Lilian one day. 'He's not the only one, either. The war's got more than the dead to account for. There's nothing you or anyone else can do about it.'

He'd been different before. Lilian hadn't known Ed. She'd taken him on faith. How was she to know what was him and what wasn't? It helped to know Iris had noticed something too. But he could be mended, surely? Look at him, he was a little better already. He'd taken to juggling eggs.

Suddenly, Sarge was there – inside Ed's hands. He was holding what looked to be a bloody lamb's tail, and his eyes were imploring them. Ed dropped his arms and got to his feet, grabbing one of Lilian's napkins. He sat Sarge down roughly on the grass and knelt beside him.

The lamb's tail was Sarge's hand.

'You've taken off the top of your finger,' Ed said. 'A clean cut. Not too much has gone but there's a lot of blood.'

'I sharpened the knife.'

'It's certainly clean, Sarge. Next time, shift your hand along a bit and you'll get the whole finger.'

He got Lilian to press the napkin on the wound to stem the flow and used the other napkin to make a tourniquet around the arm. Sarge was pale, his eyes closed. Ed used a tea-towel to wrap around the hand and hold the napkin on, and then he hauled his friend upright. There was a brief moment when Sarge staggered and looked like he was going to faint, but Ed held him up without seeming to notice.

Sarge opened his eyes and looked sheepishly at Lilian. 'Sorry for all . . .' and he tried to gesture towards the picnic basket. Lilian guessed then what the injured man had done. He'd been trying to clean the knife in a hurry so he could leave Ed and Lilian on their own.

'Don't be silly,' she said. 'It's only a picnic.'

'Come on, old soldier,' Ed said. 'It's not like you to bleed so much.' And he heaved Sarge off down the hill.

Lilian could only hear Molly on the porch now. Billy must have gone off to play. She finished her tea and got to her feet.

'So,' she said, looking around the room for a clue, 'where for the life of me was I?'

The hen house Ed built that month was just as he'd shown her it would be, and there wasn't a time she'd go into it without thinking of his hands making shapes up there with the lambs. There was a pulse in the wood, she could feel it, and a dim sense of threat that refused to go away.

11

The Friar was spooning tinned sardines and boiled potatoes into his mouth, the open door of the stove providing just enough light to see by. Not that he needed to look at what was on his plate – it was an automatic thing when a man was this weary and he'd been eating the exact same thing for a week because he'd had no energy to get the lines out for something fresh.

He'd always used a spoon, cutting his food with it and scooping it into a mouth wider and closer than it needed to be, his left arm hugging the plate. Four older brothers and an ailing mother was a good enough reason to eat that way. She'd never eaten with them except on a Sunday, preferring instead to clear up the pots and pans before her energy gave out, and taking small mouthfuls when she could. So there wasn't much she could do about the table manners of her youngest except tell him he'd have to mend his ways when he found himself a wife.

As a matter of fact, it turned out that the only woman who'd ever caught the Friar's fancy hadn't stayed around long enough to make any inroads into his manners, although she did a bloody good job on the rest of him. His mother had been long gone by then, bless her, for who knows how she would have coped with all of that.

The Friar thought about the whale steaks he'd turned down at work. Whatever the others might do, he couldn't get his head around eating the bastard after boiling it up every day that week. Every meal he ate tasted and smelt of whale anyway. He wrung it out of his clothes and scrubbed it out of his skin, but it stayed there as hard to shift as dog shit. Still, enough salt to make a meal tasty and a mug of tea to wash it down, and it did what food should. It was just coal to the boiler in the end – it was a womanly notion to make out it was anything else. And there was his mother: 'Look at your plate, Owny, I'd be wasting my time cleaning it.' The weak smile of satisfaction she gave him as if he'd done something wonderful, when all he'd done was eaten, when all he'd wanted to do more often than not just then was take himself off to the dunny. But, 'It was good, Mother,' he'd say, and she'd be waiting for the next bit: 'one of your best.'

His pipe still tasted as it always tasted and was strong enough to clear the air. The Friar picked a fish bone from between his teeth and laid it on the table top. Despite what he'd said to Gunner, he really didn't want to find someone else to tie his boat to. He'd done with women. For who knew why they stayed or why they upped and went, there was no rhyme or reason to it. And when they went, they pulled something from you that was left writhing like a fish in a bucket. Anyway, that was a long time ago, and he had Smiler now. Best leave it at that.

The Friar didn't hear the knock at the door because the dog was already on his feet barking. For a moment he thought it was Ben come over for a hand of cards. But it was Micky who pushed his way into the kitchen.

'Mate!' Friar shooed Smiler to his corner and kicked out a chair for the boy to sit on. 'Give me a minute.'

111

Micky sat with his hands in his pockets while Friar took his plate to the sink and lit the oil lamp.

'Drink?'

'A beer would hit the spot.'

The Friar looked at the teapot. 'I'm up at sparrow's fart, Mick. One beer could lead to another and then where would I be?'

The boy looked at him steadily, waiting for the answer to the question perhaps. The Friar found himself going to the cupboard and taking out a bottle. The brown paper label said *December 1937*. He had a new batch in the copper, but this would do. The Friar dried a glass and put it on the table; he poured a beer for Micky and a cup of tea for himself.

'Here's skin off your nose,' said the Friar, and they tipped their heads back at the same time.

It didn't take Micky long to drain the glass. He flicked his eyes at the Friar and, seeing him nod, poured himself another one.

'Looks like you've been picking up some skills in Wellington,' said the Friar. He leaned back in his chair and watched the boy, who finished off his second glass without a word and waited a while with his hands flat on the table.

'Is there another one in there for me?' Micky said at last.

'More than one, but you've had enough, I reckon. Get yourself on home, eh? I should be getting to bed.'

'Don't want to let that go to waste, though.'

'It won't. Now tell me what you're here for.'

'Here for?' Micky frowned. 'Just passing, saw you were up and thought I'd stop in.' He looked at the Friar closely. 'There's nothing to do here. No one to meet. It's a bloody cemetery. What else can a man do but go for a walk?'

'What about your friend Phil? You two could find something to occupy yourselves.'

'Phil's not a mate.'

'I see.'

Then there was a strange sort of smile – nothing much, a scratch. 'How do you manage?' said Micky.

'Just apples, thanks, son,' said the Friar briskly, and he busied himself trying to relight his pipe.

Micky sighed and stretched. 'You've been writing.'

The Friar turned to see the pen and ink on the bench beside the folded letter. He hadn't expected company or he'd have put it away.

'Got a sweetheart somewhere?' The boy said it without mischief, the tone more wistful than anything.

When the Friar didn't reply, concentrating still on his pipe, Micky kept on: 'I should write to *my* sweetheart, but I have no ink and no paper, and nothing to say.'

The two men looked at the letter on the bench. Micky turned away first.

'You know, in the old days, whalers discovered testicles had another use altogether.'

Micky looked up startled.

'Believe it or not, they used them to steer their sailing ships by. Balls being so sensitive, they can feel the currents and know when the tide is about to turn.' The Friar took another sip of his tea. 'I suppose if testicles are kept busy like that all day, they don't go around looking for a girl to impress at night.'

Micky looked him in the face a moment and then threw back his head and laughed.

The Friar laughed too. 'It's true,' he said.

'Why don't they like you, Friar?'

'Who?'

'My parents. When I say your name, they change the subject or ignore me.' Micky pointed at him. 'And you're funny, and they're never funny.'

'Is that why you came tonight? To annoy your parents?'

The Friar watched the boy with his fingertip now circling the top of his beer glass. He wondered, not for the first time, how much he knew. The boy could shake things up if he wasn't careful.

'I don't need to come here to annoy them,' Micky said, pushing himself on to his feet with his hands flat on the table, giving that smile again, smaller and thinner, letting the words slide from his mouth – 'Good of you' – before he scratched the dog's ears and left.

The Friar sat looking at the empty glass, unsure what it was he'd just seen. Then he started on the dishes.

It wasn't just women he was done with; it was people, really. He didn't need the trouble a kid like that would cause. Ed wouldn't have a bar of him coming here for a start, and Micky would know that. The Friar was aware he kept his arm around his life as he did around his plate of food, and while it wasn't ideal, it was what he'd come up with, and it seemed to work.

Micky exploded the last of six bottles off the wall, then he tipped his gun away from his face and sniffed. Only six left now. Already he felt the downward pitch of disappointment. What would he do after that? He'd woken late and had felt aggrieved ever since. Nothing was right. He propped the .22 against a tree and walked through the pines to the old wall. He moved slowly because he didn't like the pine needles; their acidity made his skin itch even when he wasn't touching them.

He lined up the six remaining bottles. He knew exactly where to sit each one on the rough brick so it wouldn't fall. He stood back and tipped his head as if at an adversary, and then climbed the hundred yards back up the bank to his gun. He never varied his target practice. He could do it in his sleep: lining the bottles up, the number of strides to get back to the gun, looking down the sight, firing.

When he'd finished, and it didn't take long, Micky kept the gun to his eye and moved it idly over the trees. In the V of his sight he saw a bird, a branch of a tree – partly broken off, raw-edged and hanging; and then down through the trees there was the hen house, and the sick chook let out on its own. All wedged for a moment. He would do this when he was smaller too. He remembered once watching his sister climb through the trees, calling him to lunch. He'd been shooting and, without thinking, he'd trained the gun in the direction of her voice. It was only then that he realised the safety catch was off. His breathing was so shallow it was barely there, and his head felt light and blown out like his father's shirt on the washing line. He could have put the safety on but he didn't. He saw her emerge fully from the trees, her head flicking upwards, looking for birds or cicadas. He could hear her humming. If he'd let go at that moment, if he'd continued logically and pulled the trigger, he would have stopped the singing and the girl all at once. There'd be blood of course, but how much and where? Would it be like a goat? He had wanted to know.

He'd watched his sister until she was nearly upon him and he saw the bleach of fright on her face. She'd stopped, and he'd put the gun down and laughed. 'Don't be so stupid.'

Then, without expression, without blinking: 'The safety's on.'

It was his mother, he realised heavily, not his sister who had walked into the sight now. She was small and fly-like. The safety catch was on this time. He checked to be sure and continued to watch her. She moved as she'd always moved, her shoulders slightly rounded, her chin forward, her mouth set in a straight line that could be called grim but was more unsure than that. It seemed to Micky that his mother was always distracted and he didn't know where her thoughts went when she was like that. He remembered Susan asking her over and over: 'Are you all right, Mummy?'

Micky would never have asked his mother a question like that because he'd dreaded the answer. What would he have done if she'd said she wasn't? Instead, he'd watched her. As far as he could see back then, his mother never stopped moving from when she woke until she sat in her chair in the evening. If there was any constant about her, it was this. And there were all the sounds that came along for the ride – songs she hummed, small grunts that went with clatters, knives and forks rattling, water splashing, the glug of something boiling, the big knife thudding on the chopping board, and eventually the rustle of her reading. The only time she seemed to pause and look at him was when he lay in bed at night. There'd be her cold washed hand suddenly on his forehead and the swiftest kiss. *Sleep tight, little angel.* And then, well, he never knew what would happen. Sometimes he would pray, sometimes not.

Micky was watching as his mother bent to the hen, then continued to walk through the garden. Along the rifle sight, he saw her go through the old gate. It was on a slight angle, that gate, so it always shut itself, and she always waited. Micky remembered waiting there with her when he was only half her height. 'Are you ready, shall we go?' Then her head nodding, dipping as if she needed to see her feet first, her hand tightening on his and both of them lurching forward down the track towards the beach. He used to think it was like a mother bird and baby bird flying.

Micky started forward. He slid down the bank, holding the .22 above his head, taking the same care as before, but faster on his feet somehow. She was wearing his father's trousers tucked into gumboots and carrying a bucket of fishing gear. And he knew Billy was down at Fishing Bay with Susan, so his mother was on her own.

Micky didn't know what he was doing, though. It was like with his sister that time: his head full of air and his movements involuntary. He was having trouble swallowing and he was panting without running. There seemed not to be enough air. And somehow he reached the garden fence. He fell against it, briefly winded. His mouth was dry and the thing he wanted more than anything just then was a drink. Now, that would set him on an even keel. One of those bottles of the Friar's would do nicely.

The hen was there, eyeing him suspiciously, one claw poised in the air ready to scratch the dirt. She was clearly sick, her exposed flesh spotted with blood. His mother, it seemed, was avoiding the obvious. In one single, unbroken movement, Micky lifted his rifle and shot. She collapsed into nothing, a pitiful pile of feathers.

Micky climbed the fence. He hooked the dead bird up with the .22 and flung the small body towards the trees. He misjudged the throw, though, and his arm slammed down on the top of the fence where a loose wire grabbed his skin and tore it. 'Damn!' The pain made him drop the gun and clutch his arm. He was hissing through his teeth.

But he didn't have time.

He picked up the .22 and ran. It didn't take long to cross the garden and leave through the old gate. He stopped a moment as his mother had, to wait for the gate to shut and to find his breath. His heart was thudding so hard he felt sick. He could hear her humming and guessed she was about halfway down the track by now. On her own, going fishing. It made him so angry, so unspeakably angry, that her defences were so thorough. The hum, the chores, the books she read, none of it let him in. He just wanted to be let in. Couldn't she see that? Or let out. He wasn't sure for a moment. Let out.

Perhaps that.

He started running again, not caring if he made a noise. She must have heard him: she'd stopped and turned, she was holding up the bucket.

'You coming with me, Micky?'

He stood there panting, his arm throbbing, unable to move out of her sightline. She held him there, frowning slightly, as she would at one of her troublesome chooks. He heard himself saying, gruffly and unexpectedly, 'Only if I can row.'

'Are we shooting fish now?' she said, smiling.

'No,' he said. 'I'm going to leave it in the shed.' And that was that. He didn't know what it was he'd been thinking, but whatever it was the chook had taken it out of him.

They continued on down in silence. It wasn't until he picked up the oars that she saw his arm.

'Taiho a minute. What have you done there? You can't row with that.'

'It's nothing,' said Micky, and he pulled the sleeve of his jersey down to cover it.

'It's not nothing, Mick, it's bleeding.'

'I cut it – the bottles. It's nothing.' And he felt suddenly and terribly ashamed, and looked past her to the mouth of the bay.

'You should have told me.'

'It's just a cut, I can still row.'

'Not a chance,' she said. 'Let me see.' And she managed to touch his forearm before he pulled it away.

'Leave it.'

Her eyes shifted, and she began to row. Micky leaned back and tried to let himself go with it. The pull. The pull. The pull. He'd never liked his mother rowing him; it always made him feel on edge and today wasn't any different. It wasn't that she was a woman – he didn't mind his sister rowing if she insisted – it was just something about his mother doing it.

He was tapping the seat now without realising it; finally, he reached into his pocket. 'You still fish most days?' he asked, lighting up.

She nodded. 'I can't row quite like I used to, though. Everything all right, Micky?'

'Everything?'

'You know, work, Wellington.'

Micky shrugged.

'You seem preoccupied.'

He shrugged again.

Talking with his mother could go either way. Micky could choose to be expansive or closed. It depended how much he needed it – the feeling he got, a sliver of something which felt akin to power or revenge or both. It was enough, sometimes, that sliver like a splinter under the skin, to set him up again and make the world feel less awry. Today, though, today he had gone beyond that and there was nothing to say. He wondered how long it would be before she'd notice Molly had gone.

Micky thought of what Nana used to say about his mother having an open-and-shut face. Nana always had a turn of phrase that summed up a person, not necessarily nice, but usually right in some way. Micky had never especially liked his Nana, but he had approved of the way she didn't hesitate in taking people down a notch or two. She'd have something to say about his boss, for example. Micky tried to think what it would be. 'Sly as an outhouse rat' was one of her favourites. It was either that or 'Fish Lips'. He smiled at 'Fish Lips': if only he'd had the bottle to say it. Nana would have. She'd probably have delivered one insult to his face and while he was digesting it she'd have quickly followed it up with another. She'd have had old Fish Lips out cold before he knew what was happening.

His mother was shipping the oars. Micky started readying the lines. They worked silently until everything was done and then she smiled and looked back at the shore.

'Everything looks different from here, Micky,' she said. 'That's as good a reason as any I know to go fishing.'

Micky stretched both his arms out as far as they'd go and locked his hands behind his head. He shut his eyes. It all seemed so pointless.

'I suppose so,' he said.

Lilian was out of bed and on her feet. She was blinking fast in the dark bedroom and unsure what she'd heard. There it was again. She looked at the bed. No Ed, and the bedclothes flung back. Lilian went to grab the lamp, but grabbed her dressing gown instead and ran along the dark corridor to the end and the light she could see in the kitchen. It was empty.

The back door was open.

'Drop it!' Ed wasn't shouting so much as roaring, the words lost in the need to make an alarming noise. He was standing with his back to her over by the shed, facing Micky. The boy had the axe and was holding it at shoulder height, caught, it seemed, halfway through chopping a log.

'Come and get it off me, old man!' And the boy trembled a little and looked like he was going to fall.

'No, Micky,' said Lilian.

Ed didn't even look around. 'Get back!'

She didn't. She just stood there looking at Micky, seeing the familiar blankness in his eyes. She used to say to Ed, *His curtains are pulled*.

'Micky,' she said. 'Put it down, love.'

Lilian saw the boy falter, something fire in him briefly and then go out. 'Get out of it, won't you?' he said, dragging out the words, refusing to look at her. 'I know what I'm doing.' He stepped back and as he did he teetered again and his eyes opened wider and briefly slid over hers.

Lilian smelt the beer before she saw it. There was a bottle on the ground – no, there were three or four. And they were all empty. Two more lay on their sides on the woodpile.

'Ed, he's drunk. What's he doing chopping wood?'

'You tell me.' And then, hissing, 'Idiot.'

The boy swung the axe and missed the log and only just missed his leg.

'Stop him, Ed!'

The axe came up again, Ed's eyes were on it.

It was falling and he moved to Micky's right flank, his hands out to take it. It was Lilian who lunged, grabbing Ed and forcing him away. She'd regretted what she'd said the second she saw her husband move; but now he was pushing her off and scrabbling on his hands and knees, yelling like a man possessed. Billy was there. His small face buckled with sleep, his head turned to the faintest whistle of the axe as it swung, his eyes waking up, the edges of white, the way he seemed to slip – and all that was left was the crack as the axe bit. Micky let go, and was falling back then; falling, until Ed caught him; falling, and yelling something indecipherable, until he was hard against the shed, winded, and his father holding him tight, shouting back.

Shut. Up. Shut. Up. How. Dare. You. Stupid. Fuck. Could. Have. Killed. Look. At. You. Useless. Ed's face up against Micky's face, both men snarling. Then Micky silent and Ed spitting out smaller and smaller words until they were like threads of tobacco.

Lilian found Billy sitting on the ground behind the woodpile, hugging his knees. He grumbled softly when she put her arms around him.

'He didn't see you there, love,' she said. 'He didn't know.'

Billy's eyelids flickered.

'You moved so fast, Billy. Thank goodness you move fast.'

She could hear Ed and Micky breathing heavily, and then Ed saying, 'You're on the next boat back to Wellington.'

'Mick,' said Lilian quietly, and then she started to cry into the back of Billy's neck.

What came out from Micky was hard to hear: 'I can't.'

'What?' said Ed.

'I can't.'

Lilian heard Micky slide down the shed to the ground where he let out a small hiccup, and then another. He was crying too.

'Why?'

'I lost my job.'

'Bloody hell.'

'Fish Lips did his block.'

'Fish Lips?'

'Fucking Grant Prescott.'

'You–' But Ed stopped, he sounded exhausted, his voice was leaden. 'What did you do?'

Micky lifted his voice so they'd hear it behind the woodpile. 'I'm really sorry, Billy. I'm really sorry. I didn't want to hurt you.'

'*What did you do?*'

'I hated the job. I started getting there late. He hated me, Fish Lips.'

'What happened?'

'I had it out with him.'

'You had a fight?'

Billy stood up then and walked back inside. Lilian thought how self-contained he was compared with Micky, how well he took things. Micky couldn't seem to hold himself in. There was ragged breathing and then his voice: 'I miss Ari.'

She walked around the woodpile to where they were, her hand touching the wood for support. The axe was stuck in the shed door and Ed was passing Micky a cigarette. He lit it for him, cupping the cigarette but really cupping the boy, somehow. He started rolling one for himself. Lilian didn't know what to do but Ed did.

'Finish that,' he said, 'then go to bed. We can talk about what we're going to do with you in the morning.'

Micky nodded and pulled on his cigarette, his eyes averted again. Then he leaned over and picked one of the bottles off the ground and tried to drink from it. It was empty. 'I need more bottles. For targets.' He tried to pull himself up using the chopping block, but soon slumped back defeated.

'By the way, the beer's crook.'

The next morning was like the day after a southerly storm – scoured and cold and, for a short while at least, unnervingly still.

Lilian had woken first. She lit the range, then she pulled on her boots, took the lamp and went out looking for Molly. It wasn't yet light.

Passing the shed, Lilian kept her eyes from the splintered door. She shone the light into the woodpile, around the shed and started on the garden. It was still too dark. Molly had died, she was sure of it, and she didn't want Billy to find her. In the matter of Micky, there was still a lot to feel anxious about, and she hadn't slept well. It was surely inevitable now that he would stay here and they would have to think again about what to do with him.

Maybe Molly had got back into the chook run. Lilian shone the lamp around the perimeter fence before going inside. Some of the birds rustled as if she were a small wind, but most of them were still sleeping. The smell was reassuring. Chicken shit, feathers, straw, earth. The steam from her breath. But no sign of her girl.

Molly had hatched when the older children were still small. Susan had named her Molly, and Micky had added a string of other names they'd long since stopped using. Molly Polly Wolly. Iris had sung them a song with those names in it – not Molly, but all the rest – that she claimed to have got from an American swagman. Anyway, Molly Polly Wolly had become a feisty little hen with prodigious egg-laying abilities and unexpected longevity. She'd be at least ten years old now. She must have finally had enough.

Lilian saw Russell begin to stretch. The shine on his dark feathers was green in the early light and he looked magnificent. Walking back to the house, Lilian continued to look and to call. *Molly Polly Wolly*. As if she weren't calling the hen at all, but calling her small children, the ones who had bestowed the names, who'd used the names, who'd forgotten the names, and who now slept unaware. Susan and Micky, aged six and eight. *Molly Polly Wolly Doodle*, they'd sing, *Molly Polly Wolly Doodle* all the day.

The light was beginning to spill and spread. Lilian knew there'd be a handful of people on the island waking now – two or three handfuls, perhaps, but no more. She didn't know all of them, but she knew who they were. It was hard to believe they were so few. To Lilian, the island was burdened by the weight of people and groaning with ghosts. It was something to do with the way everyone clung together, mouth to ear, ear to mouth, keeping everybody else's business and tripping over gravesites and the names of the dead. Even those who were alive carried the dead on their shoulders. Ed was named after his father, so there was a ghost right there and he'd wanted to name Micky after Jack. Thank heaven she'd held out on that one. It was difficult enough everyone saying Micky was like his uncle without removing all doubt.

Lilian had often wondered what it was like for her son in Wellington, swimming through shoals of people he didn't know and didn't care about. It would have been lonely at times, no doubt, but surely it was liberating too? He could have become a whole other person if he'd wanted to. Here, well, even she knew what every family on the island was doing right at this moment, down to the way they drank their tea. They in turn knew her movements and the movements of her family. And how, she wondered, could one move lightly knowing that? Every step was weighted, every look weighed, on the soles of each boot great clods of clay. She was astonished sometimes she could move at all.

Opening the back door, Lilian heard men's voices. She removed her boots and went through to the kitchen.

'Good morning, Sarge, I didn't hear you arrive,' she said.

'Tea would be welcome, Lily,' said her husband. 'And breakfast,' he looked up quickly, 'if that's all right.'

Sarge was standing and nodding and then sitting and fixing his eyes on the table top.

'There appears to be a solution to Micky's current lack of employment.' Ed's voice fell heavily; he sounded tired. Lilian put the water on and started the bacon. 'Gunner's sick. They want Micky on harpoon.'

Lilian could smell beer still, but there were no bottles about. It seemed to be stuck in her nostrils from the night before.

'No, he hasn't got it in him,' said Ed finally. 'I stand by what I said before, Sarge. He's still a boy.'

'He's sixteen. Same as when you started. Jack was younger.'

'It's not Micky's age, Sarge. He hasn't got the self-control. He's a hot-head like Jack – we all know that if the Turks hadn't got my brother he'd have come home and killed himself or someone else.'

'High spirits,' said Sarge, grinning.

'High spirits is one thing,' said Ed, and he was going to go on but he met Lilian's eye and stopped.

Lilian broke the eggs into the pan. She made herself concentrate on the way the transparent part of the egg whited out and the yolk started to cook. She heard Sarge clear his throat. She wanted him to leave.

'Ed, this is how it is – Micky can shoot and we need a shooter.' Sarge was speaking quickly. 'We're already a couple of men down. If he doesn't do it, the chaser stays off the water and we lose money.'

Lilian could feel Ed watching her put the pot of tea, two mugs and the sugar on the table. He seemed to have lost his tongue after that speech from Sarge.

Lilian put a plate of bread and butter down hard on the table. The plates of bacon and eggs were next. Sarge looked relieved and hoed in. Ed was slower on the uptake.

'Eat up. It will get cold,' said Lilian, but Ed wasn't moving, he was looking at her. 'Another egg?'

'No, no, this is plenty.'

Ed waited until he'd finished eating before he spoke again. He pushed back his chair and fixed his gaze on Sarge.

'Gunner can have the boy.'

Lilian caught her breath at the back of her throat. 'Ed!'

Up came his hand, palm out to stop her. 'Sarge is right. Micky should show us what he's made of. It's not working for him like this, is it? He can't hold down a job in a fish and chip shop, he's hanging around here like a bad smell, going off fishing with his mother when he's not exploding bottles and getting drunk and nearly killing his brother. I don't know what the right way is, but this isn't it, Lilian. Keeping him wrapped up.' He wasn't looking at her now either. 'Being a gunner might be the making of him.'

Lilian put her head down and tried to eat her food. Not here. She couldn't say with Sarge here.

'Good on you.' Sarge was on his feet, wiping his mouth.

'Not today, though,' said Ed. 'Micky's in recovery after

his theatricals last night. Tomorrow.'

Sarge opened his mouth, but Ed shook his head. 'And God help Gunner if anything happens to him.'

Sarge was gone. Lilian could hear him whistling to his horse and heading off down the track. Ed seemed to deflate.

'It's the right thing, Lilian. I'm sorry.'

'Ed, you said, after that time, you said . . .'

That time. Micky was only fourteen, the beginnings of a beard, stinking breath, and so angry with her he couldn't speak. Pushing her up against the dresser so hard she had handle-shaped bruises for weeks. Only fourteen. She couldn't remember what she'd done to him to make him lash out like that. She'd said, 'Micky, love,' to try and calm him, to show him she wasn't angry. She was never angry with him, because she was always making up for everything, wasn't she? 'Micky, love—' and he'd lifted his fist then and she'd seen it there above her, and she knew why, and she'd closed her eyes and shielded her face, but the fist fell behind her, on to the dresser, through the glass door. She'd heard the glass pane smash, the crystal glasses smash, she heard him cry out, felt his blood on the back of her neck.

'I know what I said. Things have changed.' Ed was looking off to one side of her. 'Will you tell him? I need to get away.'

Lilian let the boy sleep, which he did, despite Billy checking on him every half hour, hoping for someone to take him fishing. Half the day had gone when Micky came to the kitchen door and stood there watching her and Billy eat lunch. His skin was the colour of parchment, his eyes bloodshot.

'Gunner wants you out on the chasers,' she said at last. 'And your father's agreed.'

'No bloody way.' He was suddenly alert and suspicious,

advancing and retreating without moving an inch. 'Why would he, after last night?'

She saw the way he'd drawn himself up a little, though, standing without leaning on the door frame.

'It was Gunner and Sarge putting the hard word on him. Gunner's sick, and he reckons you can handle it.'

It was too big a gift dropped in his lap. Micky kept fingering the wrapping, unsure what to do with it. 'When?'

'Tomorrow, love.'

'Definite?'

'Unless you don't want to.'

He was smiling now and looking terribly young. 'What do *you* think?'

'No bloody way,' said Billy through a mouthful of corned-beef.

'Billy!'

'Shall we go fishing today then?' Billy said.

'I reckon I need a bath first,' said Micky.

He dragged it into the kitchen from the porch and filled it with Billy's help. Lilian was making bread, so she watched them come and go. At last, Micky said he was ready, so Lilian slapped the bread one more time and left it to rise.

She had work to do with the hens, and in deference to Micky's bath Lilian let herself back in through the front door. The unusual stillness that had started the day had persisted and brought with it a light that gave everything a rare clarity. The chickens' feathers had seemed remarkably fine and, here in the hallway, the blue roses of the wallpaper bloomed as if they'd been freshly watered. When Lilian passed Micky's room, she looked in as she always did, to check things were in order, and there he was, her grown son, sitting on his bed entirely naked. He was side-on to her, looking at his hands which were cupped in his lap. She paused, knocked into stillness. He was beautiful: the whiteness of the skin he usually kept covered, the leanness of his flanks, the swell of muscle in once slender arms. He looked exquisitely vulnerable in that light, but at the same time strong enough to account for himself.

Lilian hastened away to the kitchen, hoping she hadn't been heard.

For the rest of the day, when they weren't out fishing, the boys paced the garden and watched the whalers with the binoculars. Lilian could hear them as she dug over one side of the vegetable patch.

'You, too, Billy, one day. You'll be a gunner, I reckon. It's in the blood. You'll need to practise your shooting, though.'

And Billy's excited trill: 'Are you scared? Do you know what to do?'

It was hot work digging. Micky had offered to help but Lilian refused. She wanted to do it. There was sweat involved and fresh air and the task of opening up the earth. And somehow the day passed. Micky contritely chopped the wood while Billy watched from a safe distance, and then the two of them worked together to fix the broken door. At last, night fell. Micky took the maps out of the cupboard and opened them up on the lounge floor. Lilian found her sons with their shoulders touching, their attention on Antarctica.

Ed returned home and Micky jumped to his feet.

'They'll need folding and putting away,' said Ed. 'Before someone steps on them.'

'I was showing Billy . . .' But Ed had gone through to wash before tea.

Lilian served up. She watched the way Ed cut into the fish pie, sawing right across his plate so the potato split apart and the filling spilled out. He hovered over the steamy fragrance of fish and milk and nutmeg, and took a large forkful. 'Now that's what I signed on for,' he said.

'Me too,' said Micky.

'Me too,' said Billy with his mouth full.

'Well, we're a boring lot, aren't we?' said Ed. 'Don't ask for much.'

And for a moment there everyone at the table was smiling.

'You're coming out with us tomorrow,' said Ed to Micky. 'You all right with that?'

'They seem to have confidence in you.'

'And you don't?'

There was a pause while Ed chewed and swallowed. He looked at Lilian but she looked back at her food.

'Of course.'

Micky was silent. Ed continued to eat. He was looking at Lilian now. 'I didn't know you were out on the water today.'

'It wasn't me,' said Lilian. 'It was the boys. They were only gone an hour or so and got enough fish to feed an army.'

'Getting your eye in on the small fry, eh Mick?'

'No need,' said Micky.

'In your opinion?'

'Absolutely.'

'So you're aiming for a whale tomorrow?'

'One at least.'

12

The Friar woke with Annie face down on his chest. She'd been crying in her sleep. He was wet with it and the night air made him cold. He moved her back on to her pillow where her hair clung to her face across her nose and mouth. He managed to peel it off without waking her.

She looked very pale. She'd changed so much since the baby, there were days when he didn't know her any more.

The Friar lay wide awake beside her for an hour, watching the light come, hearing the birds. When she woke, she didn't remember crying. She kept to her pillow, staring at woolsacks on the ceiling and telling him her dream.

It was the whale, her whale, the night whale. It was just as she remembered it that time when it had nudged her boat. But where the real whale had been no threat in the end, the whale in her dream was terrifying. When it dived, she feared it might be coming back to tip her up. There was nothing to show where it was. She'd seen it, though, before it rounded up. That eye, the size of a teacup – swivelling to take her in. But it wasn't the whale's eye at all; it was Robert's eye when she'd woken to him that first morning.

It was a month after the baby and she hadn't talked about him once. Now the words slid from her mouth and down her chin, barely making sense. She talked about how she'd been lying so close to him that morning that when she'd woken all she'd seen was his eye. It was extraordinary, she said, to be that close to someone – to reduce them to one blue eye.

The Friar had noticed nothing about Robert's eyes. What he'd noticed, he supposed, was the baby's weight. He seemed to weigh nothing at all for flesh and bone, for a whole lifetime ahead. How long Annie and the baby had lain together after the birth, he didn't know. Could a baby be still for that long without making a noise? But when the Friar had gone to tell Annie the midwife was there, when he opened the curtains and let the sun settle on her back, he found her asleep. So he'd picked the baby up gingerly and taken him out of the room. When he looked in on Annie, she was still sleeping, her mouth wide open with exhaustion and the rest of her body tucked around the space where the baby had been.

He was the one who had to tell her what had happened – how weak Robert had been, how he hadn't opened his mouth to cry. That he'd sucked the Friar's finger until it had slipped out and fallen to his small unmoving chest.

The Friar felt he should have cried with her then. But it didn't feel like there was room for his feelings in the barrage of pain and sorrow that squalled from her mouth.

13

The sky was the colour of barely beaten egg, and the sun newly emerged from behind Arapawa Island streamed clear yellow on Lookout Hill and the men who waited there. Little else was lit at that early hour. A hundred yards below the Lookout the sea was still dark, and the hills behind were in shadow and crisp with frost. Each man on that hilltop felt privileged to be there on the edge of, the very edge of, the waking world.

It was a promising day and Sarge was heartened by it; so promising that it made him want to try a bit of mischief. Waiting for the billy to boil, he clapped his hands together and stamped his feet to stop the cold setting inside the tips of his fingers and toes. That was a good reason – if he needed any – for a bit of fun. It always got the blood moving.

Micky had come. They'd been making wisecracks about his city ways all the way up from the beach. It had started the moment he'd got water in his boots climbing out of the dinghy, and reached a peak when he'd spread his coat on the grass and started to remove the boots. They'd all watched Micky tip the water out before putting them in the sun by the lean-to.

'Thought you'd bring the sea up with you?' said Boots

without any preliminaries. He hadn't so much as said 'Gidday' to the boy.

'I guess they don't have much call for gumboots on Lambton Quay,' said Jimmy. 'It's only natural the silly bugger would mistake them for bailers.'

Micky wrung out his socks and hung them over the boots, tucking his feet into his hat for warmth before picking up his binoculars. He had sent back some of the jibes early on, but now he wrapped himself in heavy silence and the laughter petered out.

It seemed to Sarge that the other whalers didn't know what to make of Micky now. The boy had surprised everyone the way he'd been down at the whale station angling to get on the whale boats, chiacking with the flensers, giving Gunner a hand. If you asked Sarge, this was the job he was made for. Sarge couldn't say that to Ed, though. He'd had his reasons for wanting the boy off the chasers.

They'd been sitting on Lookout Hill for an hour before Micky turned to Sarge and spoke in a low voice. 'Hey Sarge, can I ask you a question?'

'You can ask me a question, son, but I'm not sure you'll get an answer.' And Sarge had a good laugh at that, as a few of the others did round about.

Micky waited.

'What am I looking for?'

'A whale, last I looked.'

Ed looked at Micky sharply, and Sarge saw the look, and the flare of the boy's nostrils in response. It seemed like yesterday Ed had talked about Micky taking his place on the chasers when he was old enough; how he was a natural gunner and it ran in the blood. Then without explanation he'd taken his son over to Wellington one day and found him a job in the fish shop. He couldn't get rid of Micky fast enough.

'You're looking for a whale spout.' That was Ed. And after the laughter subsided, it seemed the sea subsided too, hushed itself against the beach below and waited. 'It's like your breath on a cold morning.'

Micky looked at his father, but Ed's face was behind the binoculars, his elbows on his knees to keep them steady, trained on a corner of the vast pitching blueness of the sea. So he returned to his glasses again and the porthole they made. Sea, only sea.

He would find a bloody whale; they'd laugh on the other side of their faces.

Micky's eyes moved around the circle of shifting blue, paused on a breaking wave, travelled along a shiny slick, came back again to what looked like warm breath in cold air, and waited. Nothing. It was strange to have the sea filling his eyes like that. It began to mesmerise him. He liked the way boats in the far distance blended into the line of water; the further out they were, the more the water and light dissected them, eventually leaving only a shiver. And his thoughts travelled like the boats, disappearing when they'd gone far enough. He could hear the others talking; they'd seen a fishing boat coming in from Cape Campbell to the south.

'It's the *Sunset*!'

'Where are you looking, Jimmy?' That was Sarge.

'Between us and Cape Campbell straight line down from the Pyramid.' And they all knew what that meant exactly and they shifted their glasses to that spot. Micky tried to follow but got lost until into the circle of his view came a white triangle-shaped bluff on the Cape Campbell shoreline thirty miles away to the south.

'Nah, not the Pyramid, a straight line out of Mary's Bum.' That was Phil. Micky caught his eye and sniggered.

Phil wasn't much older than him and they'd had a bit to do with each other when they were growing up, but then Ed had taken Phil on as a farmhand when Micky was still at home, which had made Micky unaccountably angry. He'd had a fight with Phil, smashed his face up, and this had been added to the list of reasons why he had to be sent away. Since his return, Phil had acted like a mate again and bailed him up with questions about living in Wellington and the girls over there. Micky guessed that the farmhand was in dire need of female company.

Micky shifted along from the Pyramid to find the two round hills that made up Mary's Bum, then pulled out to the fishing boat chugging their way. It had twenty miles or so to go: how could they make out which boat it was? He squinted hard but couldn't for the life of him identify it.

'I give up,' he said. 'How do you know it's the *Sunset*?'

'It's pink,' said Phil bleakly.

'But you can't see the colour from here,' said Micky, adjusting his lenses to try for more clarity.

'Bloody girl's colour,' said Phil.

'It shouldn't be on the water,' said Jock. 'His wife chose the colour and the name too. Went down with a paintbrush to touch up around the windows. That Dave's got no shame.'

'They're coming in early,' said Sarge. 'Wonder what's wrong.'

'A lot's wrong if it's the *Sunset*!' said Jimmy, chuckling. 'Silly buggers wouldn't know a good boat if they fell over it. It shouldn't even be out there. It's a hazard to shipping.'

And they all erupted into laughter except Boots who was humming *Red Sails in the Sunset.*

'There she blows,' said Ed quietly. And Boots shut up.

'Blows?' spluttered Sarge, looking to see where Ed's glasses were pointing. 'You doing a bit of mollyhawking over there, Ed?'

'He's not poaching, you silly bugger,' said Jimmy. 'Your eye was off the ball.'

'My eye is never off the ball,' said Sarge. 'Where the hell is it?'

'Five or six mile out,' said Ed. 'Straight out from here in the first patch of dark water. I've seen six spouts. I reckon it's a pair of humpbacks. They should be up again in five.'

'Should I have a bird in the top of my glass?' asked Boots.

'No, the bottom of your glass, move it up a bit,' said Ed.

'Straight under that long thin bit of cloud?'

'Yeah, you've got it. Right at the end of the finger of cloud.'

And it was silent for a moment as they looked. Micky was sure he was on the right spot, and the blood beat in his temples as he waited.

'Blow!' said Ed, louder than last time, and then louder each time. 'Blow! Blow! Blow!'

Micky felt something spurt in his chest.

'Gotcha!' cried Sarge.

'It rounded up beautiful!' cried Jimmy. 'That's another one for you, Ed. Let's get out of here.'

Micky hadn't got it; he was moving his glasses about too fast, feeling himself a fool.

'That's it!' said Jock. 'See you fellas later.'

And that's when they knew it was all on and scrambled to their feet, grabbing lunchboxes and rain gear. That's when Micky reluctantly put his binoculars down, pulled on his damp socks and pushed a foot into his right boot; and that's when something in there shrieked and wriggled and bit his big toe, and he shrieked too and fell over backwards and tried to pull his foot out as fast as he could. And Sarge was laughing the most and Micky was swearing like crazy, holding his toe, and out shot a blue penguin not much bigger than his foot but a whole lot more furious than Micky and louder than Sarge. Its flippers flapping, waddling in a hurry, squawking and gargling, it scrambled down the narrow path to the boats. And the others ran off after it.

'You've got to watch yer boots, son, at all times! You never know what'll get in there!'

'Or who will *put* it in.'

'Move your Christmas parcel, kid,' said Old Jock, not a hint of a smile on him. 'I've just about had enough of your pissing around. I don't know who you think you are – Little Lord Fishbreath of Lambton Quay or something – but you'd better pull your bloody weight and get out there.'

Micky growled at the back of his throat and felt the colour shift from his neck to his cheeks. He stared at the dark veins on Jock's nose.

'Get a move on, Micky!' Jimmy had come back up the track to get him, his face the same colour as Micky felt. The boy let his fist unclench and turned deliberately away from both men. A fight now would stop him going out on the water. If Jock didn't say anything, it'd be all right. Micky tipped each boot upside down, pulled them on his feet and picked up the rest of his gear.

At the bottom of the track before the swing bridge he and Jimmy caught up with the rest.

'Looking for your friend, Mick?' said Sarge, pointing down at the blue penguin fast scrabbling away over the stones.

139

Boots and Phil got to the beach before the others, and were taking the first dinghy out to the *Nautilus*. The others piled into the second dinghy. That was the rule. First crew to the beach had an advantage. Within minutes, all three chasers were firing and heading for the mouth of Tory Channel.

Micky was at the front of the *Balaena*, holding the harpoon gun. It was so tight in there at the opening to his throat where he needed room for air, though. He could barely breathe. He couldn't do this.

Ed had readied the gun this time, and the hand-bombs were where they should be. *All I need to do is hang on and point.* How hard could it be? Whales were a hell of a lot bigger than goats, and he'd dropped so many of those he'd lost count. Micky held his lips tightly together as the swell rose, for his stomach was rising too, up into his chest and into the back of his throat, just where it was already tight with anxiety. Seasick. Micky hadn't counted on that.

They were through the heads and into Cook Strait heading south-east. Micky stared at the water up ahead and the sickness gradually receded, or maybe he wasn't noticing it as much. There was nothing between him and the wide sea, nothing at all. In the far distance the horizon was a dark pencil line and past that horizon was the world. Here he was as small as he was, a gunner on a whaling boat, embracing all of it. And out of the water it came, thirty feet to port.

Moving slowly and unconcernedly, the humpback whale let go a rush of wet stinking air. Micky was close enough to see the air holes like large nostrils on its back. The creature was as fine a sight as he had ever seen. At that same moment the blockage in Micky's throat cleared; his head emptied out; his body leaned to take the thrust of the gun. It was as if he'd been doing it all of his life.

It can't be this easy.

He pulled the trigger and, without meaning to, closed his eyes. He felt but didn't see the explosion inside the barrel, the harpoon bursting from it and the kick of the gun. His eyes opened again and he was sucking at the air like an old man. It was a direct hit into the whale's spine behind the blow hole; the harpoon was shuddering from the impact and as deep as it could go. Micky slammed his fist into the side of the harpoon gun and yelped, 'That's it! That's it!' His hand was sore but he didn't care. He felt his airways open and he heard himself laughing in a way he'd never done before — it belched from him. He'd never thought, not the first one.

Micky sought out Jimmy. The driver was shaking his head. Yeah, thought Micky, who's the silly bugger now? And then he looked for the other chasers. Both of them were only yards away: Boots and Phil grinning, Sarge giving the thumbs up, his father's face grim as he went for a hand-bomb to finish it off.

For the whale was still moving. It managed to lift its tail and slap the water, one hard agonised slap that flicked blood into the air. And then the bomb hit and it was over.

14

Stepping on to the wharf at Picton, Susan felt something lift deep inside her and push a small amount of air out through her mouth in a sigh not unlike one Emily would make. Susan adjusted the little one against her. Holding a baby was, she thought, like holding a stone kept from the beach after a day in the sun – all that stored energy vibrated against the skin. Susan was loath to release it into the pram Titch had manoeuvred off the boat and placed before them. After all, this was somewhere new for Emily. She'd never been off Arapawa Island, let alone to a town. But the pram it had to be; Susan couldn't carry her all day.

'She doesn't like it,' said Titch, keeping his fingers on the edge of the pram hood as Susan placed Emily into it and tried to tuck the blanket around her. The baby had stiffened the moment her mother's hold had loosened, and she was grumbling now; but Titch's close attention flustered Susan more than the baby did.

'Swaddling,' he said. 'Our mother was a midwife – she swore by it. Can I?'

Susan didn't know why, but she stepped back and let him take over. She could see his white fingers fiddling inexpertly with the peggy-square blanket, and she could also see the top of his head. The hair was scraped thinly across a bony irregular skull, and there was what looked like a raspberry-coloured birth mark right where her daughter's fontanelle would be. Susan felt queasy both at this forced intimacy and the association with the vulnerable pulse in Emily's head. She began to joggle the pram on its sprung wheels – partly to calm Emily but mostly to dislodge the boat man. The baby hiccuped and started to wail, and Titch pulled back frowning and hissing: 'Screw that.'

Not so long ago, Susan had told Ben about Titch, but he thought she was making too much out of nothing again, finding things to be frightened of. Susan had tried hard since – to see cheeriness not oiliness, and to answer back in kind – but she couldn't escape the feeling that Titch was more than he seemed. Micky said in Wellington they'd arrest him. Her mother was less quick to judge but she had questions. She'd asked about where'd he come from and who his wife was, and had run it over her tongue: 'Titch and June, June and Titch.' And then she'd shaken her head and left it.

There wasn't much Susan could tell her mother about June, except that her skin stretched thinly over her round body and she was unable to speak much due to the pins in her mouth. Her hair was the exact same colour as her husband's. Susan guessed that's what had attracted them to each other. For the first time in a long time, June had been on the mail boat. She'd asked if she could hold the baby, but the way she'd plucked at Emily with those boneless-looking fingers had unsettled Susan and made her ask for the baby back.

Susan jerked the pram away from the boat man now and set off briskly along the wharf. 'I'll be back at four,' she said.

Ben had told her with some pride that there was enough money for material for a dress for Emily and one for herself.

Nothing too costly, mind you, but dresses nevertheless. She should go to White's, he said, they had a better selection and she could take her time. And there was no Titch. Susan looked back to see him adjusting his mooring ropes in that particular way he had. It seemed to her he always jabbed at everything, unlike the fluid movements of the other men on the wharves.

'Screw him,' she said softly.

White's was the rasp of tape measures, the whisper of cloth, the slice of scissors. It was heavy bolts of fabric dropped on to counter tops like meat to be chopped. It was, in Susan's mind, a place of deep, almost reverential silence punctuated by the aggressive sounds of commerce. But when she entered the shop that day what she heard were women's voices, like layered petticoats, swishing this way and that, talking of dress lengths, trimmings, stitches, ribbons, eyelets, elastic, twilled satins, rayon taffetas, shantung silk.

There was a stand of new washable flannel folded and stacked and teamed with jaunty patterns for shirts and pyjamas, and Susan found herself standing there and stroking the warm fabric, even though the last thing she wanted was a flannel shirt. She thought about Ben and his string vest, and then turned her attention back to the shop. They'd changed things around a little in the past eighteen months. Nearby there was an arrangement of nets and gauzy materials to use for bridal and evening wear that used to be up by the counter. Pride of place was a dusky pink net with roses attached. Someone – Gloria, it had to be – had labelled the whole display, 'Dreaming of Love'.

Susan walked over and reached out to touch the roses.

'It's Susan! With her baby!'

Gloria's voice had a nasal quality that was unmistakable,

her whole face paying homage to a long nose that reminded Susan of the Romans in the illustrated Bible. All of Gloria was long and straight, in fact, and she had to fold herself up to peer in on the baby.

'Fine work, my girl,' she said at last. 'I can't see the seams *at all*.' And she honked softly.

They both regarded the sleeping child.

Gloria surfaced first. 'You're here for her, aren't you? Her first real dress? I have something perfect. The finest lawn – just in yesterday – you can barely feel it.' And Gloria was the saleswoman now, leading Susan like a lamb to the slaughter. For Susan knew even before she saw it that she'd want it so much she'd have to have it, and that wouldn't leave quite enough for a dress for herself. The finest lawn, the highest quality silk, the best wool. Her love for them was a kind of hunger. *Better than chips*, Nana used to say. She was the one who'd shown Susan how to sew, and had been the one to bring her here to White's. Susan remembered it like a visit to church. The size of the place, Nana's hushed explanations, the sounds of female worship.

The two other girls in White's were cooing around the baby, making it difficult to concentrate on the material Gloria was unrolling on the counter. It had small yellow and blue roses, and would look lovely on Emily, with a Peter Pan collar and pearl buttons on the sleeves. But Susan had been thinking of plain white with pale blue stitching.

She moved the pram away from the counter so the shop girls would follow it. She thought she could hear Emily stirring and hoped the silly chooks wouldn't wake her. There was room now to come forward and put out her hand. The material was flawless, like Emily's skin.

'It's very fine,' she said tentatively.

'And . . .?'

'Do you have it in white too?'

'White,' said Gloria. 'We do have white.' She brought another bolt of cloth to the counter and unrolled it a little. It was almost transparent.

'You could always take both,' she said. 'The white is a good deal cheaper.'

'Oh Gloria,' said Susan, 'if only I could.'

She could hear Emily making small licking sounds with her mouth which could grow into something full blown in a matter of seconds.

'One and a half yards of the white,' she said at last, her voice hushed as if Ben could hear. 'And the same for the floral.'

Emerging from the filtered light of the shop, Susan was briefly blinded by the sliding mid-afternoon sun and a car that shone like a mirror. She almost retreated back to Gloria and the girls until it was time to leave Picton. But she was hungry now, and while she had something in her bag she liked the thought of a cup of tea and a sit-down. Emily, thank goodness, had been fed out the back of the shop.

Susan wheeled her daughter to the Centennial Tearooms, where she chose an egg sandwich and a small piece of sponge cake, and carried them to a table near the window. She felt grand. The girl brought the tea and said it needed to draw, and then paused to look in the pram: 'Nice baby.'

The tea was hot, but Susan swallowed it quickly. She took longer over the sandwich – the bread was a bit dry and the egg needed more salt but it did the trick. She wrapped the cake to take home for Ben. Titch was waiting.

*

Lilian could see the whalers. There was a gunmetal shine on the water and they were out there not far past the mouth of Tory Channel: small dark fish waiting to be swallowed. She could feel Micky's excitement carried on the flood tide. *Mama, look at me!* And there he was and only ten years old, standing high on the back of the dead whale with the men, his arms folded like them, his chest puffed out like them, bowyangs made from sacking tied to his legs to stop the blood drenching his shorts. They'd printed the photograph in the newspaper, and when it had arrived by mail boat Lilian had cut it out and framed it. It was on the sideboard still.

There was something in the excitement on Micky's face that had always made her heart ache. He was up there with the men doing a man's job, but he was still a boy. He would spend hours by himself at that time, polishing and cataloguing his collection of marbles or making and flying kites. He'd disappear into the trees with Susan and play convoluted games that didn't have a name. It was those games combined with a pig of a temper and that stubborn streak of his that gave him the nickname Micky Savage. But it seemed no time at all before his vivaciousness curdled into surliness and the famous temper got out of control. When was that? At some stage Ed started saying what she'd known for a while: *Drop a match a mile away and Micky goes up like a bonfire.*

Lilian didn't have a photograph for it, but she could see it as clearly as if she did: a young Ed standing by a whale the same way his son had stood for the newspaper man. Was he posing for her? She couldn't remember. She was pretty sure there wasn't a photographer there, or she'd have the photograph. But he was certainly standing like the boy, waiting for something, posing by the whale he'd killed, full of himself, but shyer than Micky, and looking all the while at her. It was just after the war and not long after she'd arrived on Arapawa, so he'd have been about twenty-six, and still leaning towards the thin side. There were calluses already on his hands and feet, flayed skin on his cheeks. Lilian would have been twenty-three and starting to show with Susan.

That was the Tipi Bay station across the channel and they'd gone over for the season. It was pretty basic and there was no winch yet for getting the whales up the ramp. Ed's whale was partly submerged, but you could still see what a large beast it was, which was why he was so pleased. Still, you'd have thought the Friar had fastened it, the way he was acting. She'd forgotten that. Of course he was there.

She didn't see it start, but Ed had shoved his cousin with his shoulder and the Friar had grabbed Ed as he was falling and the two of them ended up on the ground, rolling on the sand and laughing and shouting. With Ed's height and his cousin's width they were probably even, weight for weight, and they'd been doing this since they were small, so they could keep on for hours until someone pulled them apart. Gunner was the one who did it that time. Both were dishevelled, dark hair in all directions, although the Friar's already had early strands of white. Ed was unconcerned, the Friar sheepish. Chalk and cheese.

Then the Friar was beside her, looking at the whale, and what was he saying?

'Have you seen a whale heart?' He'd lifted his eyebrows up and down and patted the left side of his chest. 'It's almost as big as this one.'

Lilian had laughed and shaken her head.

So he'd tied a rope to his belt, saluted her and taken a knife. He went to the large slack mouth of the whale and without any preliminaries dived into the water, into the mouth, and disappeared. Swallowed by the whale.

Ed explained later how the Friar had gone in through its gullet, cut the ribcage, and after coming back up for air he'd gone down again into the lung cavity. That's when he hooked a chain to the heart and crawled out. The facts, that's what Ed had given her, not the *heart* of the matter. Not the way of speaking that made ordinary things strain at their moorings.

Out of nowhere, there came a line of men wet to the bone, for it was drizzling and the hills were grey gauze, and these men pulled that heart from the body of the whale, pulled it out hand over hand. She was the sole audience as it emerged at last, six foot wide and the weight of three men; and they'd cheered to see it; and Ed and the Friar had looked at her at the same time to make sure she was watching, Ed smiling and frowning all at once and pushing his wet hair back to his head, the Friar laughing and shaking like a sheepdog, showily licking his lips. How astonishing it had seemed back then, the men and the whale with a heart in its mouth.

Nineteen years on, Micky was stepping up to the line of men at the mouth of the whale like they all did hereabouts in one way or another. Some survived it, some didn't. The gunner Ed had replaced had been dragged from the chaser, his foot caught in the boxline, and drowned. Tommy's Dad had died in agony after falling head first into the digester. God willing, Micky could handle himself out there like his father had done.

Lilian thought about Ed. How he'd paced up and down outside last night for an hour at least. Micky had joined him for a smoke, and she'd listened through the window while she cleared away the dishes, but they hadn't said a word. Lilian took Ed's cup of tea out to him, and there was a small smile, she was sure of it, a nod, *champion*, then he'd drained the cup and was off inside to bed.

Worried or not, Ed was sound asleep when she'd climbed in beside him and pulled the quilt up to her neck, and he'd stayed asleep while Lilian's thoughts had kept her brain from shutting down. After a while, she'd turned on her side and reached out for her husband. He lay as he always lay, showing her the fullness of his back. Gently, she'd pressed the tips of her fingers into his skin. She didn't want to wake him, or maybe she did. Finally she'd slept.

Lilian heard a small sniffle behind her, and felt a warm body land on her back. It scrabbled up her like a possum and hung on her, legs dangling.

He smelt of grass.

'Mummy,' Billy said, trying to pull her face round towards him. 'I dreamt about a whale last night – no, two whales.' It was a game they played.

'Two whales!'

'No, three whales.' He nodded solemnly, counting his fingers.

Lilian gently pulled the boy down off her back and sat on the grass with him.

'Were they as heavy as you?'

'No!' The giggles were Billy again as he poked her stomach. 'They were as heavy as you!'

'That heavy!' Lilian poked him back. 'They must have been blue whales, then.'

'One of them was! You've got two more guesses.'

'Did one of them have long flippers and a hunched back?'

Billy nodded encouragingly.

'All right, so we have a blue and a humpback. Let's see, did the third one eat whale tongues for breakfast?'

'Not an orca.'

'Was it long and thin and moving very fast?'

'No.'

'A sperm whale?'

'No.'

He'd burst out with it soon.

Lilian wrapped her arms around him, and when he didn't object she pulled him closer. There was a small silence that ended with a half-hearted reproof when Billy pinched her cheek.

'Well?'

'I give up,' said Lilian.

'It was a humpback whale *calf*. The other one was its mother.'

'Ah.'

'Where's Molly?'

'I don't know, sweetheart. She was in the garden. I think she got out through the fence. We'll find her, don't worry.'

'I've looked. She's nowhere.'

'There's Micky,' said Lilian, pointing at the distant chasers. They'd barely moved.

Billy stared. 'Which one?'

'That one,' she said. 'The one right at the front.'

The copper began to bubble behind them. Already she'd lugged water to it and got the fire going underneath, and this was only the beginning of a chore that would fill the rest of her morning and most of the afternoon. Knowing there was work involved, Billy retreated up the apple tree. It was left to Lilian to watch as the steaming water engulfed the sheets and pillowcases – grey and softened by the bodies they'd been

151

holding; bodies that had tossed and snored and dreamt, bodies so precious to her that she could smell each sheet blind and know who'd slept in it. And she knew that if nothing else, at the end of the day when the men returned, these sheets would be perfectly white and, hopefully, dry and redolent with sunshine.

15

Night after night she sat by the window and looked into the dark. Night after night, refusing to draw the curtains, sitting rigid in the frigid house, not talking about the baby, not talking about anything very much.

After a week, Annie said she wanted to talk about the whale.

Had he noticed that whales' eyes swivelled to follow you? Had he seen the glimpse of white like the white of a human eye? When it looks up at you through the water, what does it see? Are you clear or distorted? Does it see you at all?

Exasperated. Sick to his stomach. The Friar, who had answered all the questions as best he could, snapped, 'How am I supposed to know that, Annie? Unless I got inside a whale and looked out. It's like asking me what a dog sees.'

If he fed Annie up on red meat, he'd thought, he might be able to give her some of her colour back and clear her mind. She was muddy with grief, still. So he traded the last of their precious muttonbirds to get some stewing beef, and then had to sit and watch her picking, leaving most of it on her plate.

'Where are the muttonbirds?' she'd asked plaintively, and when he told her she was inconsolable. He could do nothing right. Annie's grief had become a heavy unbreachable stone which made it difficult for her to swallow or move or breathe. She was often cold. She didn't want his comfort.

When he took himself off to bed, he'd will her to follow him, but increasingly she didn't. And he'd fall asleep, as he always did, as soon as his head hit the pillow. One night, he was restless and he heard the door open and Annie go out. He supposed she was using the outhouse, but he worried nonetheless, and when she didn't return after ten minutes he pulled on his clothes and went to see. She was nowhere around, so he walked to the beach.

She was pacing by the water.

The Friar kept his distance. It was not too dark to see, and there was cloud clearing around the moon. All at once Annie dropped her coat and dived in, and the Friar gasped as much at her nakedness as at the sound of her entering the water. Summer it may have been, and the evening was mild, but the water was cold enough to stop a person breathing.

He was scrabbling with his shoes when he saw her walk from the water and pull on her coat. He dropped to his stomach and lay in the spindly grasses until she'd gone back up to the house. The Friar walked to the water's edge himself then, and stood staring, no clear idea what he expected to see. The night air slipped inside his clothes. He knew Annie would be missing him up at the house by now, but it was hard to move. Her grief had defeated him; there was nothing more he could do.

She was sitting in the chair by the stove fast asleep, her head tipped towards her shoulder and resting on the back of the chair. She hadn't removed her coat or dried herself; there were still drops of water on her legs. The Friar pulled up a kitchen chair and sat down. He'd never understood the way she could sleep like that. To him, sleep was a time to discard everything – he threw his body on to the bed as into a river. To fall asleep sitting in a chair must be like being a reed in the shallows, not properly submerged or refreshed.

The Friar slid his arm behind her back and his other arm under her legs. He picked her up without feeling it: she'd lost weight, surely? Where were those thighs he remembered? Where, in fact, was she? He'd looked at her face, which appeared to be struggling now to wake or to stay asleep, he couldn't tell which. He felt it then, both the tenderness and guilt.

Then Annie started on another hat. This one looked like it was being made for a giant, and it was in brown waxy home-spun. He didn't dare ask what had happened to the other wool or the other hat and the tiny half-finished jacket. The Friar marvelled at the way her fingers moved and her eyes barely looked at what she was doing. To be so concentrated and adept surely meant her mind was clearing.

So the Friar left her to it and went to dig over the compost. He thought it might get Annie interested in the vegetable garden again. He had been at it for ten minutes when he had to stop. There was something wrapped tight around the garden fork. A root. A worm, perhaps. Pulling at it, he realised it was a tangle of something that went deep inside the compost pile. He pulled and pushed at the rotting kitchen scraps, and what he saw at last was small and matted and pale blue. It was a garment the size of his hand, wrapped around two small balls of wool and stuck through with knitting needles, clumped like a small tumour in the leavings of the food they'd eaten that terrible week. Or barely eaten that week; he couldn't recall, in fact, eating anything at all. He removed it from the compost, took it to the far end of the garden and buried it.

The Friar saw Annie finish the hat she was making for him. He saw it the minute it was done. She bit the brown wool with her teeth and patted it flat on her lap. He saw her sit there a moment, her eyes somewhere else. She must have thought he was having a snooze. Then, without looking at what she was doing, she'd lifted the hot iron from the range, laid a clean pillowcase over the hat and pressed it. The smell of the warm damp wool made the Friar think of the shearing shed.

She must have known then that she was leaving him.

He saw her hold the hat to her cheek before she came over. She touched his head, and he pretended to wake.

'These strands of white,' she said. 'Where have they all come from?'

Then she put the hat on him and took a while adjusting it, smiling and grimacing up close to him as if he were still asleep.

'No!' she said at last. 'It won't work, you have too much hair!'

And she'd pulled the hat off.

But he was too quick for her, he grabbed it and grabbed her hand, and held the hat in his lap and her hand to his cheek. It was still warm from the ironing, from holding the wool, from all the things it had done in its lifetime. Singular hand.

'No, love,' he said gruffly. 'Leave it right where it is.'

16

Gunner was feeling better by smoko, and he was out in front of the whale station in his usual possie. It had been one of his fevers that had kept him onshore, and the urge that came with it of visiting the dunny regularly throughout the night. He hated stumbling from bed into the dark and cold with a screaming bladder, even worse getting there and having nothing to show for it. What sort of man was he? And out of the fever came thoughts that were irrational in the light of day. *I'm past it. It's time to give up harpooning. Let the young fellas have a go. Can't even piss.* But Gunner wasn't so far gone he couldn't have a laugh about it. He peered out into the clear day that had inspired Sarge to make mischief at Micky's expense.

'Can't piss, can't shoot a harpoon,' he chuckled to himself. 'What's the bloody *point*?'

Really, it was no bad thing to have a day off the water and to see to the business side of things. He'd check the equipment, talk to the men, do whatever needed doing. Gunner took a last drag of his cigarette and flicked the butt out into the bay where it fell among the mass of cape pigeons. One went to grab it but missed.

There was the thrum of an engine, and within seconds

everyone was outside as if called to come. The tug *Moana* entered the bay, a whale attached to it by the fluke.

'A cigar,' said Gunner to Ben who'd appeared beside him. 'And the tail's completely black. Haven't seen a humpback as long and thin as that in a while.'

All around him, the men were rolling up their sleeves. There was half a day's work in that one.

The *Moana* cleaved the water and the small birds cluttering its surface and came up alongside the ramp.

'Whose is it?' cried Ben through cupped hands.

'Micky's!' the skipper called back.

'Good on him,' said Ben. 'That's my brother-in-law! First day out and he gets one.'

Micky was pulling up now in the *Balaena*, seeing his whale in.

'Hey, Mick!' called Gunner. 'Do you want some chips with that?'

At the sound of Gunner's voice the men went back to work.

'C'mon, you bastards,' the Friar was saying. 'Move it, there's a whale out there.'

It was a good team.

Gunner was suddenly aware of the quick rush of a nor'wester against his skin and he looked to the sky to see what was happening. Not much had changed. The wind was always there, somewhere. Even if you couldn't feel it, it was only just around the corner. He realised then how many times he'd looked at the sky that day, or felt for the wind direction. It wouldn't be hard to go quietly mad on shore.

*

The Friar watched Ben use the scarf around his neck to wipe the sweat from his eyes. He'd attached the strop to the end of the first strip of blubber and the winch was pulling it off the flesh like an enormous banana skin that crackled as it peeled. The bull whale lay on its side, its ribbed throat spilling across the concrete, massive gashes where the flippers had been.

'Where'd he get it?' yelled the Friar over the winch.

'Just in front of East Head,' Ben called back. 'First time out. You wouldn't read about it.'

Stew and Charlie rested on their cutting spades, watching the blubber as it lifted away. Tommy came to watch too, and leaned against the wall, scratching his head. The Friar made a note to himself that when it was quieter he would tell the boys how Micky's Uncle Jack – Dead-Eye – had got a pair of whales his first time out. He was a bit of a hero among the ladies after that. Did the same at Gallipoli – off on his own raids from day one, shooting Turks, returning for ammunition and taking off again. He had eyes like a lizard's at the finish. Opaque and darting, they took in everything and gave out nothing. Didn't stop him getting shot through the head in Snipers' Gully, though.

The Friar heard a cough behind him.

'What do you think, then?' It was Micky.

'Not bad.'

'Not bad? Bloody oath!'

Micky walked past him and right up to the creature with its perfectly black tail. He put his hand on its flanks and turned to the Friar, his face a picture of triumph, then he cupped his hands around his mouth to call to Ben.

'Cut me some?'

Ben frowned.

Micky held up two fingers and yelled, 'Two steaks.'

'Can't do that.'

'Gunner won't miss them. Look at the size of this thing!'

'He might not,' said the Friar, stepping up beside Micky, 'but I will.'

Thinking of Dead-Eye had made him look differently at the boy. The eyes were the same. The cockiness. The Friar had a sudden feeling that Micky needed to be stopped.

Micky's face darkened and he turned to the older man in a sudden fury. 'Who are you to say?'

'Who am I?' The Friar moved his face closer to the boy's. 'You've got a nerve . . .'

'Are we winning?' Gunner's voice slapped the air between them, causing the Friar to step away. Then Gunner was up beside Micky, his hand on his shoulder and calling out to Ben. 'Cut the boy a couple of steaks, he deserves them.' And he dropped his voice. 'Good work, son. I knew you had it in you. You're a chip off the old block.'

'And which old block is that?'

Gunner narrowed his eyes. 'It's about time you learnt some respect, Michael Prideaux. Your father's a mighty good whaler, always has been. Your Uncle Jack was too.'

Ben pulled out a knife and cut three large steaks from near the tail. He put the dark, coarse-grained meat into newspaper and wrapped it tight.

'It's a pearler, Mick.' It was Ed. He was inside the room. The Friar didn't turn to look, but he felt a chill on his scalp despite the hat. 'I'm looking forward to those steaks.' That was Ed again, talking like it was an everyday event for him to be there.

The winch stopped. The first strip of blubber was off the animal and Ben was removing the strop. There was a silence that seemed to hang heavily around the packet of meat which Ben was handing to Micky. The Friar could hear Tommy whistling as he moved off to the digester and he knew he should be getting on too. He turned then, just in time to see Ed gesturing for his son to join him, and the two Prideaux men leaving the room.

'First time he's been around while we're cutting in,' said Ben.

'I knew he'd see the sense,' said Gunner. 'That boy's a genius behind the gun.'

The day Dead-Eye died was the day the Friar had started reading Ed's letters. The memory had come to him swift and sharp as he'd watched Ed's son admire his catch, and he was freshly ashamed of the connection. In a shit hole in 1915, one cousin dead and the other grieving, and that's where his mind had gone. The Friar had never much liked Dead-Eye, despite his being family, but that didn't explain using his death like that to get his hands on something he wanted.

Ed always seemed to have one of his girl's letters to hand – pages and pages of news from home in a difficult script, so fine and spidery, legs running into arms, tails into heads. The Friar was curious: what did Ed's sweetheart write about so abundantly? It seemed they'd only just heard Dead-Eye was killed when the mail came. Glazed by the loss of his brother, Ed sat with the letter in his hand, ignoring the way it groaned to be opened. The Friar let him alone for a while, and then he went and offered to read it aloud. He would skip over the personal bits, he said. It would cheer Ed up.

That was how the Friar found himself unfolding four clean, tightly written pages with more excitement than he'd felt in a long time.

Ed, my love

Here was a quandary immediately. The Friar looked at Ed, who wasn't looking, who still seemed not to care.

'It begins in the usual way,' said the Friar carefully.

'Ah,' said Ed.

'So I'll just start from the first bit of news, shall I?'

'Start where you like.'

The Friar scanned the first page silently.

Ed, my love

How much I worry about you, especially when I don't hear anything for so long. I assume if anything has happened we would be told, but perhaps not, perhaps a ship has been sunk with your letters on board, perhaps you do not write because you have been wounded. If you can, you *must* write to me.

On a more cheerful note, there has been sun every day for the past week – clear winter sun that shows up the dirt on my windows and the dust on my shelves, so I've been doing some spring-cleaning. A bit early, but it keeps me busy. The sun helps me imagine it is summer again and makes me think you are close to coming home.

'There has been sun every day,' the Friar began. And saying the words was like opening a window and letting the day in. She wrote in a hurry, throwing the weather and people and their doings on to the page, her eye flicking from near to far and back again. There was some sewing she had to do, the unseasonal rain, the aunt who came to stay, the owl that woke her in the night. Her life was a cluttered thing, and the Friar tripped over his tongue to get through it all. Now and then she would grapple with an idea that had arisen out of something she was reading or wonder about something that had been flushed from her life in Picton. Why, she pondered once, did women spend so much time inside? But generally they were pretty ordinary things she talked about. To be honest, if he'd read the letters on Arapawa Island, he'd have been bored. At Gallipoli, within sniffing distance of death, they were marvellous.

At the end of that first letter, a small sketch of a flower touched with blue wound its way around her name. The Friar found himself lifting the page to his face and sniffing it. He was sure he smelt perfume. He folded the four pages carefully and gave them back to Ed, then he sat whittling a stick and thinking.

The letter that came two weeks later was handed to the Friar without a word.

The trenches weren't quiet places. There was the constant low-grade hum of people, and on top of that the hissing, cracking and whining of bullets or machine-gun fire. Ed took to huddling next to his cousin so he could hear what he was saying, but even then there were times when the Friar had to raise his voice. It would start with just the two of them, and by the time they were halfway through, half a dozen men might have gathered to listen, their mouths open or smoking or chewing, and their eyes half closed.

The Friar remembered how what seemed like half of one letter was spent describing the fruit cake she'd baked.

He'd tried to skip some of it to move on to something more interesting, but the men insisted he go back. It was a recipe of her mother's, and while it had the ingredients it had none of the method. She'd listed them in the letter – the flour and the dried fruit, the eggs and rum, cinnamon and cloves – and then described her attempts to put all these things together. The result wasn't too bad; however (and she'd never make the same mistake again), she'd forgotten to line the tin with butter paper and the cake had baked with a hard brown crust. She cursed herself for her stupidity, but she said it was still delicious. *Delicious*, said Ed. *Still delicious*.

Ed hadn't had much to say about the woman who would be Micky's mother except that she was a daughter of a fisherman and she could row like a man. When the Friar quizzed him, he managed to talk about the easy way she'd tie up her hair – she'd twist it and pin it and there it would be. And one day, out of nowhere, he'd told the Friar he liked to inhale her smell when he said goodbye so he could take something of her with him. It was an ordinary smell, he said tentatively, like leaves.

Reading the letters worked. It took Ed away from his grief and it gave all of them something more to talk about. Some of the men asked if they could write to her; some pronounced they'd fallen in love. It was to be expected.

The Friar went through to the digester. He was wondering at the way Tommy's tuneless whistling could cut through the noise of a such a big machine and how he could go on doing it for so long. The Friar pushed up his sleeves and flexed his shoulders with a deep groan. He suspected that although Tommy was physically present, he was in fact absent without leave, in a place where pale come-hither girls whispered his name and baked brandy-soaked fruit cakes. The Friar stretched again, another groan. His shoulder muscles were knotted tight and he hadn't lifted a thing that day.

'Time to get to work, old man,' he muttered to himself; then, bellowing above the din, 'Hey, Tommy! Will you *shut it?*'

17

One night, after many nights, Annie woke him, shaking his shoulder. She'd found it at last: the silver edge to the waves, the electric slivers of light. She'd been looking for it all these nights while he'd been sleeping. She described how when she swam through it her skin had glowed with the phosphorescence and tingled as if she too were electric. She told him how she'd dived and surfaced like a whale, blowing the water from her mouth with a soft 'phuff'. *A fountain of light.*

Before she'd finished, he'd pushed her off him and climbed from the bed, his anger inexplicably huge, distorting his voice and making him hateful. She was being foolish; she was to stop it now. Annie had stared at him. She knew he was afraid, he could tell that much, but it didn't stop him. He wanted her to end this nonsense and be herself again.

When he stopped, she'd said nothing more, but instead lifted her hand to his face and rubbed his cheek with her fingers. Was he imagining it or did he feel a faint charge from her skin to his? Her eyes were shining again, like they used to. He expected her to kiss him and say she was sorry, but she said nothing. She dried her hair with a towel, slid silently under the covers and fell straight to sleep.

The Friar couldn't sleep. What he felt was hollow, the hollowness after anger had been poured out, and in that hollow place there was something small and rotten that was beginning to smell.

18

She was a sweet thing, Emily. Too small to play with, but if Micky held her on his knee and bounced his legs a little, her eyes would open a notch and she'd let out small sighs of surprise.

'I can't see you getting back to shop life,' said Ben to Micky, and he chewed on his sandwich, smiling at Susan when she passed him his tea. 'Not now.'

Micky started to reply, but then he cried out and wrenched his finger from the baby's mouth. 'What's she got in there?'

'She's learning to whittle with those teeth of hers,' said Ben.

'They call it cutting in,' said Susan.

'Think she's going to end up a flenser like her dad?' Ben squeezed the heel of his sandwich in both hands, grinned and thrust it into his mouth.

'Giddy up, horsey, giddy up,' sang Micky. Emily seemed riveted by him. Micky was certainly riveted by her; he felt almost proprietorial. *His niece.* 'You know,' he said, 'I think she'll be a gunner like her Uncle Mick.' Hearing his sister laugh, he turned to her. 'Don't tell me you didn't dream about it, Suzie?'

'Mmmm . . . no,' said Susan, yawning. 'Can't say I did.'

He was back to the baby, the gentle giddy-up. Emily's eyes were drooping. 'She's tired,' he said.

'She was up five times last night with those teeth of hers,' said Ben. 'I never knew they were so much trouble to sprout.'

'Hey Suzie, do you remember Dad doing this to us? Both together? He'd kick us so high I was sure we'd fall off.' Micky considered the memory that had only just presented itself. 'You bit your tongue once and it bled.' He felt Emily wriggle on her bottom, then she yawned and her whole body spasmed. 'And it was sunny and there were pikelets.' He sighed then, like Emily. He hadn't meant to. It had been squeezed from him and he couldn't take it back. Embarrassed, he stood up, thrust his niece at her mother and went to the window.

There was a cupped silence in the room.

'Dad didn't do horsey rides, Mick,' said Susan. 'It was the Friar.' And what she didn't say, and what Micky suddenly knew, was that when their father came in the room, into the laughing room with the crying girl with the bleeding tongue and the smell of pikelets, everything had stopped. Ed had stood with his hands heavy at the end of his arms.

'Well,' said Lilian. 'I think it's my turn to hold Emily. She's had enough bouncing around for today.'

'It's nearly time for her sleep,' said Susan, handing her over. 'The girls are coming around this afternoon to sew and I want her in bed.'

'I wonder how long the Friar will take fixing the *Balaena*,' said Micky. 'He's taken an hour already.'

Without Emily to distract him, Micky was keen to get going again – perhaps he'd go and give the Friar a hand. There was nothing much wrong with the chaser. The engine had been spluttering a bit in the last run: it was Gunner who insisted it be checked out.

'It's fixed, it's fixed, the chaser's fixed!' They could hear Billy before he got to the house. Micky lifted his eyebrows at Ben, and the two men went to go.

Then there was just the three of them: Lilian, Susan and the baby. Susan cleared away the plates and wiped down the table. She watched her mother holding Emily on her knee. She was running a finger tentatively over the small padded palm, and looking like she'd be happy for someone to take the child off her. She'd been such a fierce mother. Susan remembered waking sometimes to find her sitting between their beds – hers and Micky's – upright and watching them. *Sleep tight, little angel.* Susan reached for Emily.

'Of course, she needs to sleep,' said Lilian. 'She's had enough bouncing around. Time for me to go.' And she gave her daughter a quick hug and kissed the baby's head. 'I just wanted to see how you both were.'

'You won't stay?'

'Me? A sewing circle? Lord no. I still need to take my time walking so I don't put too much strain on the leg. Thank you, darling.'

Susan put Emily in her bed, then took her mother's arm and walked with her to the end of the path, their feet crunching on the shells. Lilian seemed to totter a bit and Susan steadied her.

'Are you up to this? Maybe Ben . . .?'

'I'll be fine.' Lilian moved to one side so Susan had to release her arm. 'Now off you go.'

Susan watched her mother move through the whalers' baches, slender, slightly unsteady, but mostly controlled, and then up the path towards the hillside and home. Susan went back inside, straightened a few things and brushed the floor. There was just time to read the newspaper. She'd seen a photograph over Ben's shoulder – two women in black holding babies wrapped in white. She had no idea who they were or what had happened to them, but she needed to see the photograph again. It didn't take long to find it. The caption said: *Women of Madrid watching from cave shelters in the hillside while Madrid is bombarded below.* Susan leaned close, hoping to see something that explained why their lives were being threatened in such a hideous way. But the caves above Madrid and the women and children in summer clothes could just as easily be living on Arapawa Island. She stared until the photograph became sections of colour: black, white, grey. Nobody, and nothing.

Her gaze drifted to a nearby article. It was about another bombing in a small town somewhere in Spain. Five hundred killed in the plaza, mostly women and children. Five hundred. Susan couldn't imagine that many people together for a start. What were they doing? She supposed they were shopping like she had been with Emily in Picton; she imagined there was a market rather than individual shops, and there would be mothers with one hand holding a child and the other choosing carrots and onions, thinking about what they'd make for the family to eat. And what did the mothers do when the bombs fell: did they hear them first and not know, did they look and wonder, or did they know the very second they started to fall? And did they run then, looking hopelessly for a place to hide, dropping the heavy baskets full of vegetables, laying the babies down on top of the onions, panic calling for lightness; or did they grab the small children and run as best they could, another one stumbling beside them and crying?

You're the child who's running beside the mother and you run as fast as a child can run, but it's not fast enough and you fall and your mother holding the other child looks back, anguished but knowing she must keep going so at least one of you is saved. But the other child is too heavy and she puts him down and tries to pull him instead, but other people are running too and he gets dragged away from her, and still she runs, her eyes darting, panicking but running, looking back but running. Away. And you're filled then with a terrible understanding of what made her let you both go, and at the same time you hate her for her weakness, and then you try to get up and run after your retreating mother, for she's the only safety you know, even though you hate her now with all your heart. And that's when the bombs fall, and you see your brother and you fall on him, for you must be the mother now.

That wasn't Spain.

That was a nightmare she'd had all her life.

Susan went outside for some fresh air, and almost immediately bent and straightened some of the shells. Her heart was beating as if she'd run to Stony Knob and back. She breathed deeply and looked down at the sea. It was overlapping ripple on ripple like sheets on the line, and the air above it was moving in the same way. Both were the palest shade of blue, clean and fresh, like summer. Everything was quiet, even the whale station. It had been so noisy when the coal boat had come. Later, she thought, she should stop by and look for stray pieces of coal; their bin was down to dust.

Susan went inside, folded the newspapers carefully and put them with the kindling by the range, then she got out the treadle sewing machine and unwrapped the material she'd bought. The lawn was just as creamy as she remembered it, and she smiled at the thought of what the others would say when she showed it to them.

Gunner's wife Nadine was the first to arrive. She was

puffing a little and clutching a basket spilling fabric. 'I have the perfect dress!' she said and thrust the fashion page of the newspaper at Susan. There was a pencil ring around an advertisement that took up a good part of the page.

Cut a glamorous figure for your revelries at night. Dazzle their eyes with your splendour! A swirl of net sweeping wide and romantically!

'They do it with layers,' said Nadine. 'Pink taffeta and then pink net and then black net. And the wavy pattern on the black net is in hammered gold!'

'Real gold?'

Nadine nodded and Susan looked closely. 'Where would you wear such a thing?'

'Not me, Susan, not at my age. But I think you should have one in the cupboard just in case. Just in case the Walkers decide to have a ball instead of their plain old singles dance. Just in case the Queen comes to Arapawa. Just in case your husband takes you to Wellington for the Centennial celebrations.' Nadine sat there a moment, her face blank. 'You know, the only use I would have for it, love, is if I ran out of fishing line. All that net would have to be useful.'

Nadine's daughter-in-law Jane came in the door then, her belly large under her dress, and when they showed her the picture she giggled.

'The gloves! Look at the gloves! Look at all those perfect little buttons.'

'You'd rip them into shreds in minutes!' Nadine snorted.

'Look here.' Susan had been reading an article at the bottom of the page. '*Exhale a colour to match your gown*! Can you believe it? It says an American inventor has patented a cigarette with coloured smoke. Apparently the chief enjoyment of smoking is watching the smoke, which was why it isn't so much fun in the dark.'

173

'That reminds me,' said Nadine, pulling out her pack of King's Gate and lighting up. She inhaled deeply and let out short appreciative puffs. 'You know, smoke *is* the thing I most like about smoking.'

'And which colour would you like to exhale?' asked Susan.

'The colour of my gown, of course.'

The women laughed and little Emily started to grumble in her cot, but Susan didn't move to get her; she'd rescued the newspaper she'd been reading from the kindling basket and was turning the pages to find the women in the caves.

'Have you seen this?' she said.

'Yes,' said Nadine. 'Gunner showed me.'

And the two women looked at the photograph in silence.

'We're lucky – so far away from anything here,' said Nadine. 'My mother used to say we fought the war without hearing a shot.'

'We didn't hear a shot, but the men did,' said Susan. 'My Uncle Jack for one.' She looked at Nadine's wide-set, reassuring face. The mothers in books she read as a child surely had faces like Nadine's. 'Do you think there will there be another war? I hear the men . . .'

'Men always talk that way, dear. Nothing they like better than a good fight. Now where's that material you were telling me about.'

There was knock at the door and Jimmy's wife Maisie walked in, her arms full of materials and two red-headed children holding on to her dress. Behind her was Shirley with her queen-sized quilt.

'Pleated skirts,' Maisie said, dropping her pile on the table and holding up a brand-new Butterick pattern. 'They're the thing.'

*

The Friar pulled something from his pocket and held it up to the light. 'I've made a start,' he said, and the others looked at the piece of bone he was turning in the air.

'Didn't know you had it in you,' said Gunner.

'It's supposed to be that old whale we caught with the Fyffe harpoon in its back.'

'Yes,' said Gunner. 'I remember it.'

'They say they sing,' Ben said, yawning. 'Whales do. I never heard them, but they say they sing.'

'They do, but I'm not sure I've ever heard them,' said Charlie.

'Never heard them,' said Stew.

'You've heard all right, boys,' said Gunner, 'just not known what it was. It's a moaning sound, like a man drowning.' He saw Stew and Charlie exchange looks and Tommy raise his eyebrows suggestively at Ben who missed it because his eyes were shut. 'First time I heard it I was scared out of my wits. I thought it was *fantasmi* come to haunt me.'

'Not *fantasmi*, Gunner,' said Tommy. 'Fantasy.'

And the young men erupted.

Ben shook himself.

'No, no, no,' said Charlie over Gunner's objections. 'It's not a woman, it's worse than that. It's all the poor souls who drank your beer, mate.'

'Your beer!' chortled Stew.

'Never heard them whales sing, eh?' said Gunner, clearing his throat. And he stood and held his arms as if Nadine was in them and began to sway and sing his bastard version of *Blue Moon* – a harpoon standing in for the moon, a whale swimmin' alone, no dream in its weighty heart, no cow to call its own, but the harpoon knows what it's there for – and there words failed him so he started all over again and then fell back to humming. It had been funny the first time he sang it and still raised a laugh. His eyes closed, Gunner let his body do the dancing. Finally, he sat down. 'Always liked to dance,' he said. 'First saw Nadine at a dance.'

'What does that mean,' asked Stew slowly, "blue moon"?'

'Rare,' said Tommy.

'Like what?'

'Like hen's teeth. Like you washing your neck.'

'Yes, but is the moon ever actually blue?'

'Can be,' said Tommy. 'Some nights it's a bluish colour.'

The men grunted. Some having seen it, some not, thought Gunner. Mostly, it came down to whether or not you had an imagination. That went for the whale singing too, no doubt. Tommy was a storyteller and knew how to make things up. Some men chased sardines, some chased whales, and while some of it was the luck of the draw, most of it was the way you saw things from the day you first opened your eyes.

Gunner's Papa had been a sardine man, but he took to his bed with a poor heart when his children were still young. Gunner had been taken out of school at fourteen to take his place on the fishing boat. He didn't mind too much, but the days were long. All he saw all day, all he could think about, were small shiny sardines. He couldn't eat a meal without thinking of them, or sleep without dreaming of them – shoals and shoals, spilling from the sky and slippery under his feet. And then he met Nadine and he'd stopped dreaming of fish for a while. He had that to thank her for at least.

A dozen years later, his Papa long gone, Gunner had been anchored off Point Rununder. Sardine catches were down, so he'd taken Charlie and Stew out with their rods for a bit of fun. They were only small, but truth be told neither of them loved fishing even then – both boys were farming stock like their mother. They were probably longing to pack up and get back to dry land.

Gunner remembered seeing a mollymawk drying its wings on a rock in the sun, and in hindsight there was a shimmer of disturbance that made him decide to stop there a while. So there they were, man and boys and bird and a tremble in the air and no sound to speak of but the knock of water against the boat, and below the water small fish skimming, and then no more fish. Something large and inexorable was rolling towards them and towards the fishing boat and the stretching bird.

All of a sudden the water curled in on itself and a whale rose up so close Gunner could see the criss-cross scars on its skin. He stared, startled, not believing. He had seen humpbacks and other whales going through the strait, but not a whale as big as this. It was a blue – it had to be.

Within days, he was hard at work on prototype harpoons and possible boats. The year was 1911, and the dreams were back – whales this time. He'd sure as hell caught a lot of whales over the years: humpbacks mainly, and the odd sperm, but he'd never caught a blue, not a single one.

An old man was what he was; an old man who'd never done the thing he'd dreamed he'd do. But surely it was the nature of dreams to appear to be one thing when they were in fact another, so he hadn't caught a blue but he'd got himself a few whales in his time, and run a business and raised a family on the bones of those whales. Gunner stood up, stretching his arms outwards as if embracing the scene in front of him: the water frothy with whale refuse, seabirds, a shark, all of it. One day, someone would catch a blue in these waters, they'd have to, and if it wasn't him it would be one of his men, or the sons of one of his men, or the grandsons of those men. Maybe even one of Charlie's or Stew's sons might want to be like their grandfather and get out on a chaser.

Blues were fast, but the world was getting faster, there was no doubt about that. Hell, they might go after them in the air one day. Imagine that.

19

The boy was ahead of her, running as usual, rolling on the grass, disappearing and reappearing. It was safer here; there were no rocky cliffs, just grass on all sides. He was a giant eagle screeching over her head, his arms wide, showing the whites of his eyes. Then he faltered. Half an hour from the top he started to drag back and complain. 'I'm going to die,' he said at last, and dropped on to the grass and lay there.

'You need to go slower, Billy,' she said. 'Take your time.' Lilian remembered the chocolate cake then and she pulled it from her bag. Breaking a small piece off, she held it over his nose, and when he opened his mouth she laid it on his tongue. 'There's more of that when we get to Stony Knob.'

'But why do we have to go all the way to the top? It's just the same here.'

'It's spectacular at the top, Billy. You can see the whole world up there.'

He continued to whine as he pulled himself up the steepest bit using the wire fence, crawled the very last stretch and collapsed at last with his tongue out. Lilian sat down and kissed him on the forehead. She rubbed her leg. It was a bit stiff, but it was all right. She wouldn't have felt it five years ago.

'You're a champion,' she said, and unpacked the picnic.

Ed and she had walked to Stony Knob at the start of their marriage. It wasn't a long walk for her, but it was steeper than she'd done before. She'd stopped, too, near the top and asked if that wouldn't do. But it wouldn't; Ed wanted her to climb until they could see the other side of the island and Queen Charlotte Sound. Breathless, they'd flung themselves on the windy hill, and the wire fences trilled and the air smelt of Antarctica. At last, the world was at their feet and almost all of it was water.

In the middle of the sandwiches, Ed had spoken in that tentative way he had as if he didn't want to presume. 'This isn't what you thought it would be.'

'No, it's so much more beautiful.'

'I mean the island, the house. It's not what you expected.'

'You're here. Arapawa is my home now.' And the wind in her hair made her feel bold and playful all of a sudden. 'Is it what you thought it would be, married life?'

'Yes. Of course.'

The disappointment surprised her, although it shouldn't have. It had been there from the beginning, with the postcards, but it was a small current then that she had quickly absorbed. Lilian had spent a lot of energy building up a life around Ed's postcards, imagining that one day when he knew her better he would be more generous with himself. The disappointment was as strong as it was because she'd thought his reserve would have broken a little by now to let her in. Instead, since he'd returned home, he seemed to have stepped back more firmly inside himself. And there were no postcards now to give her clues about what he was thinking.

The wind was coming at them in short gusts, all those unasked-for kisses, and her hair was twisting wildly from the clips she used to keep it up. Ed, on the other hand, with his hat on and arms folded against his body, seemed unruffled. She tried to catch her hair in her hand so she could clip it back again, but it was almost impossible. She barely heard him at first.

'I couldn't be without you, girl.'

It came out of nowhere and shamed her. Of course she knew it. It was unreasonable of her to expect him to say it. And he held her hand to the earth between them, and both were cool and firm, his hand and the earth. The sky swooped above them in its best cerulean blue, and the sea in the exact same colour seemed to be nothing more than denser air. There was the fragrance of gorse and the trilling of wire on the fence. What more could she want?

'Hi ho, what have we got here? A couple of wood pigeons cooing at the view. And lunch! I was feeling a little peckish.' It was the Friar.

He'd put down his gun and his hunting bag, and settled himself down on the grass. He'd been Lilian's view as he tucked into the sandwiches, talking about goat hunting and the bad luck he'd had that morning. His voice filled the spaces the wind left. It struck her how one cousin could have so much volume and another didn't, and it had nothing to do with their actual size. Ed was the taller man, but his reticence meant the stuff of him was reduced so it could slide easily between two blades of grass. He was the whistle you made when you blew. His cousin was shorter, but he could fill a field on entering it.

She remembered Ed pressing her hand and then letting go so he could pass the packet of cake. He didn't take her hand again, but lit up instead and walked off a little way to smoke.

'That's where the whales come from.' The Friar was standing beside her and gesturing with his pipe. 'In winter they swim all the way from Antarctica up past here through the strait to the warm water of the Pacific where they can breed.' His arm swept through the air in a wide arc ending up above her head. 'When they're pregnant, the cows swim back to the Antarctic again to feed up on all the krill, then it's north the next year to give birth to their calves in the tropics.' He sucked on his pipe. 'They just have to hope we don't get them on the way. Hah!'

'That sounds like a lot of effort. Why don't they just stay where it's warm all year round?'

'The krill's down south and it's a sad fact but everything comes down to food in the end. Look at me. It was your mutton sandwiches and sponge cake that brought me here today; it certainly wasn't the conversation!' And he raised his eyebrows in the direction of his cousin, and raised the last word too so Ed could hear, and she'd found herself laughing even though she hadn't meant to.

'It's a mighty long way to come for three-day-old mutton and an indifferent sponge cake,' she said.

'What?' he said, his eyes open wide in mock disbelief. 'That cake was easily as good as that fruit cake of yours.'

Now there was only Billy up there with her, and he was calling from behind a small rise. He'd found a dead sheep. Its thin teeth stuck out from withered lips and its bloated stomach was crawling with maggots. They both stood looking at it, and then Billy reached down and pulled one of the teeth from the gum; he sniffed it, wiped it on his shorts and put it in his pocket. Together, they braced themselves to go back down: Lilian stretching, Billy spreading his wings.

When they got home, it was nearly dark, but the lamps were lit, the stove banked up, and in the lounge Ed and Micky were looking at the maps.

Lilian paused by the door.

'Oceans have currents which are like rivers,' Ed said. 'They pour over the sea floor which has mountains and valleys of its own. You know yourself, Micky, how varied it is in the strait. There's Karori Rip – choppy water at the best of times and at the worst of times twelve-foot waves breaking in all directions at once.'

Micky didn't say a thing. He kept his head down and his eyes on the map. He looked like a character in a fairy story, scared to move unless he break the enchantment.

20

Rain was falling. Falling all afternoon and most of the night, and now with the morning barely begun the ground was too wet to hold it. Streams were filled to bursting, rock faces spilled with waterfalls and earth slid like water into the bays. There were dark pools where mud met sea and then as it spread outwards it lightened to a milky brown aureole. The cloud was so low it shrouded all but the rocky outcrops at the water's edge. When the men spoke, their voices echoed, but mostly they stood on the chasers grave and silent. In the distance they heard a rooster and it made Micky think of eggs and bacon. He could do with a good fry-up. Even after a week on the chasers he couldn't get used to getting up in the dark and eating a cooked breakfast before cock crow. He always regretted what he'd left behind on his plate as the cold seeped into his skin and his body cried out for fuel.

Despite low cloud at the Lookout first thing, Phil had managed to spot a humpback coming in close to Jordy's Rock. Without too much trouble, the whalers had herded it through the narrow entrance into Tory Channel, despatching it efficiently right there in the middle of Fishing Bay. They'd left it to float in the muddied water with the blind eels and the cape pigeons. Now they were returning to Lookout Hill, following the line between the milk chocolate of the bays and the huffing teal water of the channel. The men were wet and cold, and the day had barely begun. There was no sign of the rain easing. Micky had discovered that the first three drops down the neck were the worst – each icy slither on dry skin was as painful as a scratch – but by now he was well past counting.

They were almost to the moorings at the base of Lookout Hill when Micky shouted. The flag was up again and smoke was billowing in the beginnings of a fire set high on the hill. There was another whale and it was heading out past Wellington Head. The three chasers turned towards the channel entrance and picked up speed – and with the burst of acceleration came the adrenaline which was like any other sort of hunger in Micky's stomach. It seemed inevitable he should think of her then, Ari. Skin as glossy as a plum and those surprising crevices of deep pink. He thought of men using their balls for navigation and imagined himself guiding Jimmy across Cook Strait and straight to Ari waiting at the wharf in Wellington. Would he ever see her again?

Everything seemed to quieten for a moment, leaving a small window for the chasers to exit the channel without a struggle. Micky blinked to clear his mind and the rain from his eyes, and then he stuck out his tongue.

Cloud had cleared a little from the vertical cliffs that faced into the strait at the end of Arapawa Island, and as they went past Micky checked automatically for goats. They'd be there somewhere in the collapsed spurs and gorse bushes or hovering around the skinny waterfalls. He should have brought his gun to get himself one on the way back. He sniffed the air appreciatively and looked over at his father who was at the bow of the chaser, his head forward of his shoulders, his eyes skimming the water. Then he turned – Micky thought he was looking at him – but he was looking to Lookout Hill for instructions. He pointed for Micky to see: the fire was extinguished, they were on the right track. Ed waved his hand at Sarge and the drivers of the other chasers: *Keep going*. So they did, past Cabbage Island and Cape Tear-Arse. Out of sight of the Lookout.

There was no doubting they'd had a good morning going after the first whale of the day. It had been stuck up with porpoises and in the calm channel water the three chasers had been able to spread themselves around it like wolves surrounding a sheep. They'd worked well, he and his father, agreeing on what to do, acting without having to speak. It was a piece of cake, and Micky felt he'd acquitted himself well.

Back in Cook Strait, the sea was another creature altogether. It was dark and unnaturally glossy, and there was a six-foot swell at least. The last of the low cloud had disappeared, but the high cloud was heavily bruised and it was still raining fitfully. Micky could feel the southerly buster picking up. It would be cold rough work getting this one in.

He'd forgotten to load another harpoon, and as he hurriedly bent to the deck to pick up the iron he looked quickly at the *Chance* and saw his father do the same. Micky pushed the harpoon hard down into the barrel and felt the snugness there, then he turned to see The Brothers up ahead. The two rocks were the guards between near and far. If you were out there fishing or chasing whales, you were off the end of the long northern arm of Arapawa Island, still close enough to scuttle home if the sea got up, but with fair weather you could continue safely on from there, out through the strait, as far as Kapiti.

Ed was signalling thumbs-up. Sarge opened the throttle gently and felt the chaser pull away. Close behind were the *Balaena* and the *Nautilus*. Sarge screwed up his eyes and tucked his head down between his shoulders to ward off the sea spray. He could feel the swell heaving beneath them and his stomach heaving with it. He needed to change the angle of the chaser. Ten degrees to port should do it, give them all a smoother ride.

They were still a mile away from The Brothers. Sarge slowed the chaser right down and took deep breaths to still his stomach. It wasn't rough enough to be feeling like this – he'd better not be crook.

Suddenly, Ed was pointing to starboard and looking round at Sarge, trying to get his attention, his mouth shaping the word 'Blow!' Jolted out of his torpor, Sarge spun the chaser in the direction of his driver's arm. Ed had the whale in his line of sight and he was leaning back, using his weight to swivel the harpoon. Sarge whistled long and low – it was thirty feet away, no more. No matter how many times he'd seen it, it always got to Sarge, finding a whale silently carving its way through the water, especially a humpback – hunched over like a man ashamed of his size.

Opening the throttle right up, Sarge halved the distance between them, then he slowed and curled the chaser around so it was running alongside the whale. It didn't seem to be aware of them. They could take their time.

Then all of sudden there was the *Balaena* on the other side of the whale, and Micky at the bow, his hat gone, his wet hair blown back, his whole body intent on the whale, making not one gesture towards his father's boat or even apparently aware of it. Sarge felt a surge of irritation at the boy's foolishness at the same moment he heard Ed let loose the harpoon and felt the *Chance* suddenly and unexpectedly buck underneath them, knocking Sarge against the edge of the cockpit and Ed to the deck. What the hell had hit them? As they struggled to right themselves, Ed was shouting like a madman.

The iron arched over the back of the whale, kicked high by the lurch of the boat. The light caught it and for a split second rendered it invisible. The boy wasn't looking at anything but the whale, and can't have heard his father, or didn't want to. The harpoon hit him low and then smashed into the deck. Micky cried out as he buckled and fell.

A second humpback broke through the surface between the two boats. It was much larger than the one they were chasing. Two whales, not one.

That's the mistake they'd made.

Ed couldn't have cared less. He was still shouting, his voice hoarse, for Jimmy to help Micky and for Sarge to get alongside. Sarge did his best, struggling against a bruised arm, trying to pull the chaser over. Jimmy's face was a beacon of distress as he climbed over to check the boy and then disappeared below to pull out a tarpaulin to cover him. Micky's face, by contrast, was no colour at all and his dark curls stuck to it like wet leaves to a stone. It was hard to tell if he was breathing or not.

At last, Ed fell to the deck beside his son. Sarge had seen it before: the stricken embrace as if to suck the pain from the body beneath and replace it with your own life's breath. He'd slept with it every night as a child – a tortured painting in reds and blacks of Mary and the dead Christ. It had terrified him but he hadn't dared to ask for it to be taken down. The same terror invaded him now. The *dead* Christ. Ed was saying the kid's name over and over to no response.

The *Nautilus* had drawn up alongside the *Balaena*, and Boots was calling to Ed, but Ed wasn't listening. Sarge saw him stiffen and lean forward. Boots stopped. There was a movement under the tarp, Sarge was sure of it. Then he thought he heard a moan. The father was talking to the son now, leaning to his ear and stroking his forehead, lifting his head and laying it in his lap. But the boy's head hung loose, too loose, on his neck.

Ed looked up and called to Jimmy, then he put his hand up to Sarge, the thumb and the first finger linked in a circle. Okay, the boy was okay – or it was okay to go? The head was still lolling.

As the *Balaena* pulled away, followed by the *Nautilus*, Sarge saw Ed turn to see where the whale was, and the surprise on his face when he saw two. Left alone, Sarge was violently sick over the side. As he climbed back behind the wheel, he saw the whales slip below the surface of the sea, the fluke of the cow hanging there a moment before it was gone. The hand of God, they used to call it. All that was left was the round slick on the surface as the whales took themselves down as deep as they could go.

Over the sound of the whale station they heard them. The chasers, coming home at speed. The Friar removed his hat and scratched his head, and Ben stubbed out his cigarette and silenced Tommy. The boy had been regaling them with a description of Trixie serving potatoes, leaning close to lift them to his plate. He'd been intrigued by the gentle wobble at the top of her breasts. 'Like jelly,' he was saying, and then he'd delivered one of his best lines yet: 'my little Trixie Trifle.'

Most of the crew missed it. They were moving off to watch the chasers. They were almost to Fishing Bay: the *Balaena*, followed by the *Nautilus* and then the *Chance*. The Friar was unsure what to make of it.

'They're holding twenty-five knots,' said Ben.

The last two boats began to slow, but the *Balaena* kept its speed. Jimmy was at the wheel, but it was Ed, not Micky, on the deck, and he was crouched over. It took the men at the whale station a while to see the kid lying under the tarpaulin.

Sarge was calling out as he pulled into Fishing Bay. 'It's Micky! Get Lilian!'

Ben would go.

She was in the hen house, humming to herself, when he crashed in, trampling her egg basket, his breathing coming hard. Lilian gathered herself. 'Ben?' Her voice knew. She put a hand to her mouth, waiting for the name that would come from his.

'It's Micky,' he shouted, and then stood embarrassed. Lilian let out a small grunt. 'We don't know what happened,' he said, struggling to drop his voice. 'He's alive. Jimmy's taking him to hospital now. Ed's with him.' He moved forward with his hand out. 'Come, Lilian. Sarge'll take you and Billy on the *Chance*.'

Lilian still didn't move, except to tuck a hair absently behind an ear, all around them the chuckling of hens.

'Come,' he said firmly. 'Where's Billy?'

She gave him her hand then, and moved forward stiffly. At the door of the hen house lay the basket and the smashed eggs. Lilian let go of Ben and made a small hiccuping sound that sounded like she was going to be sick. He put his arm around her shoulders.

She shook her head. 'There's a suitcase in the shed if you wouldn't mind. I'll go and get Billy.'

Inside, Lilian pulled her apron off and held it loosely in her hands. What was she looking for? She stood a moment, unable to move or think. There was something pressing to attend to that just for a moment escaped her. She could hear something and was bewildered by it. Tiny clicks, light, like tapping on glass. Lilian moved into the hallway. Someone was tapping on the window. All of a sudden the light was too bright and she needed to shut her eyes. Her hand on the wall, she could feel the texture of the wallpaper. Blue roses, absurd blue roses. Then Lilian lifted her hand and, with an enormous effort of will, pulled herself back. Wiping her face with the apron, she walked into the boys' room.

Billy was playing with marbles. Micky's marbles. No one was tapping on the window. It could be Micky there, his dark head bent, muttering to himself and sniffing every now and then.

'Mick . . . Billy, leave those, we need to go to Picton.'

Micky had given the marbles to Billy when he'd left home. Three dozen balls of clear glass with curls of blue and green and yellow and red sealed inside. Mostly red. She couldn't look at them.

'Why are we going?'

'We're going to see Micky, love. He's in the hospital. He had an accident this morning.' She wanted suddenly to run down the hillside and climb aboard the chaser, but she had to be sensible. 'We need to take some clothes; we'll have to stay with Aunt Ada for a night or two.'

'What happened?' Billy was up in an instant, wiping his nose on his sleeve. 'Is there lots of blood?'

'No, no, of course not,' said Lilian. Automatically, she put her hand on the boy's forehead to check his temperature, but he seemed cool enough. Just a cold, then. She passed him a handkerchief before lifting shorts and shirts out of the dresser. 'He'll be right as rain.' But even as she spoke, Lilian heard the tarnished sound to her voice and there was that taste as if she'd licked an old coin. She had been practising these lines for too long. The words were old lies. She just hadn't known who they'd be about or when she'd need them. 'Now come on, let's get these into a suitcase.'

Billy put the handkerchief in his pocket and rubbed his sleeve on his nose. He looked up at his mother to assess her level of buoyancy, then he set his jaw firmly.

'I'm not going without my marbles.'

21

Oyster Bay, Tory Channel. Summer. A host of families are perched like birds upon the beach. All of them plump and sleek in the sun, replete with the bounty of Christmas. The sunlight shines on their feathers.

Wild cherries grow here, small, dark red, hanging like decorations. The children run to be the first to fill their buckets, elbowing each other, coming back with mouths dripping red and the buckets never full. One trips and cries. The young people work more slowly, choosing who they want to pick with, moving close so she has to reach over him or he has to lift her up. The cherry stones taste of almonds if you suck them.

And of course there are oysters in Oyster Bay, rock oysters shucked on the beach and swallowed down like a single ice-cold shot of seawater. All the jokes that go with it: 'You'd better watch him tonight!'

How Micky wished for that coolness down his throat, that spurt of the sea. Lying there in a white room, his eyes aching from the light, helpless and thirsty, moaning like a woman. And he was hot and then suddenly cold. His skin was flayed, letting the air in, letting the heat out.

After the food, all that eating – the cherries, the oysters, the cold lamb sandwiches, the potato salad, the mussels, boiled eggs, scones with butter, nuts, fruit cake, and beer and lemonade to wash it down – after all the food, they lie on their picnic blankets. Even the children are silenced, gasping like fish. And then one pipe is lit and then another.

Beach cricket, and young men take turns to bowl, running up with bodies hunched over the ball before sprawling into the air and heaving it at the sticks. There is a satisfying connection with the bat and off it flies into the sea. Girls watching, heads cocked, giggling. Sarah with curly hair, pretty as a picture. Eyes narrowing like a cat and kissing him on the lips like that, a cherry in her mouth.

There's swimming if it isn't too cold, but it's always cold and the braver ones swim anyway, dodging the skimming stones. Then the women boil up water for tea, and bring out the fudge and coconut ice. Well, that does for you. The men and his Nana snore like seals while those who can gather up the leftovers. If a boy is lucky he'll get another kiss.

The pain was white in the white room with curtains tight about them. Micky was aware his father was beside him on a chair, his eyes shut but not asleep, blood on his clothes and his hands shaking. He didn't know how he knew this. His mother hadn't been on the beach at Oyster Bay, but when had she ever come? His father was there, Nana too.

Having struggled to consciousness, Micky felt the excruciating pain in his leg and retreated again to Sarah and the cherry kiss. But this time it was Ari, and her tongue was as wet and salty as an oyster.

22

There were three empty beds in the room and a screen around a fourth. Ed was waiting, slumped on a chair.

He looked up blankly and didn't move.

That's that, thought Lilian. He's dead.

She put her hand on Billy's shoulder to hold him.

Ed receded; he was a continent away from her, on the chair. His hollow eyes were another continent. The shiny white walls seemed to billow like curtains.

'That hurts,' said Billy, shrugging her off.

Then a cry from behind the screen caused Lilian to stagger. But her legs moved, one and then the other towards it. Somehow Ed came across the white continent, loomed over her, grabbed her arm and said to her face, 'No.' She looked at his hand on her arm. 'The doctor's with him.'

The cry came again, but more of a bleat this time. Ed's face tightened around his jaw. 'I need to get some air.' He put a hand on Billy's small head. Held it there a moment, and then released him and walked from the room.

Lilian told Billy to stay and she'd be back. She caught up with Ed at the hospital entrance.

'You're not leaving.'

'I need a smoke, that's all.'

'You need to tell me how he is, what happened.'

'I won't be long.'

'The doctor might need to speak to us.'

'I won't be long.' Ed was losing patience, but she had to stop him. She didn't want to be alone with Billy when the doctor came through. Ed kept walking, down the hospital steps and into the grounds. He stopped and put a cigarette into his mouth but didn't light it.

Lilian followed him. 'How did it happen?'

'Can't we talk about this later?'

'I need to know.'

'I don't know.' Ed's voice was so small after hers it was barely audible. 'I don't know. I don't know. All right? Micky's a flaming fool. I've said it all along.'

'I don't understand –'

Ed's nostrils flared; he removed the cigarette and came up close. 'Sarge and I were alongside – it looked like a small cow. There was no other chaser in sight. It was a clear shot. I fired. The chaser bucked and knocked me and Sarge down. It was another whale.' He blinked. He looked exhausted. 'A cow. It turned out we'd been after the calf – almost grown. Neither of us had seen it coming. And then I saw –' She felt Ed's spit on her face. 'It was too late. There was nothing I could do.' He pulled away from her. His self-disgust was palpable.

She wiped the spit with her fingers and tried to go to him, but he was turning away now, sucking on his cigarette, holding his hand up to her as he did with Sarge: *Stop*.

She went back inside.

Billy was rolling marbles on the linoleum. Lilian sat on the chair and waited, listening to the sounds of the doctor and the nurse behind the screen. After a while, she relaxed. She realised she could sit like this all day, waiting for Ed to get back, waiting for the doctor to finish his examination, waiting for whatever tests needed to be done, waiting for Micky to wake. No news to deal with, no decisions to make. Suspended.

It was warm in the room. Lilian yawned and closed her eyes for just a minute. The face she saw in front of her was Micky's – nearly six, the quickest eyes and a milk crust around his mouth. Such a mobile face, too, always reacting to something, or looking for something, only still when asleep. Micky was untied from the apron strings and following Ed around the farm in work boots that were too big for him. Lilian worried that he'd trip over and hurt himself, but Ed had thought it amusing. He said most boys wanted to fill their father's boots when they were grown but his son wanted to fill them right now. In those days, at that time, Lilian let it go.

What could she say? When she'd returned home at last, Micky had run from her and hidden. It had been a year and he didn't know her or want to know her. It had taken two days for him to say anything, and then there he was beside her at the sink.

'Have you got a scar?'

'No, no, I don't.'

'Why not?'

'I didn't have an operation.'

He'd looked disappointed. 'Did it hurt you, though?'

'Yes, it did.'

'How much?'

'A lot. It hurt a lot.'

He'd nodded, and reached over to stroke her arm. 'Can you make chocolate cake?'

Whaling was over and Ed had been busy catching up with the farm work. The day she was thinking of, Ed had gone off with Micky at the crack of dawn to join the shearers. She watched them go, the boy in his big boots talking nineteen to the dozen, his father leaning his head to listen and looking back when they got to the gate, telling Micky to wave to his mother. There they were both of them waving and smiling the same shy, tucked-in smile, their eyes concentrated into their pupils, Lilian waving them away.

She and Susan took scones and sponge cake down to the woolshed for morning tea. Work stopped and the men wiped the sweat off their faces and dipped their hands in the bucket to wash off the wool grease. Ed was the last, carefully checking the bales as if loath to stop. Micky was nowhere to be seen, and Lilian supposed he must be hiding in one of the pens. She called his name, but she was busy with the food and serving tea; only when the last cup was filled did she put the teapot down and check the shed. He wasn't there.

Outside, she couldn't see him either.

Then something made her look up. He was walking away from her along the top of the six-foot-high concrete wall at the back of the shed, his arms out for balance, taking great care to put one large unwieldy boot in front of the other, tipping to one side and then the other, righting himself, stopping, continuing on. Lilian opened her mouth to call to him, but a hand clamped across it and another hand grabbed her arm to pull her back inside the shed. It was Ed.

'If you call out he'll fall,' he hissed. Then he let go of her mouth.

Lilian was trying to twist herself out of his grip. 'He'll fall anyway! Look at the boots he's got on.'

'Stay here.' Ed's hand gripped tighter on her upper arm and the other closed the shed door so she couldn't see.

'Let go of me!'

He pulled her away from the door and from Micky. He

wouldn't let her go until they heard those boots slapping on the floor of the woolshed. Micky was looking for a scone and a glass of milk.

Ed released her then like lint from a pocket. Lilian remembered how he'd gone immediately to tie the laces of Micky's boots and while he was doing that Micky had reached down to touch his father's hair. They didn't speak. She had a sneaking feeling then that Ed had known about Micky on the wall all along. She'd just got in the way. But all her anger was stifled seeing them there like that – joined in one continuous, contented line.

Enough.

'Mrs Prideaux.'

Lilian sat up and opened her eyes. The doctor was pulling up a chair, and she stared at him a moment before becoming suddenly afraid.

'My husband,' she said. She looked at the three empty beds and Billy curled around his marbles trying to make them into pyramids. There was no one else there. The doctor looked at his watch.

'My husband,' she said, louder, 'should be here soon.'

'Look, why don't we start?' It was a statement, not a question. He was looking at the patient notes. 'I'm Dr Hughes, the orthopaedic surgeon. Your son Michael's right tibia or shinbone fractured rather badly in at least two places from the harpoon hitting him directly in his lower leg, and then smashing into the deck where the harpoon head exploded. In one place the bone has broken through the skin.' He tapped his notes. 'We can't get too much out of him about what happened – he was knocked out for about ten minutes when he fell, and he's still concussed with a four-inch gash on the side of his head.

'We will need to X-ray the leg and then operate to realign it. We'll use pins to hold the bone in place rather than a cast because of the open wound. It will take up to twelve weeks for this leg to heal. We'll need to X-ray his head at the same time to check everything's all right in there – that's Dr Phillips' area, he should be here soon. Meanwhile, we are monitoring your son every half hour. A person's temperature drops dramatically when they go into shock and we want to see it get back up to normal levels. If it overshoots or refuses to stabilise, then it's a sign we might have a problem.'

Lilian was suddenly aware of the silence and the doctor's pitiful cough. He was a small dark man with soft hands and a fancy black and gold fountain pen that seemed to get most of his attention.

'His name's Micky,' she said quietly.

But Dr Hughes wasn't looking up. 'We are fortunate, Mrs Prideaux, that the growing use of automobiles on the roads gives us a better understanding of concussions and fractures. We will give him the best care possible.'

A man like that wouldn't have time for a man like Ed, she thought, and he would never understand what had happened out there on the water. It was the way he said 'harpoon'.

'He's a strong young man.' Doctor Hughes was standing now and clearing his throat. 'He'll need everything he's got and then some.'

His eyes shifted over to the door where Ed was standing.

'I have talked to your wife, Mr Prideaux. If you have any questions at all, we can talk in the morning. You can see your son now before he goes to be X-rayed. He's lucky enough to have a room on his own for the time being, so there's no problem with disturbing other patients.' He was looking at Billy. 'Visiting hours don't apply in serious cases but you will need to get the boy looked after.'

Lilian nodded and they went behind the screen. Micky was sleeping. There was a terrible bruise on his right cheek and another on his chin; his head was only lightly bandaged, and blood was beginning to soak through. His leg was covered. Lilian found her son's hand and held it. Billy nudged up against her and Ed simply closed his eyes.

The nurse came, and it was time to leave.

Lilian kissed Micky on the cheek without the bruise. Then she looked at his face. She could see the shine where her kiss was. There seemed to be a dip there too, as if the weight of her lips had made a dent in him. If he'd been well, she thought, he'd have wiped it off with the cuff of his shirt.

'I'm hungry,' said Billy.

Lilian felt a tug on her hand. Ed was taking her from the room, calling Billy to follow.

They walked to Ada's, their eyes on Picton Harbour and tiny Mabel Island in the middle like an upturned bowl. It was calm enough, the sky was darkening, and there was a heady smell of chimney smoke mixed with grass and alyssum and detritus from the sea. Every so often a wave fell heavily on the shore in a way that suggested it was rougher outside the harbour. Lilian saw Ed take note of this, and of the heavy cloud massing just above the circle of hills that ran around the harbour, holding everything in.

Billy stopped all of a sudden and refused to walk any further, so Ed pulled the boy on to his back.

'I'll come to Ada's,' he said. 'But I can't stay. I need to get back to Arapawa. I'll be here first thing.'

Lilian wasn't surprised. What did surprise her was how hungry she was. She didn't want to be hungry.

23

Annie was wandering the garden. She wanted daffodils but there were none, it wasn't yet spring.

With her hands, she went through the soil in the flower bed she'd so carefully dug. She threw weeds and stones and chunks of earth over her shoulder until she found a bulb. She held it up like a question.

In a basket by the washing line was a folded tablecloth and some towels. She walked towards him as if on any ordinary day, rubbing dirt between her palms. Her eyes were round, her pupils pointed and bright in a feverish sort of way. They weren't glossy with light any more; nothing outside seemed to be making its way in. She took off her shoes, unfolded a towel, put it on the ground and sat on it. She smiled so meltingly at him, as if she wanted to start a conversation or invite him to a picnic. The Friar started forward, briefly hoping, but that's as far as it went. Her voice was shrill.

'Why did you pick everything and leave nothing for me?'

That was the first day. After all the crying. After the first night when she'd clawed his face and run into the garden and stood there rigid and silent until he'd coaxed her back. So he'd decided to wait until she was asleep and bury the infant on his own away from the house. The midwife had suggested it for Annie's peace of mind.

The Friar carried the small bundle up the hill to the holes the Maoris had dug to hide from attack. Not there, for the baby, but close by. There was something he liked about the place. It felt safe, and next time the priest visited he would bring him up to bless the grave. Maybe Annie would be better by then and she could come too. They could plant some daffodils.

When he got back to the bach, he found her wide awake and accusing. Where had he hidden the spade?

Not long after that she'd started to dig.

24

Ada was serving up shepherd's pie and Jenny was setting the table when Lilian, Ed and Billy walked in. There was a flurry as they held each other, and then, wiping her eyes, Ada laid three more places.

Jenny couldn't stop looking at her mother and held tightly on to her skirt, her face ferocious. Lilian bent down and looked her in the eye.

'Jen-jen,' she said. 'How are you, my lovely?'

'I want to go home.'

There was a pause as Lilian looked briefly at her sister and then at Ed. 'And there was I thinking I'd have to carry you back crying,' she said. 'I want you home too. I . . . we've missed you.' And she hugged the girl again and then stood and hugged Ada who had to put down her serving spoon to wipe her hands.

Jenny reached in her pocket and put a tiny snail on the table in front of Billy.

'I've called him Speckle,' she said. 'He's very clever and he loves cabbage.'

Billy watched Speckle unfold from his shell. 'We'll need a box for him,' he said. 'A snail needs a special box.'

By the time Ada had found a box that would do, the pie

was getting cold. They took the plates to the table already set with knives and forks and napkins, and a jar of Ada's chutney and a jar of her tomato sauce.

'What's wrong with Micky?' Lilian heard Jenny ask Billy.

'He's smashed his leg,' said Billy, 'and he's got to eat custard.'

Lilian snorted.

'What did he say?' said Ada.

But Lilian was laughing so hard now she couldn't speak.

Billy and Jenny watched perplexed.

'Concussed,' said Lilian, coming up for air. 'He's concussed.'

When Ed had gone and they were doing the dishes, Lilian thought of her kitchen, cold by now with none of the smells of an evening meal, and the lamps and the stove unlit. She'd worked so hard to keep that wolf from the door, and the only time she'd faltered was that time, the other time. It was so long ago – yet just at this moment, after her fall and Micky's accident, everything that had happened twelve years ago seemed bright and fresh. It was as if a harpoon on the end of a long rope had been spinning out across her deck and across the water for all this time and had finally come to rest. She'd lost her fear of it and relaxed her vigilance. She shouldn't have. The small gasp she felt on those evenings without Ed was a reminder to her to never let up. Only this morning, she'd been in the hen house singing to herself: how could it be that she hadn't felt even the tiniest ripple to warn her?

Lilian didn't hold a lot of store by prayer on a daily basis, but that night in bed she turned to it. When she finished, she still couldn't settle. She knew she should be thinking about Micky, but she kept thinking of Ed outside the hospital. It had reminded her of the time when they were first married and how desperate he'd been.

This man who shook inside his bones. Who muttered and wept when he finally slept, and woke screaming. Who dreamt about Jack dying alone in Snipers' Gully and *he* was the one holding the gun. Who dreamt about rotting bodies and *he* was the rotting body clawing to get out of the earth. Lilian would always get herself up, whatever hour he needed her, and make them both a cup of tea. The next morning, she'd tell him, 'You were restless.'

Sometimes back then it spilled into the daylight. And he'd stop what he was doing and sit for an hour or so staring.

After a while, she'd started to hear the rustle among the women. Some of the men who'd returned weren't as they had been. There was a question in the air, and it was the same question in her head. She'd hung it out with the washing and folded it up later to put away in a drawer; she'd prodded it into a stew and chopped it up with the wood. *Who is this man?*

After twenty years, he had mostly returned to her. He slept better, he held himself together, he could be patient again, and kinder. Although there were still times when she met his eyes and saw the exhaustion and fear again, the wide pupils sucking in the light. She'd seen it today and it had horrified her.

Lilian was jolted back to Micky. He'd looked so young in the hospital bed. She stuffed the pillow into her mouth to quieten her crying.

Sleeptightlittleangel. How to keep a loved one safe.

Utter it.

You can only utter it.

*

Lilian dressed in the grey light. In the kitchen, Ada was waiting.

'I knew you'd be up early, Hen. Have some breakfast.'

Lilian tucked into the eggs and bacon without pausing to sip her tea. 'Ada,' she said, 'what would I do without you?' And she found herself crying again, and Ada came over and held her shoulders and kissed her hair.

'You must be exhausted, I bet you didn't sleep.'

'I did,' mumbled Lilian. 'For a little, anyway.'

'There was a storm,' said Ada.

'Yes, Ed said there would be.'

'Off you go now, or we'll start talking and you'll never get away. I'll watch the children.'

'Billy has a cold. Keep him warm, won't you?'

Lilian didn't notice the clarity of the air or the exultant cries of the birds, and when she rounded the corner and the sea came into view she shaded her eyes from its brightness. If there had been a storm there was no evidence of it. She wondered how things were on Arapawa. It was unsettling to think of the island waking without her, of the house without her. Lilian hoped Ed would remember to check the chooks.

At Seymour Gardens, her thoughts were ambushed by the past again. This time it was the Anzac Day parades here after the war and Ed always so reluctant to go. She'd dragged him along the first couple of years, and then the memorial gateway was built in 1921 and he told her he'd done his bit. He'd be staying home. Lilian felt there was something vaguely shameful about this and tried to insist. He went in the end, because she'd gone on about it, but he made sure they didn't stay long.

That time, the first time with the new memorial, they were late, and there was so much frustration stuck between them as she hurried him from the wharves to the gardens, holding her hat to stop it blowing away. Ed was holding Susan.

'Please, Ed, we need to get there.'

'There's no need to hurry,' he said, and that's when she saw the crowd in the distance and started to quicken her pace even more. Her hat must have fallen off – it was like a man's hat, but smaller and lighter, she didn't feel it go. She could remember his voice: 'Lily, the hat.' And then: 'Come back.' She'd looked back to see him standing there with Susan in the crook of his right arm, and, at his feet, her hat. Lilian stared at him. She could see he wasn't going to pick it up.

Lilian walked back towards her husband and her daughter. She stooped awkwardly and put the hat back on her head. She took the tip of Ed's elbow and felt the trembling, and felt it quieten. 'Bloody hat,' she said. Ed smiled, and they walked together the rest of the way to the memorial. As they drew nearer the trumpet began playing the Last Post and Lilian felt something crumple inside her. The crowd was dispersing, talking and laughing, released from the past. The Friar was beaming at them, his medals catching the light. Only then did Lilian realise Ed had forgotten to wear his.

'And what kept you?'

'I can't say.'

'Never can say, eh Ed?' The Friar had tweaked Susan's cheek and taken her from her father. 'Matter of fact, the speech by the mayor was dull as ditch water, you didn't miss a thing.'

Lilian saw her old friend Jeannie approaching with her husband Walter, all trussed up in his best suit and his medals high on his chest. Two rows of them. She saw the way Jeannie smoothed his hair and laughed up at him all lipsticked air.

And he laughed back, took her hand firmly in his and put it in his pocket. They walked along so close you'd think they were stitched together.

A white fury had blasted her. Why was it so difficult to have ordinary things? A husband who walked with his head up? There was Jeannie, everything for nothing.

What did 'I can't say' mean anyway?

Ed was waiting for her. He was in the chair by Micky's bed, his hair combed and his face shiny. He smiled when she came in, and got quickly to his feet.

'I didn't expect you here so early,' she said.

'Gunner's cancelled whaling today. I'll go back this afternoon, though. Got some things to see to.'

'How's Micky?'

'Sleeping a lot. His leg's fractured in three places.'

Ed lifted the sheet to show her. He pointed out the slits where the pins were inserted and the cage-like device around it.

'The other one, Dr Phillips, says ten minutes is a long time to be out for the count, and we'll find out soon enough what it's done to his head. The X-ray doesn't show up anything very serious but that doesn't mean . . .'

Lilian sat heavily in Ed's seat and tried not to listen. There seemed nothing to be gained by talking about it. It was clearly out of their hands. She touched her son's forehead with her fingers as she always did when her children were ill. It was something she knew to do. He was feverish, there was no doubt. Some of his hair hung there, still salty. She rolled it in her fingers. She wanted to put it in her pocket. Him in her pocket. Take him away.

A nurse appeared and proceeded to take Micky's temperature and his pulse. Without any preliminaries, his eyes snapped open and settled on his mother. He didn't speak a word, just stared, and then just as unexpectedly shut them again. Ed squeezed Lilian's shoulder. He went for a smoke. The nurse did what she had to and left. There was no sign of Dr Hughes.

The boy groaned deeply once and then was silent again. Ed returned. He found it difficult to sit. He paced the room. Lilian stood for a while by the window where she could see the sea. It was iron grey and featureless, and the sky was the same. Tiring of that, she sat on the chair and tried to knit. Ed went out for a smoke. The morning passed.

Dr Hughes, when he came, declared himself happy with the operation. It was up to the boy now, he said. He fiddled with the lid of his black and gold pen, then he dropped it and scrabbled to pick it up. He looked apologetic for the first time.

At lunchtime, Ed told Lilian to take a break. She didn't want to, but he was firm. So she walked to Seymour Gardens, then went to look for some lunch. At the Centennial Tearooms, Lilian chose a plain ham sandwich with white bread and mustard, and an egg sandwich with specks of parsley in it. The place looked clean enough and the sandwiches seemed fresh, but the cakes didn't look as nice as the ones Mrs Mackinnon made when the Centennial was Cook's Tearooms. That was a long time ago, though. Mrs M was probably long dead.

The girl brought over her tea.

'Nice sandwich?' she said.

Lilian's throat felt bone dry. She couldn't retrieve a single word through it. She nodded.

The girl had thin arched eyebrows that gave her a quizzical

expression, and pale nondescript hair. 'You don't live round here,' she said, sounding more bored than interested.

Lilian swallowed carefully. The tea was hot but weak, and the girl was waiting for a reply.

'Arapawa Island,' Lilian forced it out. 'Whekenui Bay. I was born in Picton.'

The girl looked at her more closely now, frowning. 'Really? I don't remember you.'

But the girl's mother did. Lilian could see her behind the counter, her head cocked, listening, that bright look to the eyes. *Have I got something to tell you.*

'The tearooms are new, aren't they? ' said Lilian. 'My sister came here the day you opened. It's a good name to choose with the Centennial not far off.'

'Mum says the name is festive, Dad thought it was boring. He wanted to call it the Cray Pot.'

Lilian smiled weakly. 'Well, it makes me feel festive.'

The girl's mother was busying herself filling the milk jugs.

'How many children have you got?' Here she was, the girl, leaning on the table, all the time in the world.

Lilian felt tears prick her eyes. It was a simple question, but she couldn't speak. The face of the girl seemed to bob up and down – frowning, smiling, what *was* she doing? It was a malevolent face asking her something that upset her like that. The child seemed to know something. *She's lost one. Another one. How many's that now?*

Have I got something to tell you.

Lilian knew she shouldn't have come, she should have stayed at the hospital and kept watch.

She grabbed her bag, clamped her hat on her head and rushed for the door. As she walked quickly along the street, she heard the tap of her own shoes trying to beat her there, and she started to run.

Bursting into the hospital room, she stood panting beside Micky. She tried to still her breathing so she could hear his. Her fingers on his neck could tell. If she could just quieten down and get her breath back.

Ed woke on his chair, and grunted. She held her hand up. *Wait.* There it was. Faint at first, coming through her fingers. His pulse, his heart, his blood.

Five. Damn that girl. The answer was *five.*

'I thought,' she said, and started to cry. It poured out from her in great ridiculous barking sobs. Ed was beside her, and then holding her hard against his chest.

'Shush,' he said softly. '*Shush.*'

25

It was like wearing a cat. Lilian was looking at herself in the mirror with the red fox around her shoulders and wondering if it would be over one shoulder for the wedding. It might even be too hot for March, and she wondered if it wasn't too ostentatious at the end of a war? Her mother would have been able to help her with things like this. She'd have told her how much lipstick to wear.

Lilian sniffed down into the fur: she was sure there were gardenias there. She had been going to air it to get rid of the stale cupboard smell – but wouldn't she lose the gardenias as well? It was a nice fox, she decided, a very soft one, and the red did something lovely to her hair. More than anything, it was good to have something of her mother's to wear on her wedding day. Her father had dropped it into her lap a week ago, and she'd shrieked and jumped to her feet so it had fallen like a dead thing to the floor. 'Your mother wore this at our wedding,' he'd said, laughing. 'It's right you wear it now.'

Lilian had wanted her own wedding dress, but there hadn't been the time or the fabric, and who would have made such a thing? Jeannie had offered to lend her a dress without a moment's hesitation – it was brand new and made from an Australian pattern. The pale blue silk georgette had puffed sleeves and a scalloped neckline. There were pearl buttons. It was beautiful, and would look fine with the fox. Lilian was very grateful. She rubbed the fur between her fingers and felt a rough spot where the moths had got at it. She'd need to remember to tuck that bit under when she wore it.

Back a step. Back a step up the path. Back up to the small gate of the small churchyard and make a decision there not to enter. To turn at the sound of the small birds, to turn at the smell of the pine trees, to turn at the first crunch of the gravel, and leave quietly, without fuss or hurt. If you had to go in, you fool, you, Lilian, you should have turned back at the first small gravestone, and if you didn't turn then, there was a point on that path where you could see him and he couldn't see you, and you knew with sudden clarity that there was nothing there that was familiar. If it hadn't been for Jeannie, giggling behind you and running into your back like that, you might have turned at last and, seeing the gate there and the small gravel path, you'd have known what to do. As it was, he'd heard that silly trilling friend of yours, and looked for her and saw you, Lilian, in your borrowed silk georgette and red fox, and come forward, trussed in his uniform, his head dipping bashfully and his large hand out. He'd waited outside to introduce you to his best man, the cousin you'd heard so much about, who had even written you a letter or two. And there he was stepping out from behind him, a shorter, stockier man, in uniform too, but filling it differently, with thick black hair and ruddy cheeks, older than Ed by a few years, his eyes an astounding blue. Ed clasped his hands together, and waited to see that you liked him.

You remember how slowly it unfolded, the cousin stepping forward and removing his soldier's hat and taking your hand in greeting and saying your name in a way you'd have usually thought of as familiar but in fact was less insolent than that. And then he said nothing more, although he looked as if he wanted to. Jeannie came forward, wishing he would smile at her like that, but he didn't. He took her hand instead and kissed it, and Jeannie chortled, silly girl, and showed her crooked teeth.

'Come on, Owen,' said Ed, looking pleased at the way it had gone. And they went inside the church, the two of them, to wait for you.

26

He stood at the door of the room, wondering if he should go in. She was asleep, the late-afternoon light blurring her outline, her head back against the chair. The boy was asleep, too, his face grey on the hospital pillow, the sheet tented over his leg. The room was a wash of stale breathing and leftover worry and pain.

He took off his hat and pushed it into his pocket.

She opened her eyes.

'Hello, Annie.'

She stared as if she were still asleep.

'Annie?'

'Owen.'

'I came.'

She stood and moved to the window. He didn't know what he'd expected. He had no idea what to say or really why he'd come. Except that he liked the boy, and she was here.

Stepping up to the window, he saw there was something else out there besides the vacant sky. A small silver triangle was opening and shutting like a small window or a door. It flashed in the light. As it came closer, he realised it was a seagull and when the wings were up the white of its body shone. He could feel her watching it too.

'How is he?'

'The pain is terrible sometimes, he gets very restless. He sleeps almost all the time and when he's awake he forgets everything. We don't know yet what it's done to his head.'

'Will he pull through?'

'They think so.'

'I hope so, Annie.' He was looking at her now. They were the closest they'd been since she'd left him.

'My name is Lilian.' Her eyes were still clamped on the sky.

'No. Not Lili-*an*, *Annie* to me. Annie to *me*.'

There was a short bright silence like the winking bird. The sky was clear now, the seagull had gone. The day was wrapping up. He could hear her mouth opening and shutting.

'You shouldn't have come. Ed might come any time. Micky might wake up.'

'Ed came in this morning. I saw him get back after lunch.'

'Or someone else.'

'And what will they think, Annie?' He found it hard to keep his voice neutral. Everything he'd felt over the past twelve years had been stuffed back into his mouth.

'They will think I'm leaving Ed again, they'll keep the children away from me – again.' Her voice was tired too. There was all that hair – paler, greying – and out of it a tear falling unstopped down her face.

He felt in his pocket but there was nothing he could use. The tear reached her jaw. Quickly, he reached forward and pressed it with the pad of his thumb. He held it there a moment. She didn't move. She said nothing, but he heard a small sound like a kitten. As gently as he could, he pulled his thumb up her cheek, holding the tear, taking it back. He was sure he felt the muscles of her face yield, but just then she turned and he dropped his hand down to his side. She was looking at him for the first time since he'd come into the room. Her eyes were different, soft on the eyelid and stretched at the edges. Older, but still as dark as he remembered. Lovely.

'Good catch,' she said.

'I thought I was.'

When she smiled, he saw the fine lines on her face radiating from the eyes and around her mouth. They were lovely too.

'You know,' he said gently, 'we would have sorted out the children. They could have come to us.'

She stopped smiling, her face suddenly severe.

'The court . . .' he said.

'*That* fairy story? You still believe it? That we'd fetch them back to Tar'white and all live happily ever after?'

Of course he believed it. He saw the puzzlement in her face, and then he saw it slip away suddenly and her with it. She wasn't looking at him any more and her voice was small but unassailable.

'Everyone was telling our story at bedtime,' she said. 'All those people tucked safely in their beds, imagining us in Tar'white, telling the story as they'd heard it – husbands worrying that their wives might one day do what I did, and women wondering silently why they didn't – but before they fell asleep they'd hold hands and agree on the same version, the only version they could stomach: I was the evil witch, the *adulteress*, and Ed, who was full of devils, was the good father who'd been terribly wronged. You, Owen, were the man who had been led astray. ' Annie was barely speaking; she released the words and left them there to look at like breath on a mirror. 'Astray,' she said again. 'Nobody would let me have the children, Owen, least of all the courts.'

The whaler thought to grab her and hold her, to stop her drifting further from him, but he feared what she would do. His hand went to his pocket instead. He pulled out his pipe and started picking at the bowl with his fingernail.

'Why did we think it would be different?' Her voice was plaintive. She wanted him to say something.

We.

The Friar tried to pull his thoughts together.

'We were overwhelmed,' he said at last. 'We couldn't see the wood for the trees.'

He'd been down on the beach cleaning the dinghy one day and Dick had sidled over, making that sound he made when he sucked on his bad tooth. He'd said something nice about the boat, and then he'd cleared his throat as if he'd come with something else on his mind. 'She's unhappy, that girl of yours. Moping like a wet hen. She misses her kids like you or I would miss a leg.' He'd kicked a stone then and it had hit the side of the dinghy. The Friar saw the small chip in the paint and felt a burst of rage. His hands closed into fists. 'Shit, sorry mate,' said Dick, and he came over and stood close enough for the sour smell of rot from his tooth to make the Friar turn away. How did Annie stand it? 'I just thought you should know.'

One punch, thought the Friar, one punch in that putrid mouth of his for every word he had to say to him. Shut him up. 'You've got a bloody nerve. Don't think I don't know what you're up to, you old goat. Been hoping she'd let you stoke her while I'm in the next bay stoking the boiler, eh? Ever heard of love? Annie and I *love each other*. That's why she stays with me.'

'Love? Hah. What's that all about then? You overwhelm each other. Neither of you can think straight. You're *bad* for each other, you two.' And he'd turned to go. 'Oh well, it's your picnic.'

The Friar slipped his pipe back into his pocket. It *had* been his picnic. Dick was right, the dead bugger.

'It was like Susan and Micky died that year,' Annie said. 'They were so little – Micky wasn't much younger than Billy – I hated to think how much they were missing me, and Ed's not the sort of father to have given them much to be going on with. He left it all up to Iris.

'When I went back to them, I hoped that being so small they'd forget what had happened. I tried to mend it, whatever it was – a rent, a rift, a piece of them that hadn't grown as it should. Susan was more tentative at first, and overly concerned, always watching me. She knew something but she couldn't quite work out what it was. She's got Ben and Emily now, and has become more certain about what she wants, but she still can't move away from me with any confidence. There she is at the bottom of the hill and I fear she'll stay there all her life.

'Micky was different. He got angry. He banged into everything; he kicked walls and yelled a lot. Ed kept telling me the boy was like Jack, but I believe it was more than that. It was directed at me, you see. He was always baiting and goading me as if he was trying to catch me out, and he continues like that today. I kept watch over him so he wouldn't hurt himself or do something stupid, but he kept on doing stupid things – he still does. And when he left home, what could I do? I took my eyes off him. And now this –' She nodded towards Micky, his face drawn but soundly asleep. 'This is my fault. I have to live with that.'

'No, Annie.'

'Yes. I did what a mother should never do. I left him

behind when he was small and vulnerable. I let him down, I let Susan down, both of them were damaged by what I did. Their lives were changed.'

'But if they don't remember . . .'

She looked at the boy. 'The whale, Owen, the whale had something to tell me, remember?'

'No, Annie, it had nothing to say.'

Her eyes were closed. 'You weren't there. You don't know what happened.' She stopped, her face in a grimace. 'I tried to tell you.'

'Tell me now.'

'No.'

'Tell me.'

She held his gaze and appeared to be thinking about whether to trust him or not.

'Tell me,' he said.

'When I saw the whale, I was in Whekenui Bay, not Tar'white as I told you. I'd set out at the end of ebb tide and intended coming back with the flood. I did that sometimes when it got too much for me. I could get a glimpse of the children in the garden or on the beach, or I might not see them at all. That day, I hadn't seen anything and I was disappointed. I pulled the lines in at dusk and was rowing towards Wheke Rock and home when the whale came. I tried to row to the beach, but it followed me. Before I got there, it turned and left, all lit up with phosphorescence. By rights, I should have passed Wheke Rock by then, but because of the whale I was still in the bay, up close to the beach. I could see the house, my house, up the hillside. I could see the lamps were lit and the curtains not yet drawn. Then there he was.

'He'd slipped under the net curtains and was climbing up

on to the sill. I strained to see more, and waved my hand in case. I could see the loose shape of his pyjamas and the way his hair had been flattened by a brush – perhaps he was fresh from a bath? There was no more detail than that, but I could paint the rest without any trouble. The way the whole house would wheel around that small miracle and his sister and the smell of their hot baths and clean skin.

'I knew if Micky had been at the window moments before he'd have seen the whale. But then it occurred to me that he might have been looking out and I just hadn't seen him. If that was the case, he would probably have seen me too. The whale spout was so tall and so bright it was like noon in that bay. I could see his fingers, he was tapping on the window, then he managed to open it. He leaned around and called out. The words were barely audible: "Is that you, Mummy?"'

She swallowed and waited a moment.

'I wanted to call back but I couldn't. To say anything would have frightened him – what was I doing there? To say nothing must have frightened him too. I saw Iris shut the window, remove him from the sill and pull the curtains.'

The Friar went to speak.

'I called out,' she said, 'but it was too late: *Micky, it's me.* Like I was returning from a day trip to Picton. Could anything be more pathetic? I didn't decide to go back then. I really didn't. I still – I wanted to stay with you, Owen, but my heart was so sore. I would push down on it with the tips of my fingers at night while you slept, trying to stop the ache. I had small round fingertip-sized bruises on my ribs but no rest from the pain in there. I knew in the end the only way to feel better, properly better, was to go home.'

He felt her touch the knuckles of his right hand with the knuckles of her left. She'd always been so gentle with him.

He looked down and realised he was holding tightly on to the window sill as if he might fall.

'Let go,' she said softly, and he did. His hands hung heavily. Could he have been more gentle with her?

'You said nothing all these years and I know what that cost you. You kept away and you gave me my family back. I'm sorry, Owen.' *Own. Own. Own.* 'Thank you.'

He snorted then and reached up suddenly, grabbing her chin and turning her face towards him. 'Did you think about me at all?'

What did they see, those eyes of hers resting on his face? An old man she didn't know? He knew her all right. It was her hands more than anything else, and her lips. He remembered the way she'd kissed him that day they'd gone muttonbirding, scooping the tenderness out of him.

'Oh.' She said nothing for a moment.

'Did you think about Dick?'

'Dick?' Annie looked genuinely amazed. 'No, I didn't think about Dick.' She reached up and touched his hair and where the hair gave way to skin. 'What you'll do to make a hat fit!' Then her hand slid down to briefly cup his jaw. 'I thought about you.'

He felt something burn inside his eyes. He shut them tight.

'Every day for so long,' she said. 'And I thought about Robert, too. But I had to put those things away, you see. You do see, don't you? I had to keep going. My treasure, my boy, and I forget what . . .' She seemed to sniff the air as if retrieving something. 'I remember his birth: the surprise on his face, the creamy coating on his skin, the tiniest nails. I remember the way you looked at him.' She slid her hands across her eyes. 'I remember the smell. But the rest is gone. His death and his burial. There is nothing there at all.' Her mouth was pulled back from her teeth, like Smiler when he was going to be sick. There was something oddly fastidious about it. She licked her lips and looked at him squarely again as if challenging him to say something.

'You went back for the sake of the children,' was all he could manage. 'But what about you? You deserve to be happy.'

'I love my husband.'

'Do you?' The question was sharp and brutal and hopeless, he knew as he said it. It was as irrelevant as his thumb on her cheek.

'I love my family.'

Her eyes were elsewhere, her face set. The Friar squeezed his hands together. There was no room for him here; she'd allowed him no room. His hands were sticky with sweat. He needed to leave.

'It was a blue whale, you know. The one I saw. I asked Gunner. One had been spotted that day coming into the channel – they thought it had come and gone. It might have been a pygmy, a young one. It wasn't very long for a blue. He couldn't explain why it followed me.'

The Friar nodded. She looked at him square in the eye, searching for something, and then looked away.

'Sometimes,' she said, 'it all just wears me out.'

The Friar made his way towards the door and felt for the handle. There was a hollow space in his ears and a wind rushing past. He needed to go from the room, but he also needed to ask one more question.

'How did you know he'd take you back?'

She refused to meet his eye now.

'You owe me that.'

'It means nothing now. Just leave it alone.'

'Let me decide if it means nothing or not.'

She looked briefly frightened and then defiant. 'For goodness' sake.'

He controlled his voice. 'Annie,' said softly, firmly, for the last time.

'Gunner.'

'Gunner came to Tar'white?'

'Yes.'

'Gunner?'

'He cared about you, love.'

Love. The Friar closed his eyes.

'But he could see Ed was suffering,' she said, 'and his work was suffering, and that meant the business was suffering. Gunner had to think of that too.'

'He brought a message from Ed one day when I was working.' It was a statement, not a question. He'd suspected it all along.

'Yes.'

'And you sent one back.'

As the Friar left the building, he thought of the letter he would write when he got home. It wouldn't be like the ones he wrote when she first returned to Ed, because he wasn't angry any more, not with her anyway. But neither would it be a letter shot through with wonder like the ones he'd penned while she was sleeping in his bed. There'd be some of all of that, though, for she still lit something in him, whatever she said and however much she kept her distance.

It had been so long and there had been so many letters written since the first one in Gallipoli with its ridiculous need to impress. There was the note he'd slipped to her on impulse, to cheer her up really. She'd looked so sad one day up at Stony Knob, sitting having a picnic with Ed, and him just smoking and saying nothing. The note had been a bit of fun and she'd responded in kind, and then he couldn't help replying and had let it run on a little, talking, he remembered, about the daffodils he'd planted. And of course she had something to say about daffodils, for she loved her garden, and back came a letter from her, longer than the last and slipped under his door while she was passing. It didn't take long for them to be writing to each other once or twice a week, using the old gate up at her place as a post box. There was a knot in the middle plank of the gate, and with a bit of whittling Annie had made it big enough to fit a letter, folded once and rolled as tight as a cigarette.

He'd become so used to writing to her that he didn't stop when she came with him to Tar'white. He'd leave them for her to find when he was gone for the day – inside a book she was reading, pegged to the clothes line or even, controversially, rolled up tight and left inside a large spider web in the corner of the kitchen. It was three weeks before she found that one, and because it was dated she'd accused him of trying to show up her housekeeping. She never replied to those letters, although he knew she folded every one and put them in the drawer beside her bed. Once he found her ironing them in front of the stove. One by one with a hot iron, trying to get the creases out. That was not long before she left him. She'd left the letters too.

After she'd returned to Ed, the Friar had begun delivering his letters again to the knot in the gate. He'd replace one with the other, and hope each time, but she didn't touch any of them, so after four weeks he'd stopped delivering.

But he didn't stop writing. It was reassuring in a way he couldn't entirely explain. Sometimes he'd write once a week, sometimes less, but the letters had filled the drawer beside the bed and then been moved into his old kit bag, and still he'd kept writing. It was as if the tension in him built to a point that he had to release it. Fishing helped, or even just being out on the water, but by far the most useful thing he could do for himself was to write it down. To her. One day, he used to think, one day she'd be back, and he'd pile them all in her lap and she'd read them. Then she'd know how much he'd loved her, and what she'd done.

Of course, he'd take her back. At the drop of a hat.

The Friar had always imagined Annie had returned to Ed without knowing if he'd want her or not. He'd thought of her walking home, terrified her husband would throw her back like an undersized fish. The Friar had been uncompromising: if she ever went back to Ed – even if it didn't work out – that would be it. No return, ever. How proud he'd been, how sure of himself. But of course Ed had taken her; he was expecting her, his mate Gunner had passed the message on.

When did Ed notice the fingertip bruises under her blouse? Or, and the Friar closed his eyes as he thought it, maybe the bruises weren't there to see. It had been hard to tell with Annie. It seemed he was always trying to steady her to have a better look, but as soon as he'd done that she'd started moving away again.

And Gunner was wrong the way he called her the wharf and him the boat. That was the idea with women, the Friar supposed, that they were rooted in the ground, or anchored in the water, and there for men to come and go from as they pleased. Not Annie. Unmoored, that was the word for her; not tied up, but not out catching a wave either. That was the unsettling truth of the woman he loved. It was the death of her mother that had let her loose, and the death of the baby that had done for them. The tangled jersey in the compost. Cries he'd never heard before nor since. He knew now that when Annie had recovered a little and could look at the world again, she'd seen what she'd managed to avoid: she had children already and left them motherless – the very thing that had been visited on her. She knew then, if she hadn't before, that she had to go back. It wasn't a choice between Ed and the Friar at all. He wondered if Ed knew.

Life at Whekenui Bay had folded around her as if she'd never left. Folded was too gentle a word – they'd closed ranks around her, stiffly and at attention, to keep the scandal out. Not one person spoke about Lilian's adultery or the Friar's betrayal of his cousin, not in public, anyway. Led by Iris, they'd decided to act this way to protect the children and the family. The whole island needed protecting, in fact, for it was too small a place to let a scandal float around unmanaged. And neither Ed nor the Friar could be expected to leave because both were members of a family that had lived on Arapawa Island for nearly a century.

Life continued as if nothing had happened. Susan and Micky were too young to remember properly, and with no one to prompt their memories it was assumed they would simply forget. In time Jenny and Billy were born.

There were times, though, when the Friar saw two of the whalers' wives talking, leaning one to the other, the lips of one almost brushing the other's hair, the eyes of the other darting up the path that would take you to the house on the hill and then back to him standing there foolishly watching. And he knew what they were talking about. But those words scuttled quickly from mouth to ear like insects. Maybe they were just referring to the reclusive behaviour of the wife of the whaler at the top of the hill – untenable to newcomers, but to the people of the whaling community just good manners. Maybe they'd heard something more about her, something that had slipped out and needed telling.

The letter the Friar would write to her now he would put in the old kit bag with the rest of them. He made a vow to himself that this would be his last. For Gunner was right, there was no future in it.

Annie my love,

When you're home, I can see you. Not all the time, but often. I see you working in the garden or tending the chooks or doing the washing or digging up vegetables. I see you walking the hills. And when I don't see you I still know you're there.

With you away from Arapawa, my eyes shift from the sea to the house, and there's nothing. It's not much I ask, Annie. Bring your son home.

Your loving,
Owen

27

Annie had her back against the ribs of the *Periwinkle* and her eyes shut. The Friar was netting a fish he'd speared, shouting out how big it was, a kingfish, a blessed kingfish, as big as they come. They'd eat like kings tonight and, if he smoked it, they could eat kingfish for the rest of the week. He knew he was making a fool of himself, but he wanted Annie to open her eyes.

They had enough fish. The Friar knew he should start rowing back, but he was tired too and he didn't know why. It was the weight of this thing in Annie; it seemed to be weighing them both down.

The oars knocked against the rowlocks and the fishing lines tugged and stretched, and the rocking of the boat was like their small house in a heavy wind, or the bed rocking and Annie holding him so tightly, too tightly sometimes. Rocking, he would hold her, his whispering voice breaking into threads, and then he'd hold her until she slept, terrified she still might leave him.

The Friar had taken her to live in Tar'white to be away from Whekenui and Fishing Bay. Even so, the earth that was under their house was the same as the earth under the whaling houses elsewhere on the island, and he knew Annie could listen sometimes for the sound of those houses creaking on their foundations and still lingered over thoughts of the people inside them.

The Friar lit his pipe. He took deep draughts of smoke mixed with the salted air and held it inside for as long as he could. Annie used to joke that when he died he'd stay perfectly preserved like a giant smoked cod. She'd been such a fanciful woman when they'd first met, full of funny things to say like that – not belly-laughing funny, just smart. But it seemed to him she'd begun to set. Her mouth, her face, her body had lost their fluidity. She didn't smile any more.

He started rowing back.

28

Lilian woke unearthly tired. She was whittled out. There were rough-hewn spaces in her head. She could feel the splinters and the shavings when she moved. Everything ached. She kneaded her temples with her fingers, but then the splinters seemed to shift to her mouth and she couldn't get up from the bed for a glass of water. Her muscles and bones had been whittled away too; there was no strength left in them. She lay there like the wooden doll her mother had played with as a child. Tiny painted lips. It was there standing in the corner of the room looking at her. Why had Ada kept it?

Lilian lay there for so long that the light of the morning was full blown and the bellbird that fluted by her sister's washing line had retreated under an onslaught of gulls. It must be stormy out on the open water, she thought. I can hear them gathering on the land, shrieking at me, telling me to come home.

Jenny and Billy joined in outside her door.

'You let the snail out!'

'I did not, she got out.'

'The lid was off. You forgot to put it on and you're not owning up.'

'I didn't take it off. And anyway, I'm going home today. I'm sick of staying here and sick of you.'

Billy came into the room, his face defiant. Jenny tried to push him aside so she was first.

Lilian closed her eyes – her eyeballs had splinters in them now – and she waved her hand to dismiss them. 'I'm not your mother today, I'm a wooden doll called Charlotte. I can't help you with the snail.'

'But Mum!' Jenny's voice was pitched high with indignation. 'Sparkle could be anywhere, she's lost in the house. She'll be so *scared*. And he doesn't *care*.'

'It's not like she's a pet,' said Billy. 'You've only known her . . .' Lilian knew he was trying to count the days, 'a little while. Not like Molly. We've had her for . . . hundreds and *hundreds* of days. I bet she's scared. I care about that. I care about that a lot.' And he burst into tears.

Lilian used one arm to pull him over to her, and held his shaking body. And Micky too, she thought. You care about Micky too. She had no idea just then what to say to the little boy. How was Micky? She didn't know that either. He seemed much the same to her. The hospital was worried, though. She could tell by the nurses' refusing to talk about it. They were waiting for his temperature to stop rising and to fall back where it should.

Jenny climbed into the other side of the bed and laid her head on her mother's stomach like she used to when she was small.

'I'm sure we'll find Sparkle,' Lilian said, wrestling her eyes open to the glaring day. 'The very good thing about snails is they don't move very fast.'

When the children had left her, she got up and dressed. It took an age but there she was at last, ready to go, her coat and her hat on. The children were waiting at the door.

'We want to see Micky,' said Jenny.

'No,' said Lilian. 'Not now. I'll take you when he starts getting better. I promise.'

And she hugged them both tightly, and Ada too. If only Susan could come. She'd take Susan with her. But Emily was sick with a cold.

Lilian walked quickly. She'd taken so long to get ready, and it seemed important suddenly that she get there in a hurry. She was angry with herself. Nothing seemed right this morning; even the light seemed to cling to her in an irritating way. It flared on her eyeballs and made her feel nauseous and a little faint.

She was in the park when she saw the chaser. It was Ed. He was manoeuvring through the other boats, then pulling up to the jetty and throwing the mooring rope out to someone she didn't know. She saw the man laugh at something Ed said, throw his head back and laugh upwards and outwards like throwing a ball. She could hear it bouncing off the water and coming towards her. Then Ed was joining in and waving goodbye and walking towards her. It felt peculiar to see him like that, in a different place and at a distance. What had he said to the man?

Lilian waved. She meant it to be friendly, to share somehow in that laugh that was still flying around, but instead what she gave was a tentative flap. Ed stopped and squinted. She waited. He waved back – he might even have smiled.

'How's the patient?' he said when he joined her.

'I haven't been there yet,' she said. 'I'm on my way. I was feeling a bit crook first thing. It slowed me up.' She saw him frown. 'I'm better now.'

'Good,' he said. 'I can't have two patients to look after.'

He took her arm and they walked a little before he leaned down close again. 'You're sure you're all right?'

Suddenly, she wanted to cry. She clawed at it, though, and held it in. No good getting upset again. 'Yes, yes, I'm fine,' she said, sharper than she meant to, and quickened her step.

At the hospital, the boy seemed unchanged, the nurses less helpful, the doctor nowhere to be found, and there was another patient in the room now. A man in his forties with a broken thigh bone. He'd been cutting down trees and got in the way. He was crying blue murder now, and a nurse pulled a screen around him.

Lilian and Ed sat by Micky and waited.

Another nurse came in, a girl just out of school by the look of her, who'd confided earlier that her name was Margaret. She took Micky's temperature without his waking. 'It's peaked,' she said. And she was smiling at them, and smiling at their son, her face a sun. 'Look.' She held up the thermometer while she wrote down what it said.

The moment she left the room, Micky groaned and started moving his head. Ed moved swiftly, grabbed the boy's shoulders and heaved him on to his side where he vomited bile all over the pillow. Ed held Micky like that until he sighed and his face went slack. His eyes stayed shut but his hand moved across the blanket. It reached his father's fingers and stayed there. Ed's eyes were locked on the boy. No one moved.

Lilian smelt the vomit and felt the air inside her expand outwards so she had to open her mouth to let it out. She didn't feel any better even so. *It was the shearing shed again.* There was more and more air inside, pushing between her ribs. *It was clear, now, all of it. How stupid she'd been.* Lilian stood swaying and then ran for the door. Like Ed making the man laugh. There it was in front of her, what Iris had called 'a bloody epiphany'. They'd managed. Ed and the children. And the Friar too. She'd imagined a mess when there wasn't one. They'd all *managed* without her. Somehow.

Lilian stumbled into the toilets, found an empty cubicle and locked the door behind her. She was gagging on her son's vomit, on hospital bleach and the oily smell of the linoleum. She sat on the toilet lid, shuddering and gripping herself around her stomach. A tender thing. How it ached when she cried like that.

They'd managed without her. It was all she could have hoped for.

When Lilian returned to Micky's room, her son was lying on a clean pillow, looking at his father through half-closed eyes. The blinds were drawn. They'd been told he'd have difficulty with bright light. The vomit had been cleaned up, but the smell still pricked Lilian's nostrils and made her want to run. She took out her handkerchief and held it up, ostensibly to wipe her nose, but it was the lavender smell she wanted.

Ed was saying, 'Now tell me what you remember.'

The boy took a while. Lilian went forward to say something but Ed shook his head.

'We were nearly on to the humpback,' said Micky at last. 'I had it lined up, it was in my sights.' He closed his eyes tight and sighed. 'No. I don't remember . . .' He paled suddenly and swallowed.

'Did that hurt you?'

The boy nodded. His face was moist and grey. He groaned then and his body moved as if trying to push something off.

'It will take a few weeks yet to get you back on the chaser, that's for sure. But it could have been worse. I'd say you're a bit lucky.'

Micky groaned again.

'I know it doesn't feel like it, but it will.'

'Tell . . .' said Micky, and he swallowed, 'tell me how it happened.'

Ed went to speak, but Lilian put her hand on his arm. 'It was an accident,' she said. 'The cow knocked the chaser. We'll talk more about it when you're stronger.'

29

'Wash Rock,' said the Friar, the words hissing out around the stem of his pipe. 'I swear there was a white whale spotted out by Wash Rock. I can't recall when exactly. Not long after the war.'

'Nah,' said Tommy. 'It was out at The Brothers. It was Ed who spotted it about ten year ago. Bloody great whale and white as the Angel Gabriel.'

'And you'd have been nine years old when it happened,' said the Friar. 'Remember it well, do you? That was a shark, my boy. Nearly took Ed's leg off. I'm talking about a white *whale* out by Wash Rock.'

'With respect, Ahab,' said Charlie slowly, 'far as I know we don't get any Moby Dicks round here.'

'They're out there,' said the Friar. 'Moby Dick was based on a real whale.' He refused to be ruffled by these kids, and the beer was helping. It slowed things down nicely as a matter of fact, made him feel mellow. Of course Gunner's boys, Charlie and Stew, weren't kids any more. They must be in their early forties, round the same age as Ed. Tommy, Ben and Phil were the young ones, happy with hearsay, even happier blowing a story up so it resembled the original only in its geography. There they were laughing together, rocking back on their heels. History was like a story to them anyway. Who cared if it was ten years or twenty, a white whale or a white shark? Boots was a bit older than them and inclined to a sceptical silence, so no one knew for certain what he thought. The Friar saw Charlie shake his head at Stew and the two brothers lapse into their beers.

After just over three weeks of whaling, the station had put through twenty-five whales – almost all of them humpbacks – and the men's bodies were aching with it. This was one of the few times they'd opened some beers together. The only thing that took the edge off it was Micky's accident.

'You do see freaks in nature,' said Ben, 'animals the wrong colour, and they always make for stories and songs. Moby Dick, Baa, baa black sheep . . .'

'. . . have you any wool?' chirruped the Friar, tipping back his glass and then filling it again. Everything was moving nice and slow.

'And how about white elephants?' said Tommy.

'Yessir, yessir,' sang the Friar.

'Or white sharks,' said Tommy.

'What is it about white?' The Friar wiped the beer froth off his top lip.

'You tell us, old man,' said Tommy.

The Friar spluttered.

'I think it's because it's so pure,' said Boots, blinking slowly.

That shut them up. They waited, but he didn't say anything more.

'White is untouched,' said Tommy. 'Like snow. That's why brides wear it.'

'Brown's pretty pure too,' said Ben, tapping his cheek. 'Many a young lady's had to touch this to see I'm for real.' He pushed his face up to Tommy's. 'Want to try?'

Tommy stroked Ben's cheek with his thumb and then he held it up to have a look. 'Damn, I hoped some of it would come off on me. Get the attention of the girls at last.'

'Afraid not, mate.'

The Friar turned to Charlie. 'How's the fencing going?'

'We're finished. All done.'

'You weren't tempted to hold off and see what the government decided about electric fences?'

'Nope,' said Charlie. 'Dad reckons they're too expensive.'

'They reckon it'll revolutionise farming,' said Tommy.

'And electrocute half the farmers in the process,' said the Friar.

'That too,' said Charlie. 'I was saying just that to Stew the other day. Where's a bloke going to lean his arm when he wants to say gidday to a neighbour?'

Ben leaned back, his mouth slack now, dribble on his chin, looking at the sky. 'And a cockie caught short, decides to have a piss beside the fence post.'

'One fried farmer!' bellowed the Friar. He was pleased with his new brew.

The Friar saw Ed first. He was coming from the whale station with Sarge and Jimmy, his face set in neutral. It had been a long hunt that day with nothing to show for it except a crook chaser. The three latecomers had been working on it, but it was hard to tell whether they'd been successful. It was Ben who called out to his father-in-law to join them. The Friar watched Ed's face, saw his eyes flick over the drinkers.

'I could do a beer, Sarge, I don't know about you,' he said.

'A beer would hit the spot,' said Sarge.

The Friar filled two cups and brought them over. 'Can't go to a glass, I'm afraid, Lucky.'

Ed looked at the Friar then, sharply and quickly. Not a single drink had passed Ed's lips after a whale hunt, not one word of loose conversation these past twelve years.

'How's the *Chance*?' said Ben.

'Getting there,' said Ed stiffly. 'Jimmy here spotted the problem and found the part in his shed. We'll be out again tomorrow.'

Jimmy blushed and started to say what he'd done, but the Friar interrupted. 'And more importantly, how's Micky?'

Ed said nothing for a moment. He looked into his beer. The other men looked away. 'It's still touch and go,' said Ed. 'He's better than he was.' And he took a long deep draught from his glass, coming up with an edge of surprise to his mouth. 'This is good.'

'Will he lose the leg?' asked Tommy. And the Friar couldn't help thinking that the boy would be drinking at The Federal in a couple of months' time, telling the story of a whaler who'd fired a harpoon at his own son and shot off the boy's entire leg. He flashed a look at Tommy, but his attention was on Ed.

'We still don't know. It'll be a long haul.' Ed was looking at Tommy as if he'd only just noticed him. 'Not so sure about his head, however.' Was that a smile?

'You should be there, Ed,' said Sarge.

'I've been there. Lilian's with him now, there's not much we can do. He's been out of danger for four days now. '

There was a short silence.

'Well, hopefully, the accident has knocked a bit of sense into him,' said Sarge.

Ed said nothing. Then: 'If it hasn't, he won't be at the end of a harpoon as long as I have any say in it.'

'Have you talked to him about this?' asked Ben.

'Since he started hunting goats for dog tucker,' said Ed.

Tommy was leaning forward earnestly. 'But he's a good shot, Ed.'

'You can be a dead-eye, Tommy, but get too cocky and you're just dead. No one benefits from that.'

'No one,' said Stew mournfully.

The Friar poured some more beer into Boots's glass and spoke near his ear. 'Have you got over missing the big one today?'

'Anyone can hit a big one,' said Boots. 'It's the little ones that are hard to get.'

'How's the leg?'

'It's still there.'

'Well, we'll just make sure you're comfortable then,' said Margaret, plumping up his pillows and tucking the sheets in. 'Bed pan?'

Micky snarled and turned his head away. The girl smoothed the blanket. 'I'll need to take your temperature again then.'

Lilian noticed how pretty Margaret was with her heart-shaped face and blonde hair. She seemed pleased with Micky's temperature and with him. She tipped up the small watch pinned to her apron. 'I'll come back later then,' she said brightly, and waited a moment, but he didn't look her way.

Micky wouldn't let Lilian hold his hand after that and he wouldn't speak. At last he said quietly, 'My foot is freezing.'

Lilian put down her knitting and looked at her son. He was staring at her and she could see he wasn't joking. 'But Mick, it's so warm in here.'

'Can you check it?'

Lilian went to the end of the bed, lifted the sheet and reached for his foot. She touched it gently. It didn't feel cold at all; it felt warm.

'Is it there? They haven't chopped it, have they? It's so cold.'

'Micky, love, it's there. You have both your feet. Maybe I should call the nurse.'

'She wouldn't know a foot if she stepped on one,' said Micky. 'But the foot is there?' His voice was querulous, childlike.

Lilian went back to the head of the bed and held his hand until he slept.

30

Gunner's body was revolting him the way it refused to hold the line. There was no doubt he was 'a leaky old boat' now, like the Friar. To think they'd once taken it for granted they could piss like horses at the drop of a hat. How careless.

The doctor wanted tests done – he suspected something more than a disobedient bladder – but Gunner was holding out. No tests. Not now. He preferred to keep what he had left as intact as possible. But then he wasn't thinking straight, he hadn't been thinking straight for a while now. He found himself crying sometimes, for no reason, but then suspected it wasn't really crying at all, just another ridiculous symptom of age.

The other thing he was doing too much of lately was thinking back to earlier times. What a time-waster that was. One thing he'd come to realise, though, when he heard his mates chewing the fat, was the few regrets he had. Like his father, he'd lived by the maxim 'Look after your own'. His family, his cobbers, his workers – he'd done his best by them all. It hadn't always been straightforward, but most things had turned out satisfactorily.

One of the memories he liked going over was the first time he'd visited Nadine. He'd got her brother Dave to take him home not long after he'd met her at the dance. They'd turned up and she was in the kitchen, sitting in the sun, sewing. Graceful, bathed in gold. Like a queen. Queen Nadine. She'd got to her feet, blushing, and asked if he wanted some apple pie, and she'd cut two pieces, one for Dan and one for him, and told them to go and sit outside under the apple tree and she'd bring it along. Well, she did just that (this in itself was enough to surprise him) and then went back inside to make the tea. It took Gunner a moment to notice, for there was a lot of cream, but while Dave had a perfect wedge of apple pie on his plate, on Gunner's plate there was a wedge with a large bite taken out of it. You could see it as clear as day. That's all the encouragement he'd needed. Nadine, he thought, my toothy love. How simple it had been.

If Gunner was honest with himself, though, there were one or two things he would have done differently. There was that business with Ed and Lilian and the Friar which was a difficult situation in anybody's book. All the whalers had been furious and humiliated on Ed's behalf, and wanted the Friar taken off the job, but Gunner couldn't do that. Where else could the man go? This was the Friar's island as much as Ed's and whaling was an important part of his livelihood.

Nadine worked on him too. She didn't condemn Lilian outright at first – she was a friend and had known how difficult it was for her living with Ed – but then she'd started talking to the other women. Where the men felt Ed's humiliation and were concerned their wives didn't follow Lilian's example, the women felt the betrayal of their whole way of life. Their judgment was swift and harsh. Who was Lilian to think she could up and leave like that? Abandon her children, make a cuckold of her husband, break apart cousins, divide island loyalties – *who was she?* These women worked every hour God brought them, fulfilling their obligations to their families as they should, and Lilian didn't. This simple act was seen as treachery. The women, including Nadine, refused to have any dealings with her or the Friar from that moment on. Which made it hard for Gunner, but he had a different sense of what was right and less anxiety about his own position. He kept the Friar on, and when he needed to step in, he did. Nadine just had to put up with it.

Gunner stood now and felt everything in his body that had been reliable and invisible for so long groan and settle uneasily into place. The problem with his plumbing was the thing he resented the most, though, because it had stranded him at home and rendered him comical. He knew they all had a laugh when he had to drop everything and rush for a piss. He'd have done the same once.

Gunner stretched his arms up over his head and felt his skin stretch tight. A shiver behind his eyes made him blink. The *Wellington* would be coming soon to get the first barrels of oil and that, at least, made him feel the King of the World. He needed to check everything was in order, and then he'd look over Nadine's paperwork. The fact was he needed to get back out on the water as soon as possible. He knew without looking at the books that he couldn't afford to have the *Balaena* off for much longer. The thought set off a small buzz in his chest.

The Friar straightened up the table for his meal. He moved his book to one side and set a single place with a spoon and fork and a linen table napkin. In front of it went the salt and pepper shakers and a plate of bread and butter. He opened a beer and poured it carefully into a glass. While he waited for the stew to finish up, he went to his kit bag.

How many letters were in there he couldn't guess. Over twenty years of letters on and off – almost half his life – and it struck him then as it hadn't before what a sterile thing this collection was. It wasn't sending news or sharing his life with another; it was dead leaves marked with dead thoughts. And he knew now that he'd never show them to Annie.

The Friar picked up the bag and took it into the kitchen. The stove was nice and hot. He opened the door and looked at the coals. Maybe he should just throw the whole thing in and be done with it. The impulse was strong. But no. It would be a bit of a shove and make too much of a stink. He put his hand in and pulled out a sheaf of letters. He didn't mean to look at them, but the one he'd just written her was on the top. *Your loving Owen*. He considered keeping it, but stopped himself, thrusting the handful into the range. The thin paper took immediately and the flames licked and chewed. Another pile then, and another. He tried not to look at the words on the paper or to imagine what they'd do now, ashy things released into the air. Nearly twenty-three years of letters, from the first one at Gallipoli, 5 August 1915, to the one today, 20 June 1938. Annie's too, not just his. He'd been so meticulous with the dates and with spelling out all the things he'd done, as if some day someone would read the letters and need to know the why and how.

Outside, there was the stutter of a seagull and beyond that the faint clapping of the sea. The pile was getting smaller and smaller. He poked at the ashes and let each handful burn down. He was near the bottom of the bag now. The Friar was moving more slowly. He felt around for the last letters. These would be the ones from Gallipoli, the hardest to throw away.

His hand felt something else. He pulled out an envelope. *Lilian Brookes, 20 Wellington Street, Picton.* Her address, and the envelope. It was the one letter he'd sent her from Gallipoli. But it shouldn't be here, it should be with her. The Friar let out a long sigh then, like the air rushing inside the coal range, and the seagull cried, and he felt such terrible desolation. He ran his finger along the raw edge where she'd used a letter opener.

Gallipoli
Turkey
5 August 1915

Dear Miss Brookes

The longed for letters finally arrived today and in the bag was the usual door-stop letter from you to Ed – he's a lucky man all right – and this time there was also a card for me. Ed told you I don't get a great deal of mail and that was enough for you to put pen to paper. I know you are a busy person so I am very grateful to you for taking the trouble.

We have never met, but I feel I know you through the letters you send to Ed. When the days are especially long and tiring, he sometimes asks me to read to him. I hope you don't mind, he is careful only to let me read things of general interest. We all look forward to your stories about life in Picton and the patriotic things you are doing to support us so far away. You complain that you don't hear from Ed enough. Well, I can tell you he writes you a postcard twice a week every week and I am his best cobber and his cousin too so I should know. I reckon many of them must get sunk. This last letter of yours took so long to come we thought it must have been submarined too, and Ed was beside himself. Now it's finally come, I heard him whistling this morning.

We're still in a hole in the ground and it rained today so you can imagine the mud. At least it's warm. The tedium is the worst thing. Our trenches here are only about ten yards or so from the Turks. Sometimes they call over to us and we strike up a conversation. The other day one of them who spoke English told us they had a lot of tobacco but no papers and could we do a trade. You won't believe it, but we did. He came over with a white flag and Ed did the swap. What a laugh we had, Ed and I, when he got back, and we all clapped him on the back for his bravery. He was the toast of the trenches, or the smoke I should say. A few days later they wanted to trade vegetables for chocolate. So that's what we did. Don't know who did the best out of that.

Ed and I still talk about your fruit cake which arrived last month in perfect condition in its soldered tin. He shared it with all the fellows so it didn't last long but not one crumb was wasted. Some of them got down on their hands and knees to lick them off the ground, and when the chaplain came and took prayers the other week, he asked what we should pray for, and Jim Thompson said, 'Lilian Brookes' fruit cake.'

Trusting this letter finds you well,

Regards,

Owen Prideaux

He sat a moment. *Ed and I.* He'd forgotten about Ed trading cigarette papers for tobacco with the Turks. *Ed and I.* He'd forgotten about the fruit cake. *Ed and I.* He'd forgotten Ed whistling when her letters came. What he'd seen that day at the church, what had blotted *Ed and I* out of his mind, was a woman in a pale blue dress that clung to a fine figure, bare calves with small muscles under the skin when she moved, and over one shoulder a fur the colour of her hair. And such wonderful hair, such shiny, fresh, wonderful hair, escaping from a hat. He saw the way her eyes moved, looking at him curiously, then looking to Ed and seeing his nervousness and reaching out to squeeze his arm. He saw her stand on tiptoes to whisper in Ed's ear, and still he had to bend.

At Gallipoli, when a man went forward his mate went too. That's how it was. As Ed had moved to greet his bride, so Owen came: two soldiers striding between the gravestones, the shape of their eyes the same but nothing else, one tall and aloof and spare of face, the other as tall as he was wide, a muddle of features and a grin from ear to ear. The Friar knew Ed was terrified, so he'd nudged him and winked: 'She's a pretty one, Lucky.' For a brief moment, the Friar felt he was the one walking to be married, he was so happy to see her there after all this time. To know she was real.

One day up at Quinn's Post they'd been picking the lice off with their fingers. They'd removed the clothes from their upper bodies and were starting with their singlets. The Friar reckoned he had picked off a good number already, but Ed declared that with no question of doubt he'd killed two hundred. That alone said a lot about the man – not that he had so many lice, but that he could carefully count them like that, one by one, and not lose track. It was unlikely he'd exaggerated or rounded the figure, that wasn't Ed's way. Whatever way you looked at it, there they were, the two of them side by side, carefully picking lice off their clothes, and then Ed had leaned over: 'If you ask me, we'll never get on top of these fellows. Let's pick off some goats instead.'

That was their code for talking about home. Side by side with their rifles cocked, one of them would start on something like the dance at the Walkers' farm or the whalers' rugby game and they'd go from there. Who they'd seen, what they'd eaten, the moves that won the game. That kind of thing. They stopped when one of them fell asleep or fell silent or the firing started up again. Ed had never tired of it, not that he did all that much talking, but he liked to listen. They saw how some diggers ended up hating their trench mates because they never got away from them. *Ed and I* were different, thought the Friar. We started off as cousins and we ended up the best of mates. We wouldn't let each other go.

31

Susan stood in her mother's kitchen and looked out at the back garden. In her hand was a rag she was using to wipe the benches. Everything was immaculately clean now, and the smell of the white vinegar was like the fall of sun on the bench. A gleaming thing. Behind her, the range was shiny with boot black, and newly lit. It had been so cold when she'd come in, shockingly cold. It had stopped Susan at the door, stopped the baby chuckling. It felt like a premonition of death.

Emily was asleep now, tucked up on Susan's old bed which was now Billy's. Outside, the chooks picked their way through the garden. Her mother should be here. She would be here, soon. Meanwhile Susan was the one wiping the benches, feeding the range, starting the meal. Like Lilian, like Nana had been.

Susan had been able to see where her father had tried to tidy up a little, and it touched her to think of him so uncertain, holding something in his hand and wondering where to put it. But no one had given the kitchen a proper going-over since Micky's accident, that much was obvious, and there was an odd smell that no amount of cleaning could shift.

She took the meat from the safe and began to chop it into cubes to make a stew. Then she sliced an onion and melted a lump of lard to fry it. Susan thought again of the women in the caves in Spain, wearing white and holding their babies, looking out at everything they knew, changed and silenced.

Susan concentrated on what was in front of her: inhaling the smell of the browning meat and feeling the warmth of the range on her legs. She peeled and chopped the potatoes next, taking greater care than usual to remove the skin and the eyes, and put them in the pot with the meat. Then carrots and water. Salt and thyme. The heavy fall of the lid. Her mother used to call a stew like this a rib-sticker. She said it would keep you warm for days.

Susan had been fighting a feeling of melancholy ever since she'd arrived at the house. She'd put it down to its being empty, but now she knew. It was not because the house was cold and empty in a way it had never been before, but because it *had* been that way once that she remembered. She'd been the first one up that morning: the one to wake and find the silent kitchen. To find the note. She could barely read but she'd managed 'Ed' on the front before she'd given it to Nana. Their mother was sick and she'd gone to the hospital in a hurry, that's what Nana told them. But while Susan had believed it for a while, she began to worry about this piece of information as she grew. If her mother was so sick, how could she go to the hospital on her own? Why didn't her father take her?

Susan polished the bench one more time and hung the rag up to dry. The mail boat wouldn't be far away. She put on the kettle, opened the cake tin and pulled a piece of fruit cake off with her fingers. She could name the ingredients one by one, and the exact proportions. Micky's favourite. How she wished he was coming back now too, the old Micky, not the crushed one. She'd ask for nothing else.

The doctors said it was hard to tell how bad the injury was. His thinking seemed fine enough, and he could still laugh at a joke, but there was a flatness there, too, and the headaches, and the way he kept forgetting things. The doctors said he would improve but they couldn't say how much and when.

Susan found herself in the main bedroom standing in front of the cupboard. She opened the door and pushed her way in to the back. It was there as it always had been, wrapped in a pillowcase and hanging on a hanger on its own hook.

The fox.

You couldn't tell it was there if you didn't know, but Susan knew. Susan knew, because this is where she hid when she was six and missed her mother. When she couldn't breathe for gulping. When she needed to be surrounded by the clothes her mother had worn, and that still, if you held them close, smelt of her. Sometimes, Susan would take the fox fur from its hanger and remove the cotton cover. She would lie on it and close her eyes and breathe in its cloying, perplexing smell. The fox was the secret she'd shared with her mother. She'd spoken her own secrets to it, breathing them into its brittle fur.

Emily was waking. Even deep inside the cupboard, Susan could hear her. She went, brushing off the clothes and the stale air, feeling the delight that never failed to catch her at that moment. She picked up her daughter and held her. She was getting heavy – would the dresses be too small? Susan had cut them both out and tacked them, but she needed to get on and finish them off.

Susan rolled on to Billy's bed and propped Emily up on her stomach. 'Emily,' she sang. It was like being under-water with the light shining green through the curtains. 'Lovely Emileeeee.'

It would have been like this for me, thought Susan. Before Micky, before Jenny and Billy, it was just my mother and me. But it was too far back and she could only guess at it. Although there was one time she held tight to herself.

They'd gone together in the runabout to visit a sick friend, leaving Micky with Iris. Susan remembered getting out on a different wharf, a narrow one that seemed to go on forever, but she couldn't quite place the bay. It was summer so she had bare feet and there was a splinter in her big toe and she was trying not to cry. After delivering the food and getting the splinter out, they'd sat together on the wharf looking at the water. There was a picnic. Cheese sandwiches and boiled eggs and cake. No, Susan didn't know that, she was just imagining. But she could remember sitting, just the two of them, eating and looking out at the water, and talking about things. She couldn't remember what they talked about or what they ate, but she remembered how she felt having all of her mother's attention. Like sunshine.

Her mother had stood, too soon after eating, cake crumbs still on her teeth, and pulled off all her clothes except for her underwear. 'Race you!' And she'd run along the wharf. 'Come in!' she'd called. 'Come on in, Susan! Come with me!'

Susan didn't move. She'd looked over her shoulder at the house they'd just visited. When she turned back to see what her mother was doing, Lilian had disappeared, like a trick. No noise even. Silence. Susan had jumped to her feet and started to run herself, lopsided because of the splinter. She looked over the end of the wharf to perfectly still water, and then – an eternity of time later – she saw the seawater bulge, and there was her mother, breaking through the skin of it, gasping and laughing and waving and wet.

So Susan had taken her clothes off too. She'd stood at the end with her mother below, calling, 'I'm here, Susan. Jump, love.' And even though Susan couldn't swim, she'd jumped. Out into the transparent air. Into the deep water. So deliciously cold and shocking. And she'd smashed down into it, to be there where her mother was. *I'm here*. Down, down. And her mother had yanked at her, pulled her upwards and held her to herself. Tightly. Slippery. And they'd paddled like that a while. The water was so clear they could see the bottom; they could see their toes.

'What a brave girl you are,' her mother had said in that way she did as if her children were a surprise to her. And then between them they'd ripped two dozen mussels off the wharf to take home for tea.

'Emileee,' sang Susan in the green room, bouncing the baby on her stomach high enough to make her laugh.

32

The mail boat was waiting and so was Titch.

'Gidday! And what a pleasure to have you on board.' He took the bags off Lilian and led the way up the ramp, Billy running up after him, Lilian following, Jenny and Ada staying on the wharf to say goodbye. They'd decided Jenny would stay at her school until the end of the year – what with Lilian having to go back and forward to visit Micky for a few weeks yet, it would be less disruptive for her. It wasn't long to go.

Titch went back down to collect the boxes of groceries and the new hen. She was still a chick, really, a bantam from Ada's coop. Molly Too, Billy had named her. 'Not Molly *Two*, because she'll think she's not as important. Molly *Too* means she's almost the same.' Surprisingly, Jenny had agreed to this.

Titch threw the last box on the deck, took hold of the rope tied to the bollard and started the engine. But first he had to ring the bell. 'People like to know when I'm coming and going,' he said. Lilian rolled her eyes down at Ada and Jenny, and both of them laughed.

One minute the boat was chugging in the water and then without warning it had surged from the wharf. Almost immediately, Lilian regretted leaving Jenny behind.

She went to sit under cover with Titch while Billy ran along the boat waving goodbye. She was too tired to do anything but sit. It was good to be going home, back to a semblance of normal life. Ada and Jenny would be there for Micky, and Ed had come every day since the accident and talked with the boy. Talked. Lilian had seen it with her own eyes. It was as if her husband had saved up everything from a whole lifetime to talk to his son about. Every detail of the weather was relayed, along with anything to do with boats and whaling and farming. Ed opened his hands and gave it all to Micky, and Micky began, very slowly, to talk back.

One day Lilian came down the hospital corridor at visiting time and wondered who the patients were making all the noise. The laughter and shouting were making people stop what they were doing. When she opened the door she saw them there: Micky in tears and Ed with his head back laughing, and Joe, who'd fallen under the tree, joining in.

Micky had waved her into the room just as Susan arrived, so there was no time to ask what they'd been laughing about. After a while, Lilian and Ed left them to it. They walked out into the grounds and stood looking down at the marina.

Ed was frowning and shuffling his feet. That usually meant he wanted to say something. She waited.

'I hear the Friar came to visit.'

Lilian thought she was falling. She grabbed Ed's arm.

'I didn't – I didn't ask him to come, he just came, he was concerned about Micky.'

'I don't think that's right.'

'What do you mean?'

'I think he came to see you.'

'No, that's not true, Ed.' Her voice was clawing at him, trying to find a handhold. Ed was looking at the harbour, his face impassive and his hands in his pockets. 'It was all so long ago,' she said weakly.

'But not long enough.'

'Who told you?'

'Gunner. The Friar went to see him as soon as he got back from here. You told him Gunner went to see you when you were in Tar'white, took the message that I wanted you home.'

Lilian could think of nothing to say.

'They didn't have a fight if that's what you're worried about. I think they got hammered.'

'Oh.'

'And the stupid buggers set fire to his hat, danced around it singing their heads off. He's cold now, doesn't appear to have another one.'

Ed started to walk away.

'Is that it?'

He stopped but he didn't look at her. 'No, that's not it, Lily. I just don't know what else to say.'

'It's just–' They'd never talked about the Friar and what had happened. It was too raw at the start and best forgotten at the finish. Lilian had put it away. And so, she thought, had Ed.

'It still bothers you.'

'Yes, it does.'

'But it was so long ago. I wouldn't, I couldn't ever. You have to believe that.'

'I reckon–' He stopped and his face withdrew, then he started again. 'I used to think you'd come home only until the kids had grown.'

'Oh Ed, no.' Lilian felt sick. 'Listen to me, I am not going anywhere.'

His head bobbed up and down for a while and he made

to go. But then he was back beside her, awkwardly squeezing her shoulders, not saying a word, his nostrils flaring.

That was Ed all along.

Lilian noticed Titch looking at her expectantly.

'What?' It was hard to hear above the noise of the engine.

'Home! Bet you're pleased to be heading back.'

'Oh yes.'

'Funny what you miss when you're away.'

Her kitchen, her bed, the view, the chickens.

Ed.

'*Palgrave's Golden Treasury*,' Titch was saying. 'You borrowed it for the Browning.'

'Did I? Oh, yes.'

'You like Browning?' Even raising his voice like that, Lilian could hear the pinched nasal quality that Susan regarded as prissy. What was he saying now?

'All's over, then: does truth sound bitter

As one at first believes?

Hark, 'tis the sparrows' good-night twitter

About your cottage eaves!'

She caught only some of it, but enough to know. Browning's *The Lost Mistress*. He was smiling now, his lips puffed with self-satisfaction. *Have I got something*. She knew his sort. Nastiness dressed up. She knew now that the gossip would never go entirely while there was someone who remembered. For so long, whenever she went out, she'd hear something, even just the tail end of something. Time would pass and she'd feel confident again, and then without seeing it coming she'd slip on a word or a look and gape stupidly, not knowing where to put herself. This time, on the mail boat with Titch, she'd thought she'd be safe. Susan had tried to warn her, but Titch was from out of the area and a more refined sort of person, and Lilian had trusted him. And now here he was looking at her with that look men had when they knew. She felt hot at the back of her eyes, and before she knew what she was going to say she'd opened her mouth to let it out,

'Tell me, Titch, how's your sister?'

His face froze.

'Your sister June? Or have I got it wrong? I remember going on holiday once to visit my cousins – it was a small farm near Masterton – I'm sure it was you and your sister June we saw down at the swimming hole every day. You were skinny and white and very high-pitched. Screaming like a girl. You showed us the veins on your arms to make us run away. They were like worms under your skin.'

'Stop that.'

'June was a tubby girl, skin like lard.'

'Stop.'

'There can't be many Titches and Junes that go together in this world. And you're still very close, I believe. Susan thought you were married, in fact. Hah! That's it. Titch and June. June and Titch. I'd forgotten, but now I remember it clearly – it was such a perfect swimming hole with a swing rope.'

Lilian tipped her head sideways and studied Titch for a moment. His skin was moist. His eyes were murderous. He seemed to be having trouble breathing.

'Just think, that was over thirty years ago. Are you all right?'

Lilian knew what she'd done. This would be her last ride on this boat, and there'd be no more sightings of Titch and his sister. No more meticulously sewn dresses for people to buy, or books to borrow, or newspapers and mail delivered to

261

the sound of his bell. It was despicable, but all she wanted to do now was to laugh. How dare Titch and June pretend like that! She'd had all these years of hiding herself away, avoiding people's eyes, pretending not to hear. She had suffered with the truth of what she'd done, while Titch and his sister/ wife had lived a disgusting lie. She couldn't stop herself. She wasn't going to be pushed aside any more. She'd done her time.

Billy was laughing and yelling at the spray and Lilian went to him, smiling. 'Billy! You're wet through!'

It seemed an age before they passed Dieffenbach Point and turned into Tory Channel. Titch was silent and pinched, his eyes glued to the water. Then there was Tar'white and the bach she'd lived in for a year, crushed by channel weather into not much more than firewood. She didn't look, she knew it was there, propped up by all that longing and loss. No wonder the Friar had left it behind and moved to Fishing Bay.

The steep hills that crowded on either side of them parted at last to show, in the distance through the narrow heads, Cook Strait and the open sea.

Lilian closed her eyes and kept them shut, letting the sun settle there, and flecks of spray. When she opened them again, she knew she'd be home.

Since the day had begun, Micky had been beset by nurses with rattling trolleys, muted footsteps and occasional bad breath. What he wanted was a cigarette. The craving seemed to coincide with the quietness in the room and his headache easing and knowing she'd gone. He was suspended here by the leg and suspended from living, and his mother had gone home. It was easy to feel sorry for himself.

Around his neck was the red scarf she'd knitted. He couldn't remember her giving it to him but he knew somehow it was one of hers. Everything his mother had ever knitted him was red. There were so many things about his mother that irritated him, and that was one of them. He'd liked red when he was ten. Red marbles were his favourites. Of all of them – pee-wees, stonies, alleys, bully-taws, cat's-eyes – it was the red ones he'd treasured. He used to hold them up against the fire in the coal range and the two reds would merge through the glass. They were tiny blazing worlds he could stare at for hours. Billy had them now. Micky didn't know why he'd given them away. Before he'd left home he'd been so angry.

Was he angry still? It felt like it sometimes. And he didn't know why his mother angered him the most. When she looked at him there was no shred of judgement there, but the rage he felt would come out of nowhere and lay siege to his common sense.

Micky had a memory. He was running up through the pines and getting bogged down by pine needles. The trees seemed darker and taller than usual, so he must have been small. He was calling his mother, but he wasn't running towards the house where surely she'd be, he was running away from it. In his head he was going over what he'd do if he found her. He'd give her all of his marbles for one thing. He could hear them tapping together in his pocket. He didn't have so many then – a few glassies, a stoney or two – but they were all hers. She only had to ask.

Micky shifted his leg. It wasn't painful any more so much as bothersome. He had another month or so of this in the hospital, and more time in bed when he got home. The whale season would be well and truly over, and he'd have time on his hands before the next one. But he wasn't going anywhere. He'd get back on that chaser again if it killed him.

33

She'd taken the *Periwinkle*. The full moon was sinking but it still gave her enough light to see by, and it had transformed the sea and sky into a rare luminous beige. It didn't penetrate the hills. They were still hunched and unwelcoming. Iris would say it was like in the beginning when Rangi and Papa parted and everything in the world held its breath. There was no such thing as colour then, nor sunlight nor warmth. There were no humans, no animals, no birds, no names. These would come.

If you let the tide take you, out of the channel and into Cook Strait, if you trusted it rather than fought it, how long would it take? *No time at all, give it a try.* That was Owen. *Once you're out of the bay you're on your own.* That was Ed. She was tempted sometimes. But today she would only go with the ebbing tide as far as Whekenui as she used to do once, and then she'd have to row like mad to get to the beach. Everything she needed was in a bag. Owen's hat was on its hook up at the bach.

Returning in this extravagant moonlight would be the reverse of her leaving – it had been opaque on the track that night; she hadn't been able to see Owen at all.

She'd thought about it often since, and tried to make sense

of what she'd done, but it was difficult after all this time for her to recall the exact events that led up to the decision to go. What she did remember with startling clarity was the rush of sensation when Owen reached out and touched her arm that night. With one touch she was plundered. It felt like everything had fallen from her, all the perplexities and concerns of her former self, and she'd left them in amongst the gorse and the grass and the sheep dung. She'd let another man take her hand and walk her away.

Where things with Ed were complicated, with Owen they were simple. She'd loved Ed, but he was ruined in a way she couldn't understand, and what she felt for him seemed somehow pitiful and useless in the face of that. Owen had listened. He'd leaned into her and given her some of his warmth. He'd batted his own voice in the air around her until she'd started to listen. He couldn't explain why he'd come out of the war relatively unscathed, except that he hadn't lost a brother there, and he'd been a different sort of person from the start. Gradually, she'd begun to yearn for this different person to the point where she felt physically sick. She'd had no choice, or that's how it felt at the time, and she'd told herself the children would follow when the place was halfway decent.

After a week at Tar'white, she'd started to feel them tugging, gently at first and then harder and harder, but there was nowhere yet for them to sleep. Over the months it became clear the children wouldn't be joining them. The tugs became fish-hooks in her skin. She'd gone and exchanged one pain for another.

And Ed. The man she'd never properly understood, the whistle between the grass. Away from the turmoil, alone in Owen's bach all day, she'd begun to feel ashamed of herself for wanting what her husband had offered before the war, for seeing the possibilities and then spurning what had become too difficult a thing to grasp. Both were decent men, but one was her husband, and living with shame is a terrible thing.

Her arms were feeling it now and she hadn't even rowed as far as Fishing Bay. She'd grown weak after the baby, in all sorts of ways. She imagined Owen waking in the bach alone, his disbelief, calling her name into the unfriendly scrub and then down over the water. She'd seen the way he looked for her, the way he needed her and was so desperate for her to be well again. She couldn't bear that sort of responsibility.

He should have told her where the baby was.

Eventually, he'd notice the *Periwinkle* had gone. She couldn't let herself think what he would do then or how he'd feel. But eventually, surely, he'd realise it was the right thing and he might even feel a little relieved.

A year was a long time in the life of a child. The Susan and Micky she'd left behind would be gone forever, replaced by older, different children. Could they trust her again? She wondered if they knew they were reeling her in.

Of course Gunner might have got it wrong, or Ed might have changed his mind, but that didn't bear thinking about it. What she knew with all certainty was her time was up. She wasn't Annie any more.

34

Riding the squally air above Lookout Hill, for this was a time of flight, remember, of men and women pushing machines to do the unthinkable, would reveal seven men sprawled on the brow of a hill as if they owned the spot. Their bodies would be poised, though, rather than relaxed, their faces concentrated on the sea below, their elbows firm to the grass, the soles of their feet planted hard, so they could push away from it the second the cry went up, and run, down the narrow track and over the swing bridge, to the beach, to the boats and away to open water. The poise was the hunter honed to evidence of his prey; and although they seemed earth-bound, these men, when watched from the sky, they were floating, in fact, half an inch above the grass, buoyed by the seltzer of anticipation, ready to take off.

Sometimes things moved too fast, even for the most experienced whaler. When Sarge first saw the spray, it was so tall and emphatic, he took it for a williwaw. But no, it didn't take long for him to realise it was too far out from land for that, and all on its own in the calm sea. He waited at the same spot, but there wasn't another one; he shifted his glasses, there was still nothing. A single spout like that. He continued to move in a line from where he'd first seen it. If it was a spout, it was too long and narrow for a humpback, but definite enough, tall enough, to be a finback. Or a blue. Sarge was beginning to doubt he'd seen it now, or the exact proportions of it. Did it taper like a finback? Or was it more of a column?

The familiar fizzing began in his chest, and then the restlessness began in his right leg. Sarge was flat on the grass, his elbows supporting the binoculars to keep them steady, but he had to kick his legs, and that disturbed his concentration and made him lose his place on the water. Squeezed with irritation, he calmed himself enough to mark the far shore, the horizon, the water, the seabirds, the clouds, to get back to the approximate point he'd been before. The sea stretched in front of him so glossy and elastic it was like the membrane of a giant eye, but Sarge knew, as they all did, that there were still many irregularities on the surface that could mask the presence of a whale.

Sarge tried to flatten his breathing because he could feel it coming fast and shallow and he knew the others would hear it and know. Where was that spout? The fizzing in his chest had broken through to his skin and he was prickling all over, his forehead damp with sweat. It was a blue whale, he knew it, a sulphur-bottom, and he had tickets on it. Bugger me if anyone else was going to spot it. His legs were really starting to bother him now, and when he moved them his whole body moved and his glasses were shaking and he was losing position. No one else had noticed his agitation yet. He needed to do something.

Sarge put down the glasses and stood up, as casually as he could, yawning and stretching his arms and then his legs, walking up and down, stamping his feet hard on the grass. Enough. They felt better. He tried to smile at Jimmy who was looking over, and to sit down nonchalantly, picking up his glasses again and cradling them against his face. Without any trouble, he found the line he guessed the whale would be following, though his hopes weren't high. There was every chance it had gone off somewhere else entirely. He'd never find it now. Never on a frosty Friday.

She blows! The excitement punched him in his throat. He couldn't call it, he just gasped. Forty feet at least, the spout was as straight as they come, an astounding plume of vapour. And in the low sunlight of the afternoon Sarge glimpsed a pale rainbow.

It could only be a blue.

They had to move fast, but now when he needed to Sarge couldn't shift himself. His legs were leaden, his throat was dry. But it came at last with all the rage and pain and amazement of a wounded bull. 'Thar she blows!' And it was all he could do not to leap to his feet and point and shout and dance like he'd had a few. He had to keep his eye in.

'Where are you, Sarge?'

'In a straight line out from Karori Rock just behind the dark slick of water.'

'There's a single seabird above it?'

'You've got it. It's moving nor'west on its way to The Brothers. Again! That's another one.' And there was a mutter and shuffle around him as everyone shifted their glasses to the spot. Sarge calmly dealt his last card. 'It's spouting over forty foot. My guess is it's a mother of a whale, gentlemen. It's on its own and it's in a blinding hurry. I've got myself a blue.'

'Could be a finback,' said Ed. 'Or a sei.'

'Not with that spout,' said Sarge. 'I haven't seen one like it.'

'That's why all the jumping around before, eh Sarge?' said Jimmy. 'Those legs of yours were going up and down like a bride's nightie. I should have known something was up.'

'Dark water or light water?' asked Boots. Even he sounded excited.

'At the back of the dark water was where I saw it last,' said Sarge.

There was a charged silence as they all looked and waited for the cry of confirmation. 'I've got him,' shouted Gunner. 'You're right, Sarge, you're bloody well right! It's out of the dark water and running along the edge of the rip like its tail's on fire. If it keeps on like this, it'll be out past The Brothers in no time.'

'Get a wriggle on,' roared Jock.

No one from the whaling settlement saw them leave Tory Channel. All three, the *Balaena*, the *Chance* and the *Nautilus*, were able to slip into Cook Strait and cut across it like light on the edge of a knife. It helped that the afternoon was brimming with brightness, so to look you had to squint or shade your eyes, and even then you couldn't be sure they were there.

At an agreed point, ten nautical miles straight out from the Lookout, closer to the North Island than the South, they slowed. It had taken half an hour to get there. All six men scanned the water. No one spoke.

It was on its way. Sarge was sure of it. It was fast but not that fast. He indicated the chasers should turn to the south and work their way along the coast. The others didn't question it; it was Sarge's whale. They formed the three tines of a trident: the *Chance* in the middle and slightly ahead, the *Nautilus* out to the west, the *Balaena* to the east. Sarge hoped he'd got it right. With a top speed faster than a chaser, a blue could shake them off with no trouble. At least after a dive there would be a number of good spouts and, in weather like this, with the sun as low as it was, they should be easy to spot.

Another fifteen minutes and they slowed again. It could have gone past them. Sarge shut his eyes and rubbed them. It had been a long day. When he opened them again, the sea was still empty of whale. All of them were straining to find something and there was, quite plainly, nothing there. Sarge let his eyelids drop again.

'Hey!' That was Boots. He was doing a little jig and pointing at a column of spray about a mile off. It was astonishing. Boots dancing and the spout which was easily the height of a tall tree. Phil let the throttle out, and Sarge and Jimmy did the same.

He was waiting for them. An enormous fellow – close on a hundred foot and carrying about a hundred and thirty tons. It could be nothing but a blue, an old pig of a blue, its mottled flesh scarred many times over. It became clear to all of them one by one that what they were seeing here was one of the wonders of the world. Ed saluted, Boots bowed, Gunner took his hat off and wiped the back of his hand across his eyes. All the better to see you with, thought Sarge. Or was the bugger crying? He remembered Gunner going on about how a blue whale could yield around twenty tons of oil, more than twice what they got from a humpback. That was enough to make anyone cry.

Ed was bending briefly to check his hand-bombs when the blue spouted again. It was only a matter of yards away and going slow, they'd be on to it soon. Then Sarge saw the water curdle. And, before he could do anything, it rounded up and was gone. He slammed his fist on the wheel, but Ed was already rotating his hand. *Turn. One-eighty.*

Sarge wrenched the chaser around, but he was also doing some calculations. The whale could dive for up to fifteen minutes but it couldn't stay at top speed all that time. It was probably scared now, which made it harder to predict, but at the same time more likely to come to the surface. He followed the line the blue had taken. Slavishly. He refused to veer.

Over half an hour later and three miles out from The Brothers they slowed a little. No sign of the whale. Nothing moved on the surface of the sea or seemingly under it, and the afternoon was fast dropping away. If they didn't get it soon, they'd be out of luck. And then there was Gunner. Sarge wasn't sure how much longer he could keep going; he wasn't a well man. He was leaning heavily on the gun, his eyes fixed and his face oily with sweat.

The sun was so low and so bright, Sarge used his hand to block it. They were all like that, holding their hands above their eyes and doing their best to scan the water and go forward. It reminded Sarge of the story Jock told of Maoris blindfolding strangers while they passed by The Brothers so they didn't offend the spirits there. The rocks were close at hand now, the late light throwing into relief the ragged surface, the steep cliffs, the lighthouse. No wonder they spooked people.

The chasers slowed. Ed was turned towards Sarge and shrugging his shoulders when, behind Ed, as if from the top of his cap, came the spout. Not once, but twice, and as high as a spout could go. The blasted whale was trying to create columns to hold the heavens up.

The three chasers closed in, spread like a net to catch it. The *Chance* got there first but the whale shifted direction slightly. It was ploughing towards the *Balaena*, a gift to Gunner. He rallied himself enough to fire, but they could all tell the moment he loosed it that the harpoon would fall short. The whale was powering forward faster than any whale they'd ever seen, past the *Balaena* and Gunner, and out into the evening water of the Strait which would soon take it away past Kapiti and on to the north. Gunner was no longer able to do the deed. He slumped, seemingly no strength left in his body, a sick and dejected man. Jimmy was calling to him, telling him he was turning back, but Gunner raised his hand, forbidding his driver to go. Grimly, the old whaler hung on with one hand and stared Jimmy out. The driver's face reddened with the effort of deciding what to do. It went against the grain for him to countermand his boss; they'd been on the same boat for twelve years and he'd never done such a thing, but Sarge could see Jimmy feared he may not have a boss any more if they kept going. Sarge was glad, not for the first time, that it wasn't him who had to drive the old Italian. He saw Gunner steady himself against the gun and then slowly but surely begin hauling in the boxline to retrieve the harpoon. He still had it in him – pulling like a man half his age. Jimmy grimaced at Sarge, and then turned his attention to giving Gunner a hand.

The three chasers came together one more time, the *Balaena* lagging slightly while Gunner coiled the rope and slid the harpoon back in the gun. He was painfully slow. Every man was aware that any minute now the sun would drop behind the earth.

The picture would be clearer from the air. There'd be the obvious stillness of this slender neck of water known for its turbulence; and then the sharp eye of an aviator would pick out the four white lines drawn on the polished surface. Fast boats. And something else.

From that distance, there'd be no evidence of the misfired harpoon or the man who fired it, and none of the sounds he let loose when he saw what he'd done. There'd be very little colour. Bled by distance, the scene would be shades of grey, molten where the sun was spilling the last of its light. It would be a case of patterns and shapes, blocks of light and dark, knuckles of land, clouds not white any longer but black shadows on the water, and a pewter sea that would seem further than it was and then suddenly closer, the height of the waves impossible to judge. And, watched closely enough, it would be apparent that three of the fast boats were moving together in formation – a string bag, a net – and the fourth was in fact something quite different. Shaped like a torpedo and just as fast, it was three times the size of those boats, and clearly not a boat at all. The hunted.

Suddenly, the boats cut free and set off together across the arc the whale was making, and whether its instincts were blunted by panic or it simply wasn't aware, the creature inexplicably – given the size of the ocean – swam straight into the net they'd made.

Gunner let loose the iron using instinct rather than judgement. It would pierce the beast, he was certain, but the whaler was drifting now to one side, coming up against the side of the harpoon gun and resting there. He couldn't pull himself back up. His cheek was flat to the metal. His exhaustion profound.

Gunner blinked to try to clear his eyes, and looked back briefly for confirmation of a hit. Jimmy gave him the thumbs-up and yelled something Gunner couldn't catch. He was in a fog, and in his fog he had speared a blue whale. Unbelievable.

His father would be proud. But his father was dead, wasn't he? Or was he? A small man who never wanted more than a good catch of sardines and to get home in time for tea.

Nadine, my toothy love, this is for you.

Gunner was drifting. There was no time. The whale rallied and broke through the chasers, the boxline fleeing after it, the friction on the loggerhead sending sparks on to the deck.

Gunner held on to the harpoon gun, shaking so hard he couldn't lift a finger to do anything else, his eyes on the rope running off the front of the chaser. He refused to look at Jimmy. He gestured for the boat to accelerate and follow the whale in the wide circle it was drawing on the darkening water. All he needed to do was to take things slowly and ignore the lassitude in his muscles and the terrible ache in his groin, but he was scared now, truly scared. He knew he was done for. The clarity of his thought blinded him. At the end of this lot, he and the whale would be dead.

They needed to hurry. The sheer power of the beast meant there was a danger the harpoon would come loose. He saw the *Chance* moving obliquely to try and cut the whale off, Ed with a bomb at the ready, Boots doing the same thing.

Ed got there first. He threw deep, and hit the base of the neck. Explosives ripped its flesh, and the whale shuddered deeply and the ocean groaned. Then slowly, as if nothing had happened, the creature seemed to let go its hold on the surface and disappear.

The men could only watch and wait.

It surfaced a matter of yards away. The whale was still for a moment, then it turned and swam straight at them. There was no time to think. Boots was yelling at Sarge to clear out so he could throw his bomb and still yelling as he finally got it away. Ed threw. One fell short; the other hit home. Ed threw again, and with the second charge the blue convulsed.

Boots put it all to rest.

Gunner was down, breathing as if he'd run a marathon. The whale's death flurry was short. There was a rush of blood the height of a tall tree.

35

'It's a blue.'

There she was, that woman with all the hair and it was flying around her face as she spoke, and she was slapping it back and the words got snapped away from her. It had been so long since she'd been down to see what was going on. The people around the whale stepped back to give her room.

'Yes.' He took her by the arm and pulled her gently forward to the front of the crowd. 'A blue. A sulphur-bottom. Look at that yellow belly, Billy. It's a ninety-eight footer.'

'Nearly a hundred feet!' cried the boy. 'It's a giant!' His mother put a hand on him but he twisted and slipped from her, falling on to the whale, both his hands flat to the pale blubber. 'It must be the biggest in the world.'

'We reckon it's probably the biggest in the Southern Hemisphere,' said the boy's father. He was still holding her arm, keeping her by him.

'But the blue whale's the biggest creature in the world,' said the boy. 'Bigger than anything. Why isn't this one the biggest ever?'

'There must be more of them where that came from,' said Ed. 'We'll fasten a hundred footer next time.'

'It's not very blue,' said the boy.

'When you see it just under the surface it looks blue enough.'

The man's gaze turned back to the sea. He didn't see Billy picking at the whale's stomach and then, after a time, losing interest and running off to play on the beach. He didn't see the way she used him for shelter.

'How's Micky?' he said at last.

'He's getting sick and tired of that bed.'

'That's a good sign. Leave it to me to tell him about the blue whale, eh? I'll go in tomorrow. See Gunner, too, while I'm at it.'

She touched him on the hand. 'Molly Too crowed today.'

'No! How did Billy take it?'

'Billy was fine. It's Russell whose beak is out of joint.'

She smiled and he smiled. Her hand was still on his.

'You've done well,' she said.

'Good enough.'

She walked away, through the gathered families. So many people and she didn't know half of them. There were small children she'd never met. One of the women nodded in a friendly fashion, another leaned to her neighbour to say something, and a young woman with a baby tucked down her front came forward to hug her.

At last she cleared them, and stood a moment to get her breath back. The door to the digester was open and she could see inside, but no one was behind it.

She continued walking now, brushing the hair from her mouth and looking around for the boy. She saw him without too much trouble, out on the rocks spearing kelp. Before she could call, she heard someone behind her. He'd run to catch up.

'I'm buggered, Lily.'
'You need to come home then, Ed.'
And she called Billy from the beach and he came running.

ACKNOWLEDGEMENTS

The Blue treads where real people have trod and while it tips its hat to them and shakes their hands it is still fiction and its characters the stuff of invention. Having said that, the whaling communities of Arapawa Island are inseparable from the place they made their home and are, I believe, present in *The Blue* without mention. Lilian talks of the ghosts that live on the island – these are her ghosts. I acknowledge the Arapawa whaling families and thank them for the inspiration they've given me.

I also want to give special thanks to:

Former whalers of Tory Channel – Joe Heberley, Peter Perano, Tommy Norton, Johnny Norton, Basil Jones and Neil Henderson – who welcomed me to the Lookout for the Department of Conservation's 2004 Cook Strait whale project, and happily shared their abundant knowledge. Peter especially put in the yards answering my subsequent emails. The 2004 DOC crew, led by Simon Childerhouse and Nadine Gibbs, who didn't think twice about including me in their project to record whale data and were exceptionally cheerful about getting me up to the Lookout on the back of a farm bike, and out on rough seas to follow the whales.

Heather Heberley whose books *Last of the Whalers* and *Riding with Whales* (Cape Catley) were my bibles, along with Don Grady's *The Perano Whalers* (Reed). The National Library of New Zealand Te Puna Mātauranga o Aotearoa, the Seahorse World Aquarium in Picton, and Pete and Takutai Beech of Myths & Legends Eco-Tours. Mike and Antonia Radon who put me up at Arapawa Homestead, scrimshander Robert Weiss, Mike Donoghue, Jerome Cvitanovich, Dr Rob Griffiths, Trev Easton, Terry Webb, Alison Parr's *Silent Casualties* (Tandem), and the websites with heartbreaking World War One stories, letters and photographs, especially nzine.co.nz, pukeariki. com, nzetc.org, and anzac.govt.nz.

All my family and friends, especially Ian, Paul, Adam and Isabel whom I love more than I can say and who lived with and supported this book for four years – barely uttering a complaint when it dominated the computer if not our lives; my mum and dad who gave me a love of stories and made me believe I could write them; my brothers Peter and Andy and their families; my grandparents Elsie and Owen and Jeanette and Jim; Mary; Chrys who told me a story one night in Athens; my in-laws Heather and Ian Stewart who introduced me to whales; Alastair and David and families; Ruby the canine muse; Alexandra and Quentin; Heather; Laura; Nat; Deb; Christina; Hilary; Kim; Michelle; Timothy; Whena; Maggie; Colin; Micky; Fi; the Ponders and my remarkable bookclub: Carrie, Mia, Andrea, Ayliffe and Pip.

My friend and writer Penny Walker, the Lilian Ida Smith Award and Geoff Walker at Penguin – all three were crucial in keeping me writing.

Damien Wilkins whose brilliance as an author and tutor at the International Institute of Modern Letters turned my 'book' into a novel; my MA class for their talent and insight: Anna Sanderson, Airini Beautrais, Amy Howden-Chapman, Stefanie Lash, Susannah Poole, Ben Sparks, Vana Manasiadis, Jennifer Smith and Kerry Hines. Peter Whiteford for his generous supervision, Dame Fiona Kidman for her belief in *The Blue* and Fergus Barrowman for wanting more stuff.

Bill Manhire, Katie Hardwick-Smith and Clare Moleta of IIML; Stephen Stratford; Harry Orsman's astonishing *Oxford New Zealand Dictionary*; Rebecca Lal at Penguin; and Jane Parkin for her sensitive editing.

My brother Peter again for his love of fishing, and for sometimes taking me with him.

And dare I? The whales.

2007